ANOTHER ENDING

Blessings,

Sara Whitley

ANOTHER ENDING

Sara Whitley

TATE PUBLISHING
AND ENTERPRISES, LLC

The opinions expressed by the author are not necessarily those of Tate Publishing, LLC.

This novel is a work of fiction. Names, descriptions, entities, and incidents included in the story are products of the author's imagination. Any resemblance to actual persons, events, and entities is entirely coincidental.

Published by Tate Publishing & Enterprises, LLC
127 E. Trade Center Terrace | Mustang, Oklahoma 73064 USA
1.888.361.9473 | www.tatepublishing.com

Tate Publishing is committed to excellence in the publishing industry. The company reflects the philosophy established by the founders, based on Psalm 68:11,
"The Lord gave the word and great was the company of those who published it."

Book design copyright © 2013 by Tate Publishing, LLC. All rights reserved.
Cover design by Allen Jomoc
Interior design by Joana Quilantang

Published in the United States of America

ISBN: 978-1-62510-420-5
1. Fiction / General
2. Fiction / Contemporary Women
13.01.31

Dedication

I can think of no other people to dedicate this work to than my wonderful parents, Kevin and Marcia. With their help, this dream has finally become a reality. And to Jesus Christ who saw my need for them and put me into their arms.

Acknowledgments

This project has not been an easy one for me. I faced fear and uncertainties at every step. Simply sitting down to write the first words on this book terrified me because I worried that I would get stuck in the middle with no hope of ever finishing. Luckily for me, that never happened, and now, here we are! This is only because I have been blessed with the most wonderful support group imaginable. God is good.

First of all, I must acknowledge my wonderful husband to be, Ben Whitley. With your undying love and support, I was able to tackle this project with everything in me. I can't begin to explain how much your encouragement has kept me writing when my fears began to tell me that getting published would probably always remain a dream, never a reality. And your genuine interest in my work has been wonderful! When we talk about the plot and characters, I know you really care. Even though reading is not your favorite pastime, I know you'll read my work. And that means the world to me, love. Thank you for being my rock when everything seems so crazy. I couldn't do this without you.

Another thank you to my parents, who loved me through thick and thin and encouraged me to pursue my dream. Thank you for always reading my sloppily put together books—I wonder if you had to hold in laughter as you read them. Thank you for understanding my desire to go into social work and then encouraging me to keep writing. You always have my best interest in mind, and I am blessed to call myself your daughter.

Thank you to my wonderful sister in Christ, Deb Stevens. God knew we needed to be friends when he paired us up as mentor and mentee when I was still only in middle school. I still think back to the time we spent together fondly, and I still use the advice and encouragement you gave me. I think of our friend, Ordinary, all the time, and of course, all the messages from the *Dream Giver* have encouraged me and made me smile over the years. Your insight and advice with this book has been such a blessing. I appreciate you reading over my manuscript and offering up your advice and feelings. It has really reassured me that this book will reach more than just young adults. Thank you for being the support I needed in this crazy time. You're truly a blessing.

Many thanks to my grandparents, Robert and Doris Watt, and to my aunt Brenda and uncle Clint. Your financial support is beyond appreciated. Without you, this dream would be stuck a dream. And thank you for all the love and support throughout my life. It never hurts to have such a dedicated fan base cheering me on and bragging me up in Wyoming and Minnesota. I can't thank you enough.

Finally, a shout out to the best church family a girl could ever ask for. In my skit writing days, your support and encouragement made me believe that, perhaps, God had a bigger plan for my life than I had. Your response to my writings made me believe that I could make it in the writing world. And now, with this first book, your response has been amazing. I know you are all eager to read what God has put on my heart, and that means the world to me. So enjoy, friends. And please use this book as a tool to bring others to Christ. That has always been my goal, so if this work speaks to you in any way, pass it on to a friend who needs to know the love of Christ.

And finally, I must acknowledge the one who made this all possible—Jesus Christ. He has put the love of writing in my heart, and now, he is opening up doors for me I never thought would be opened. He deserves all the glory, because without him, I am nothing.

I have used the New Living Translation
of the Bible in my manuscript.

Prologue

September 2009

Heavy, angry raindrops pelted my windshield, and my wipers were having a tough time clearing them away before another wave of rain washed over. I squinted hard and leaned forward, trying my best to focus on the road as the wipers furiously slashed the rain from my view. My knuckles were white from my death grip on the wheel, and I wondered when my life would stop feeling like a movie. This weather matched my mood perfectly, something that only happens in movies. The heartbroken young hero would be in crisis mode, and suddenly, the rain would start pouring down and the sad music would play. Well, the rain was pouring down, and the sad chords of some country song were softly playing in the background. Sooner or later, everything works itself out in the movies though, and there would be sunshine and happy music.

Probably no sunshine and happy music for me though. And while in the movies it always rained when something tough happened, it felt like just the opposite for me. Yes, it was raining outside, but I wasn't slogging my way through the rain; rather, I was dragging myself through a desert. One that stretched on for miles with no hope of rain to soothe my cracked and dry heart. At this point, I would relish the rains flooding into my life. But the only rains that were falling were outside, and it was getting heavier. Lightning slashed across the dark sky, and I shivered. It was bad enough driving at night without having to worry about heavy rain and lightning.

The smart thing to do would be to pull over and wait it out, but I was exhausted and just wanted to reach the next town. I'd just spent the last year and a half living in Minneapolis, working at a junky little dinner. I had been staying in an apartment with a girl who worked there and some of her friends, but I couldn't handle it anymore. Being around them brought back too many horrible memories of the day I was trying to erase from my mind forever. All I wanted was a fresh start in a place where nobody knew me or my awful history.

So I packed up my little car with all my belongings, which were few. When I left home the first time I only took what was absolutely necessary. I left all of the sentimental stuff back in my childhood bedroom as I furiously packed. Back then, I was on a time crunch; I needed to get out as soon as humanly possible. When I finally reached Minneapolis and looked through what I had grabbed, I wished I had taken a little more time. Spread out on the tiny bed in Melissa's apartment was everything I had left in the world. All on a tiny bed.

This time, the story was about the same—my car contained everything that was only absolutely necessary for survival. I hadn't been on a time crunch this time around, but in the year and a half

I had lived with Melissa, I hadn't collected many belongings. The whole time I'd been there I'd felt like a machine, just doing what I needed to get done and nothing more. I didn't feel anything anymore. So I hadn't bought anything to make my tiny, shared room feel homier or purchased many new clothes. I simply survived.

I squinted at the green sign as I drove past; the rain was making it hard to read. It told me I was just pulling in to the tiny town of Green Lake, Kansas, with a population of 1,782, quite a difference from the almost four hundred thousand people who lived in Minneapolis. Maybe a small town would do me good though. Maybe I'd get a real do-over here.

I'd gone for a city the first time I ran—because I figured it would be easier to disappear—to become invisible. I didn't want anyone to ask me about my past or even care about me, really. I just wanted to live, to escape what lay back in Oak Ridge, Iowa, for good. That hadn't panned out for me though. I lived every day trapped by my past, unable to share my pain with anyone for fear of judgment and condemnation. But after a year and a half of just existing and trying to disappear, I wondered if I was ready to be found. It was easier to be found in a small town; it was almost impossible to blend in and disappear. To really move on—to heal—maybe I just needed to be found.

It was late, so I pulled into a small motel and got a room for the night. It was tiny but clean although it did smell a little musty. Cheap paintings hung on the walls, and a small boxy TV sat on a dark brown dresser. A table with two mismatched chairs pulled up to it sat in the corner. The bed was small but surprisingly soft, so I pulled my shoes off my tired feet and collapsed into it, exhausted from the long day of driving.

When I awoke from another nightmare in the morning, sunshine was streaming in through the blinds. I blinked and rubbed my eyes, taking the room in once more in the sunlight. It didn't look any less gloomy than it had last night.

Today I'd look for a job—if there was one to be found in this tiny town. Otherwise it would be another day of driving, which sounded less than appealing. I took a long shower, however, letting the hot water relax my tense muscles. Melissa used to pound on the bathroom door and yell at me to get out, saying that I was wasting all the hot water. So I relished this shower and stood under the steady stream of water until my fingers turned to prunes.

It was one o'clock in the afternoon by the time I was all dressed and ready to go. I wanted to make my face look less harsh and hopeless since I was trying to find a job, so I worked some gel into my hair and tousled it a bit, giving it some waves. I also applied a little makeup, although I found that no amount of concealer could hide the dark circles under my eyes. My face had hollowed out since I had left Oak Ridge almost two years ago. I bet Tanner would hardly recognize me now. I shook his image out of my head though. Memories of Tanner were much too painful, so I pushed him out of my mind.

I decided not to take my car because it was low on gas, and I didn't feel like shelling out thirty dollars to fill it up. Walking would do me good anyway, and it was a beautiful day. I'd get to see more of the town this way too. I figured I could walk most of the town from start to finish anyway; it was that small. I passed by what seemed to be the only elementary school in town and paused for a second to watch the little kids playing outside for recess. What a simple age. That was where I wanted to go back to, a time where life was simple and Tanner was my protector and playmate.

No sense wishing though. We could never go back now.

I walked on and passed the post office, a tiny grocery store, and some little shops downtown. Their downtown was actually very quaint with thriving little craft and clothing stores. I walked through some of the shops, chatting a bit with the cute little ladies who owned them, putting on a good face for them. I love Midwest charm, the hospitality that locals give out to visitors without thinking twice. I considered applying for a job at an adorable bookstore, but that type of work was too slow for me though, so I kept searching.

Later that afternoon, I found myself in front of a diner. I swore I'd never work at one again after Minneapolis, but there was something about this place that drew me in. There wasn't a flashing neon "open" sign in the window. Instead, "Welcome Family and Friends" was hand painted on the front window. Dark green shutters graced all the windows, and flowerpots still bloomed with cheerful, colorful flowers. I peered inside and saw that all the tables were spotless and shining. The floors probably weren't sticky either.

I walked in and a friendly chime sounded. A plump older lady turned around at the counter and smiled at me. She was wearing a light blue-collared dress with a clean white apron protecting it. Her graying hair was pulled back in a loose bun, and she pulled a pencil out of it.

"Hello, darlin'. Can I get you a table?" she asked in a sweet voice as she came around the corner and onto the dining floor. I couldn't help but smile and nod. "All right then. Here ya go," she said as she laid a menu down on an empty table. I slid into the booth and started scanning the menu.

I ordered coffee, a sandwich, and soup that I could tell was all made from fresh ingredients. The bread was homemade, and the soup had never been frozen. She had probably made the bread herself this morning. The woman amazed me, and I continued to sit through the lunch rush to watch her run her diner. Besides a cook and one elderly bus boy, she pretty much ran the show herself. And she continued to bring me coffee, even though I was still occupying one of her tables during the bustle.

I lost track of time sitting there, thinking about the past few years when, all of a sudden, the woman was sliding into the seat across from me. I looked up with a start as she poured herself a cup of coffee and refilled mine. When I glanced up at the big clock she had hanging on the wall, I saw that it was nearing seven o'clock. How had I sat here for the entire day and not realized it? The diner was quiet now, most of the tables cleared and ready for the next day.

"You okay, little one?" she asked in a concerned voice. "Ya been here all day long just staring out that window."

"Yeah, I'm…I'm fine," I lied. I could hear my voice quavering though. Clearly, I was not fine, and this woman could tell.

"Well now, you look like you been through quite a storm. Ya just passing through, sweetie?" Seemed like she had a new name for me each time she spoke, making me feel like a child. But I was okay with that; I was tired of being an adult even though I was barely twenty years old. Hardly an adult. And there was something about this woman that made me trust her. Was it her eyes?

My middle school Sunday school teacher had said once that when someone truly loves Jesus with all their soul, you can tell in their eyes. They just shine with the love of Christ. I could see that in this woman's eyes. I glanced around and sure enough, crosses and Bible verses hung framed on the walls. I had somehow missed that. So here I was in the presence of a Christian when I had spent the last two years putting as much distance between myself and the Christians who had hurt me most.

I surprised myself by blurting, "I'm looking for a job, actually. Just moved from Minneapolis. Kind of a need a new start." It was surprisingly easy for me to open up to this woman. Her kind eyes sparkled as she took in this information. She glanced around the diner, nodding her head and murmuring something I couldn't understand.

"Hmm," she said and took a swallow of her coffee. "Well, I could probably help ya out with that. You're hired." She stuck her hand out to me and grinned.

Startled, I protested. "But you don't know me! I'm just some person whose been sitting here all day doing nothing."

She shrugged. "I know. But there is something about you, little girl," she said as she wagged a finger at me. "I can see it in your eyes. You don't have anywhere else to go, do you?"

Tears burned my eyes, and I blinked them back furiously. She smiled and shook her head. "Yeah, I can tell. You need this, don't you?"

"Yes. I do," I whispered. "I've worked in a diner for the past year and a half," I added as she stood up (my attempt to assure her she wasn't hiring a lazy bum, even though she seemed to have made up her mind about me already).

"Well, just perfect!" She beamed. "Can you come in tomorrow 'round nine o'clock?"

I nodded, stunned that it had been this easy to land a job here. I just hoped this woman didn't see me as some project, a lonely girl led here by God for her to fix up and change. God hadn't been leading me for quite some time now. And I wasn't a project. I didn't want to be fixed.

But a thought kept nagging at me—maybe this was finally my fresh start. Maybe here, I could finally escape the demons of the past, the nightmares that had terrorized me for two years.

Maybe I was finally getting my long awaited do-over.

Part One

Endings

For everything, there is a season,
a time for every activity under heaven.
A time to be born and a time to die…

—Ecclesiastes 3:1–2

One

August 2007

On the morning of my first day of school senior year, I woke up to a text message from Tanner. 6:44 a.m., exactly one minute before my alarm was set to go off. I'd be mad, except I like Tanner way too much, and this is typical Tanner behavior. Once he found out what time I set my alarm to, he started texting me exactly one minute before it would go off. He knew how much it bothered me, which was exactly why he did it. This was the type of relationship Tanner and I had, and I loved it. Only best friends can do this to each other and know the other still loves them.

Wake up, sleepyhead. Don't want to be late for our first day as rulers of the school!

I smiled and slid my phone shut. We were both beyond excited for senior year, not because we would be "rulers of the school," but because it meant we were that much closer to college. Both of us were highly amused by the immature—almost childish—behavior of our fellow students, but we were ready to move on. The year couldn't go by fast enough.

The first day of school was the most fun for us because we loved watching the cliché behaviors of high school play out right before our eyes. Everything you see in the movies about high school is true, surprisingly enough. All the cheerleaders stick together, the band kids have been there practicing marching way before any of the rest of the students arrive, and the football players clump together in the hallway talking about how hard pre-season training has been. It's loud, it smells weird, and it's mass chaos—just like the movies.

I didn't even bother texting Tanner back; he knows I'm never late for our carpool. Never in the four years we've driven together have I been late. I remember driving to school together for the first time our freshmen year. My mom stood in the driveway, waving good-bye as tears fell off her cheeks. She had driven us to elementary and middle school every single day, but Tanner had gotten a car that summer, and my mom was no longer needed. She still had my younger brother, Josh, and sister, Savannah, to drop off; but something about watching me drive off to high school with Tanner tapped into her mysterious mom emotions and made her cry. I will never understand my mother.

I could also picture Tanner's face perfectly that morning. He was so thrilled; he couldn't stop that goofy smile of his from taking over his whole face. He drove so carefully the entire way, relishing the freedom that his car gave us.

Four years later, his little car was still getting the job done. In forty-five minutes, I would climb into the front seat—my seat—and we would swing though Starbucks for mochas on our way to school. Tradition on the first day.

It was funny how almost every memory of my growing up years included Tanner. He had been there for every big moment of my life, and I knew that I would never have another friend in the world like him. People asked all the time if we were dating, to which Tanner would respond by ruffling my hair and saying, "Naw…Molly and me, we're just buds. Right, Moll?" I'd smile and reassure our wondering classmates that there were no romantic feelings between us at all. Not everyone bought that though, especially not Kristina, my closest girl friend.

"Are you kidding me, Molly?" she'd ask. "Tanner is crazy about you. Crazy! I can read people pretty well, Moll, and judging by the way that boy looks at you, it's obvious to everyone in the world but you: Tanner is in love with you."

I was adamant that she and everyone else were wrong. What Tanner and I had was different; no one understood that, but us. Our very first meeting sealed us as best friends, and anything deeper than that would ruin everything.

Tanner and I were five years old when we met. My family moved to our little Christian Iowan town of Oak Ridge the summer before I started kindergarten. Seven hours in the family minivan was starting to wear on me, and I was beyond excited to get to our new house and go exploring. I remember watching the sun filter down through the leaves of the enormous trees that lined every street. I pressed my sweaty face to the glass and soaked in every detail of my new neighborhood. I saw a group of boys my age riding their bikes and felt a twinge of sadness at the lack of girls out playing. But I was determined to become friends with them anyway.

We pulled into our new driveway, and my parents parked me and my two-year-old brother Josh on the front porch. My pregnant mom instructed me to stay and watch Josh while they began to unload all of our boxes into the garage. I went into instant-pout mood. All I wanted to do was go exploring; instead, I was stuck watching Josh pick his nose and drool. Grossly unfair. I watched the boys go whizzing by on their bikes, and I sighed loudly.

A man, who I later found out was Tanner's dad, came walking across the grass separating our houses to offer his help. After a firm handshake from my dad, Brian Walters rolled up his sleeves and got to work hauling boxes into the garage. When the boys came whizzing by again, I could stand it no longer. I ran over to my mom and begged her let me go riding too.

"Sweetheart, mommy and daddy are too busy to walk with you, and I don't want you riding alone. You might get lost or hurt. And who will Joshy play with?" Mom was always a worrier.

Brian chuckled and said, "You just moved into one of the safest, kid-friendliest neighborhoods in America, folks. Look at all the moms out in the yards! Everyone looks out for each other here, Julie." Brian crouched down to my level. "If my wife, Evelyn, watched your brother, Josh, for the afternoon, would you feel better about going out to ride your bike, sweetheart?"

I nodded my head.

"Well, that settles it then, Julie. My wife would be happy to watch the little guy. What do you say?"

After a little coaxing, my exhausted mom gave in and let Brian haul Josh over to his wife for the afternoon. Dad dug around in the moving van and placed my pink bike on the ground. They wrestled me into a helmet, and I was on my way.

Sweet freedom.

I pedaled along happily, soaking everything in. We lived in a beautiful neighborhood where all the houses looked happy and nice. I didn't even see the group of boys on their bikes until they were right in front of me. For some reason, I panicked and quit pedaling.

"Look!" one of the boys shouted. "New girl!" They were snickering, and my heart started pounding. The way they were looking at each other was really starting to freak me out, but I wasn't about to turn around because, then, they would start following me. I took a deep breath and began pedaling again, and the boys pushed forward too.

Suddenly, I was painfully aware of the fact that my bike still had training wheels, and all these boys were riding two wheelers. My dad had promised me that as soon as we got settled into the new house, he would teach me how to ride a two-wheeler. My face burned with embarrassment, and I stared at the ground as the boys rode past.

Out of nowhere, an arm flew out and shoved me hard, and I went sprawling onto the ground. I landed under someone's evergreen tree where sharp rocks and needles pierced my little hands. I was too stunned to cry and just sat there with my little pink bike, its wheels still spinning, pinning me to the ground.

"You okay?" a frantic voice called out. I looked into Tanner's deep blue eyes for the first time and sniffed. He jumped off his bike and ran over to where I sat and lifted my bike off my legs. He helped me up and said, "I'm Tanner. Sorry that Blake was mean to you. I don't know why I play with them sometimes. I would never do something like that. What's your name?"

"Molly," I answered timidly.

"Hi, Molly. Where's your mom?" Tanner didn't even know me, but he was instantly protective and wanted to take care of me.

I pointed to the moving van, and Tanner beamed with excitement. "That's right next door to me! We're neighbors!" He left his bike lying in the sidewalk and walked my bike home for me where I threw myself into my mother's legs and sobbed. Brian took me and Tanner to his house to play for the rest of the afternoon where I sat at Tanner's counter dunking Chips Ahoy cookies in milk while my parents and Tanner's dad continued moving boxes and unpacking. I cried when my dad came to bring me home, and Evelyn convinced my dad to let me spend the night. Both my parents were too exhausted to argue, so my first night in Oak Ridge was spent in Tanner's bed, my feet in his face and his in mine. It was the first of many sleepovers throughout the years.

We later discovered that our first-floor bedroom windows faced each other, and at night when I had nightmares or I got lonely, I snuck out of my window and snuggled up in Tanner's bed.

My mom panicked the first morning she found me gone from my bed. A call from Evelyn reassured my mom that I was safely eating waffles in her kitchen. My parents weren't keen on the idea of those sleepovers, so from then on, I always snuck back into my own bed before morning. It was our little secret, and I got a thrill every time I climbed out of my window and crept into Tanner's bed.

Tanner was my hero from the day he rescued me on. He stuck up for me all the time and never let any of the neighborhood boys beat up on me. We became best friends and were hardly ever apart. Our friendship had stood the test of middle school drama and survived the awkward night of junior prom. Twelve years later, we were still best friends.

With those fond memories still playing in my head, I slid into Tanner's car and breathed in the familiar musty scent that no amount of Febreeze could exterminate. "Starbucks?" I asked as Tanner backed out of my driveway.

"You bet," Tanner replied. "Can't end the tradition now, can we?"

"Nope. But what are we gonna do next year?" I whined. "It's a little sad that this is our last time doing this."

"Well, I'm sure they have coffee at Iowa State," he reassured me. "We'll just grab some before class. And I bet they even let us drink it in class. No more stuffy rules in college!" Tanner grinned at me and winked.

"Yeah, you're probably right." Tanner and I talked about the future as if we had it all figured out, as if we had a clue at all. Iowa State seemed like the perfect option for both of us. The small Christian town and school were beginning to close in on us; we couldn't wait for the opportunities and freedom of a big state school.

Ten minutes later, with mochas in hand, we entered Oak Ridge Christian High for our last first day of school. We were ready for the best year of school together.

Neither of us knew that in just a few short months, nothing would ever be the same for the two of us. But we relished this moment for all it was worth, and together, we walked into the start of the most difficult years either of us would ever know.

Two

September

"Ugh, I hate math! It needs to die!" I yelled as I threw my pencil across Tanner's kitchen table. We had been working on our calculus homework for well over an hour and weren't even halfway done yet. I get frustrated easily and just wanted to give up, but Tanner wouldn't let me. Both of us were struggling with this assignment, but Tanner was determined to figure it out. He smiled and said, "Come on, Moll. It's not that bad. We just gotta keep working on it. Looks like you have a good start on number fifteen. How did you get that answer?"

"I have no idea! I don't even know if it's right! And I couldn't care less at this point. I hate math!" I got up to go retrieve my pencil, which had scared Tanner's dog, Patches, half to death as it went whizzing past his little dog bed. I apologized to Patches and plopped myself down beside his furry little body and buried my face into him. I loved Patches, and secretly, Tanner and I both knew that Patches loved me more than him. He always freaked out when I came over, and when he had the choice of snuggling up beside Tanner or me, he always chose me. I was flattered by the undying love and devotion that Patches had for me.

"Can we please take a break?" I asked. "I honestly don't think I can handle another minute of this torture right now."

Tanner laughed. "You are such a drama queen sometimes! What should we do on this break from torture?" he asked teasingly.

I suggested that we go take a walk. September was winding down, and I knew that in probably just a few weeks we could have frost, or even snow. Tanner agreed and we grabbed our sweatshirts, hooked Patches up to his leash, and took off. We lived in a pretty developed area of town, but there was a little bike and running path just beyond the fences of our yards. It was our favorite place to go walking. During a rebellious streak that both of us hit when we were thirteen, we would sneak out at night and go walking this path together. The path was always scarier at night, but I felt safe with Tanner.

Tanner isn't a huge muscular guy, but I knew that if anybody tried to hurt me, Tanner would kill them. Once he hit fifteen, his arms started developing more muscle, and Tanner decided to start working out a little to build them up. He never talked about his weight lifting, but I could tell he was pleased at the way he was filling out. I'd noticed this summer at the lake the beginnings of a six-pack too. From the first day of school, I could tell that girls noticed this change in Tanner too. He had been turning heads all day, which, to my surprise, caused jealousy to well up in me. I was protective of Tanner, and I wanted all these girls to know that Tanner was *my* best friend. If they wanted him, they'd have to go through me first.

I had to agree with the girls at my school, though. Tanner was pretty good looking. Along with his newly toned arms and abdomen, he had the cutest head of tousled blond hair. His eyes were clear and deep blue, and his perfectly white and straight teeth were the product of two years in braces. His acne was starting to clear up, and he kept his face clear of any stubble. He was adorable, and I could understand why girls turned and stared as he walked by them at school, his attention fixed on me.

Tanner breathed in the fresh scent of fall in deep appreciation. Patches struggled at his leash trying to run but was almost choking himself in the process. We usually let him off the leash if it seemed like there weren't that many people out on the trail.

I relished the feeling of walking next to Tanner in the warm sunshine of fall. If our plans worked out, we would both be at Iowa State next year together, but I knew that everything would be different. We'd live in different halls and have different schedules, and there probably wasn't a cute little trail to go walking on together when things got crazy. I wanted our friendship to stay this way forever. I was feeling torn between emotions lately: I couldn't wait for the adventure of college, but I didn't want me and Tanner's relationship to change in any way, which I knew college would do.

"Patches, take it easy!" Tanner called out. "Stupid dog is gonna choke himself if he doesn't calm down."

"Let him run! We haven't seen a single person on the trail today." I always stuck up for Patches; it was my way of paying him back for his complete devotion to me. Tanner crouched down and unhooked Patches from his leash, and he took off like a shot and ran to the grass to sniff and mark his territory. He circled back every few minutes to make sure we were still following him. "It's okay, bud, we're still here!" I reassured. He trotted on in front of us until he saw the shirtless boy running up ahead on the trail.

The boy had an even more defined six-pack than Tanner had, and he was a good two inches taller than Tanner and had an amazing body, complete with a full head of dark wavy hair. He must have been running for a while because the sweat was pouring off his perfectly sculpted body. He ran with an easy gait, like it was completely effortless for him.

Patches ran straight toward the boy, who seemed to be so in the zone that he didn't see Patches until he was jumping up his leg. Pulling out his earbuds, he yelped in surprise.

"Patches, no! Stop!" I ran toward them and began pulling Patches away. "I am so, so sorry. He just gets so excited to meet new people. He's harmless, really."

Tanner was laughing behind me. I whipped around. "What? What's so funny? Patches just attacked him, and you're laughing?" I could feel my cheeks burning with embarrassment.

"I'm laughing because you're apologizing for my dog. Sorry, man. I shouldn't have let him off his leash. You okay?"

The boy nodded. "Yeah, no big deal. Just surprised me, is all. Cute dog." He knelt down to scratch Patches behind the ears. "Patches, right?"

"Yup," Tanner said. "Crazy little fur ball. I'm Tanner by the way, and this is Molly. You new to town? Haven't seen you around before, which for a town this size is strange."

"Yeah, actually I just moved in this weekend with my dad."

Wow, I thought. This boy sure was cute as he scratched the dog that had just attacked him. Patches was just soaking up the love of this adorable stranger.

Tanner stuck out his hand and said, "Well, welcome to Oak Ridge."

The boy chuckled. "Thanks. You know it's crazy how you two don't remember me. Jason Moore? We went to elementary school together, but I moved away at the end of fifth grade. I must have changed more than I thought!"

I snapped my fingers and jumped up and down. "No, I totally recognize you! You're definitely taller, that's for sure!" Gosh, he was cute.

He chuckled again. "Yeah, I guess I did grow a couple inches." More like a couple feet, really. "Well, it was nice seeing you guys again. I'm starting at the Christian school on Monday."

"We go there too! Oh, it'll be so great to have you there again!" I gushed.

"Yeah, definitely." Jason agreed. "I've heard it's a small campus, so I'll probably run into you guys again."

"Yup! Everyone knows everyone. It's great! See you Monday!" I waved as he jogged off.

I turned to face Tanner again and sighed in contentment. "Well, that was cool. I would hate to start at a new school during senior year."

Tanner was quiet.

"What's wrong?" I asked

Tanner shook his head. "That was just…weird, I guess. Seeing you flirt with a complete stranger."

"Hey!" I protested. "I was not flirting, I was being friendly! *And* we know him! Kind of."

Tanner's protectiveness was cute at times, but also a little annoying. We weren't a couple; I could flirt with a cute boy if I wanted to.

"Whatever you say, Miss Flirty." Tanner gave me a playful shove. "Don't you remember him at all? He was a jerk to us and teased us constantly. He would make kissy noises at us during recess all the time. You hated it!"

"Hmm. Yeah, I don't remember that at all. Besides, people grow up, Tanner. He's probably a nicer guy now."

I didn't want Tanner just deciding that he disliked Jason before he got the chance to really know him. I had been *boyfriendless* all my life because of three main reasons. First, in my small Christian school, most kids in my class had already paired off and would most likely be married within three years. All the cute, nice guys were snatched up. Secondly, the remaining boys were clearly not interested in relationships. They were either athletes focused on getting scholarships, obsessed with good grades, or crazy about video games. Not exactly the types of guys I was interested in. And last, but not least, Tanner. Tanner was so protective of me that when any guy paid me attention, he wanted to make sure their intentions were pure. He usually scared them off before anything got too serious. Usually, I was grateful for this because a lot of creepy guys from the public school took interest in me. He had saved me from rejecting guys on my own. But, for some reason, I thought that maybe Jason could change my single status, and this time, I wasn't about to let Tanner chase this guy off. I would make my own decision about this one.

"Sure, sure," Tanner said. "Maybe he's a changed man. We'll find out soon enough. Let's head back. Our calculus homework won't do itself. Break over."

I was on the lookout on Monday morning. Tanner and I walked in the building together and went our separate ways down different hallways. I had American government first period; Tanner had literature. We'd meet up second period and suffer through calculus together, shooting each other pained looks the entire class as the Mrs. Leeson lost us at the very beginning of the lecture. It was absolute torture, so I hoped and prayed that maybe Jason would be in my first period class and get my day off to a good start.

To my complete shock, I saw Jason sitting in the desk directly behind mine. I tried not to grin but couldn't help it. I thought back to Thursday afternoon when I had seen Jason shirtless.

I shook the image out of my head and went to my seat. "Hey, Jason!" I sang out. "How are you?"

I saw a few girls in my class send me curious, almost jealous looks. I basked in the delight of being the only one to know about our long-lost classmate. Jason smiled and said hey. We chatted for a bit before Mr. Johns came in and started class. What was once a boring government class suddenly became much more exciting.

At the end of class, Jason walked with me out to the hallway. "Anyone recognize you?" I asked him.

"A few guys," he answered. "But it's nice to kind of start over, you know? I'm excited to make new friends, reunite with some old ones. I'm meeting Matt and Tyler for lunch. We used to play football together during recess."

"Well, that's good. I'll see you around, Jason. Good luck with the rest of your day!" I didn't want to give my little crush away, so I kept our conversation short. He grinned and winked at me.

"See ya," he answered. My heart did a weird flutter as I walked away.

I didn't tell Tanner about my wonderful conversation with Jason because he would probably think it was less than wonderful. And so we suffered through calculus together just like every other day. He had a student council meeting over lunch though, which gave me a perfect opportunity to tell Kristina about my new crush on Jason.

Kristina's reaction was much more satisfying than Tanner's. She agreed that Jason was completely adorable but also remembered him being a little mean in elementary school. We chalked it up to the fact that he must have had a hard home life and that he was probably different now. "Just don't get too carried away now. You don't want to break Tanner's heart," she advised. I rolled my eyes. She was still convinced that Tanner was in love with me. I told her that nothing would probably happen.

"Guys as cute as Jason don't fall for girls like me," I told her.

"Whatever, girl," Kristina retorted. "You're totally gorgeous and nice. Jason would be lucky to have a girl like you."

I knew that was just a phrase that best friends were obligated to say. In the world of high school, guys like Jason really don't end up with girls like me; "nice girls" was the stereotype. Girls who went to church and Sunday school and who still felt naughty watching R-rated movies long after they turned seventeen. Guys like Jason wanted excitement, and I didn't feel that exciting.

I shrugged. "We'll see."

The bell rang, signaling the end of lunch. At the end of the day, I walked out of the building with Tanner and climbed into his little car, exhausted from another Monday. But instead of dreading the rest of the week like I usually did on Mondays, I looked forward to seeing Jason's dimpled face in government tomorrow.

Three

As the days passed, I grew more and more discouraged as Jason's popularity grew. I should have seen this coming. He was cute, charming, and easy to get along with. He gained friends easily and seemed to have a new girl on his arm every week. I gave up hope that he would change my single status and tried to forget about him. Not an easy task in my small Christian school where I saw him multiple times a day every single day.

I never told Tanner about my little crush, but he was smarter than I gave him credit for. He knew I was smitten but never said anything when I sighed as Jason passed us by with girls hanging all over him. He could have teased me and lectured me about my poor choice of a crush. But he never did. Tanner was bigger than that.

The flu hit our school hard that fall, and Tanner came down with the worst fever I ever remember him having. He missed a full week of school, and I hated suffering through calculus without my best friend and ally. Whenever I was sick and missed school, Tanner would go to the store after school and pick me up a bottle of Gatorade and some saltine crackers. Of course, I had to do the same for him, so I headed to the store after school the first day he stayed home.

I wandered the aisles and picked out his favorite flavor of Gatorade and a box of crackers. I also picked up a package of Swedish Fish, his favorite candy. Our little grocery store was surprisingly busy for a Tuesday afternoon, so I scanned the checkout lanes and headed for the shortest one I could find—didn't want to keep Tanner waiting. I unloaded my arms on the belt and then found myself looking straight into Jason's eyes, causing my heartbeat to quicken. He was wearing a blue polo and a green apron, standard uniform at our local grocery store. These outfits were ridiculous, but Jason somehow made it look good. It was funny how every time I saw Jason all I could think was *Gosh he's cute.*

"Well, look who it is! How are you, Molly?" Jason looked genuinely pleased to see me, which instantly made my day.

"I'm good. I had no clue you worked here. What a surprise." *What a stupid thing to say,* I thought.

"Yes, well, I'm full of surprises," Jason answered with a shrug. His smile was making my stomach do strange little flips.

"I guess."

He began scanning my groceries, and for some reason, I felt compelled to explain why I was buying these items. Why did I lose the ability to think clearly around Jason? I always ended up sounding ridiculous.

"Tanner's home sick today. Must have caught whatever's flying around school. So I'm picking him up this stuff." I tried not to make this sound awkward, but that was hard for me. I'm naturally an awkward person. It runs in my family.

Jason smiled and said, "You're such a nice girlfriend."

"Oh no!" I said quickly. "Tanner and I, we're not dating. At all."

Jason cocked his head to one side and looked confused. "Oh. I guess I just assumed. You guys are always together—"

"No, we're just good friends. Really good friends. But I'm happily single. Well, not happily, I'd love a boyfriend." *Did I just say that?* I really wished I hadn't said that; I sounded terribly desperate.

Jason laughed. "Well, you're a very nice friend, then. Sorry."

"It's fine. We get that a lot, actually. People always think we're dating. But nope, both of us are very single."

A slow smile spread across Jason's face. "I'll remember that, Molly. And your total is five dollars and seventy-four cents."

I swiped my card, and as Jason handed me the receipt, his fingers barely brushed up against mine, which sent chills up my spine. I thanked him, grabbed my grocery sack, and turned to leave.

"See you around, Molly," Jason yelled as I walked to the door.

I pretended not to hear, resisting the urge to turn around and say good-bye again. I wanted to play it cool as best as I knew how. So I just kept walking, a ridiculous smile plastered across my face, and my heart pounding.

Just as Tanner has always done for me, I continued visiting him after school the entire week he was sick to fill him in on the drama and chaos he was missing out on. I whined about how awful calculus was without him there. I told him which couples had broken up and how some sophomore girl fell down an entire flight of stairs and broke her nose. He laughed at my stories while he drank his Gatorade and ate his Swedish Fish, thoroughly enjoying our time together—it was tough for both of us to be without the other for this long. I bought him a new flavor of Gatorade every day, and I always went through Jason's line at the store. Jason commented on the fact that I had a new flavor each time I came in, and I wanted him to know that if we were dating, I would do this same thing for him as well. Of course, I never told him this, but I wanted him to know. I bet none of the girls who hung around him would do the same thing. I hoped he could see how sweet and caring I was.

When Tanner would fall asleep, I'd sneak out and quietly shut the door. Evelyn would thank me for stopping over, and Tanner's little sister, Ellen, would run and give me a long hug before I was allowed to leave. She was twelve and absolutely idolized me. I tousled her hair and told her I'd see her later. She grinned up at me and said she loved me.

Tanner's family was more of a family to me than my own. Things were strained at my house much of the time. Both my parents were strong Christians and would never think of getting divorced, but I could see that the spark was gone from my parent's marriage. They tolerated each other, at best, and tried their hardest to hide it from us—which they failed miserably at. Their anniversary passed by unacknowledged year after year, and we could hear their muffled arguments at night from our bedrooms. Savannah used to climb into my bed and sleep with me because their fighting bothered her so much. Mom and dad never mentioned their fighting in the morning, but we all felt the tension in the air.

Mom started picking up extra shifts at work to escape her loveless marriage. Sometimes, when I was up late at night looking for a midnight snack, I could hear my dad's snores coming from the guest bedroom. I started creeping past that room every night to see if he slept there often, and to my dismay, he was there each night.

Tanner's house was my refuge. I ate dinner there at least once a week, sometimes twice if it was a particularly rough week with my parents. Their house was filled with love and laughter. His parents kissed in front of us all the time, which made me a little uncomfortable and extremely jealous at the same time. Ellen adored Tanner, and Tanner made sure she felt loved and wanted. We played board games and watched countless Disney movies with her. She could quote more movie lines than anyone I knew.

"Don't ever take your family for granted, Tanner. What you have is special. I wish my family was like this," I told him often.

"I promise," he would always answer. He listened to me talk about my parent's fights and how I worried about Josh and Savannah being scared to love. He never complained about my venting sessions, which were often, but always listened. He seldom gave advice, which I appreciated because he had no clue about what I was going through. We prayed together, and he let me cry out my feelings. When I thought I couldn't handle it anymore, Tanner was there to pick me up and help me through it.

With Tanner sick this week, I was stuck at home. So I logged into Facebook to ease my boredom, and to block out the petty argument my parents were having this week, and saw that I had a friend request. My heart about jumped out of my chest when I saw that it was from Jason. I quickly hit "accept" and began to investigate his profile. Facebook is a great way to get to know people; you can pretty much stalk people without them ever finding out. I was a huge Facebook stalker, so I hated when people put only a little bit of information about themselves on their pages, it made them seem so boring.

I was delighted to see that Jason's page was filled with information about himself. I spent the next half-hour looking through all his photo albums and every single picture he was tagged in. I memorized his favorite TV shows, movies, hobbies, and styles of music. Under his "About Me" section, it simply read "I'm learning how to maneuver through this thing called life. If you want to be a part of mine, just let me know."

I totally wanted to be a part of his life.

Four

Early October

Tanner was back in school the next week, and things fell back into their normal, comfortable rhythm. It was nice having a friend to suffer through calculus with again, which was kicking my butt at the moment. I struggled to understand why I needed to learn all these formulas and rules. *When would I ever use this in real life?* I wondered. We quit asking our teacher this question though because she usually went off on a tangent and class would drag on longer than usual.

I did have a pleasant surprise in government, however. Our latest assignment was to come up with mock bills and debate them in class. We would be approving or rejecting our class-mate's bills, which sounded pretty cool, actually. Our teacher was encouraging us to fight with each other! It was a partner project, and everyone paired off almost immediately.

I panic when teachers tell us to pair off. If I'm not in a class with Kristina or Tanner I usually get stuck with someone I'd rather not work with. Plus, the old feelings of rejection and embarrassment of not being picked would well up inside me—too many years of being picked last for kickball and dodgeball. Luckily for me, Jason asked if I wanted to work with him.

I turned around in my chair, smiled, and quickly accepted. We had two weeks to work on this project in class, which meant that I would have fifty minutes of uninterrupted time with Jason every day for two weeks! I was elated.

We spent the remainder of the class period throwing around ideas for our bill. We wanted to be original and funny but serious about the assignment at the same time. Mr. Johns was a pretty easygoing guy; if you could make him laugh and get on his good side, you were golden in this class. We didn't come up with a good enough idea in the short time we had left, but I couldn't have cared less. I was just enjoying my time with Jason, and I knew we'd think of something eventually.

After three wasted class periods trying to think of unique ideas, we gave up. We spent most of the class laughing at the other's ridiculous ideas, and Mr. Johns told us we needed to get serious about the assignment. We settled on a bill that required elderly people to retake their driver's test.

"You know, this really isn't a bad idea," Jason said as he looked at me with those adorable blue eyes. "Old people on the roads are a danger to society. They can't see as well, they drive ten under all the time, and they never know when it's their turn at a four-way stop. So frustrating."

I giggled. "Yeah. Plus, they shrink and can't see over the wheel anymore."

Jason laughed. "What? They shrink?"

"Yes! My grandma is seriously shrinking. She looks a little shorter every time I see her," I replied.

"You are so full of it, Molly. Maybe you're just getting taller." He grinned at me—getting teased by Jason was so much fun, and I was beginning to feel much less self-conscious about what I said around him. Instead of playing it safe, I let my guard down and teased him too, wanting our fun banter to keep going.

"No, I swear!" I protested. "I haven't grown in years! She's shrinking!"

Mr. Johns glanced over at us again and shushed us, which made me giggle even harder.

"Well, I'm not sure we can use that argument in our debate because I think you're just making it up. But our other points are excellent."

I shook my head and pretended to be sad. "Meanie head."

"You'll thank me when we get one hundred percent on this assignment. Just you wait, Molly girl. Just you wait and see." My heart jumped when he called me Molly girl. Using nicknames was a sign that he might be thinking about me as more than just a friend. You don't give out a nickname to just anyone! I tried not to outwardly show how much I was freaking out on the inside. I still wasn't ready for him to know about my crush on him.

Our presentation went smoothly, although it lacked that humorous twist that we had originally wanted. I was getting discouraged by the glazed over looks of my classmates, but then, Jason started wrapping up our proposal. "So in conclusion, ladies and gents, the elderly are a threat to the overall well-being to all who travel on our Iowan roads. They don't see as well as younger drivers, tend to drive slower, drive everyone crazy, and never know when it's their turn at four-way stops. Plus, they're shrinking and probably can't see over the wheel as good anymore."

I tried to hold my laugher in but failed miserably. My classmates and Mr. Johns just stared at me as my loud guffaws echoed in the room, but Jason was grinning. I loved that we had an inside joke all our own to laugh at.

"Thank you, Molly and Jason, for your…wonderful proposal. Shall we debate?" Mr. Johns asked.

The class passed our bill with little debate. No one was quite getting into this assignment, which was disappointing. I didn't really care that much, though, because I had gotten to spend so much time with Jason.

We got our grades the next day, and we ended up getting a 95 percent on the assignment. "You're just a bunch of talk, Jason," I teased, waving the paper in front of his face. "You were sure we got hundred percent. Not quite!" I poked him on the shoulder and continued waving the grade in front of his face.

"Hmm. Must have been because I added your argument onto the end. I thought we did a pretty solid job until I said that," Jason retorted.

"Oh. I see how it is. But I never told you to say that. So, really, it's your fault."

He threw up his hands in defeat. "Okay, okay. Fair enough. I did promise us a hundred on this assignment." He rubbed his chin, which I noticed was sporting just the right about of stubble, and took a few seconds to think of an appropriate way to make this up to me. "How 'bout I take you out tonight? Would that make it better?"

Was I hearing this right? Did Jason seriously just ask me out? I was sure he could see my heart pounding underneath my shirt. But I smiled and tried to play it cool. This was definitely an appropriate way to make it up to me!

"Yeah. I think that would more than make up for those five percentage points." I was shaking, so I clenched my fists together to keep him from noticing. Why did he have so much power over me?

Jason smiled. "Cool. How about I pick you up at six thirty? We could go to that little diner—I think it's called Emma's? I loved going there when I was little."

"Yeah, that sounds great." I took out a pen and scribbled down my phone number and house address. "Just text me if you get lost. It's pretty easy to find though."

"Cool. Yeah, I should be able to find this. Six thirty?" he asked again, his blue eyes sparkling at me.

"Yeah. Sounds great."

When class officially started, I tried my hardest to pay attention, but it wasn't working. All I could think about is what I would wear and how I would do my hair. Emma's was a pretty casual place, so I couldn't get all dressed up to impress Jason. I'd probably just go with a dark wash pair of jeans, my favorite navy blouse that made my eyes look great, and some ballet flats. I'd wear my hair down, maybe pin a little bit back. I would take it easy with the makeup—I didn't want to look desperate.

Class finally ended, and we parted in the hallway with Jason saying, "Can't wait for tonight. See you at six thirty."

Suddenly, I was being jerked into the library. Tanner must have gotten out of class a little early and heard me talking with Jason.

"Want to explain to me what's going on, Molly?" Tanner demanded.

"Wow, take a chill pill, Tanner," I said, trying to fix my shirt that Tanner had crumpled with his uncalled for yank. "Jason and I are going out tonight." I looked up at him defiantly, hating that he was so much taller than me. He was really starting to annoy me with his overprotectiveness, but I would stand my ground this time. There was nothing wrong with me going out with Jason.

"Are you serious, Moll? I thought this was just a little crush that you'd get over when you saw what a jerk he is." Tanner's face was beginning to turn red, and I hated the way he made me feel like a silly thirteen-year-old with a crush.

I jerked my arm free from his tightening grasp and pulled my backpack over my shoulder. "It's not a big deal! We're just going out to Emma's for dinner." I didn't even try to explain to him that Jason wanted to make up for our lower grade because Tanner wouldn't buy it. Deep down I knew that it was just a clever, easy way for Jason to ask me out, but who cared? He had asked me out, that was all that mattered. "It'll probably be the only time we ever hang out, so relax."

He huffed and rubbed his neck. "Sorry. I know you hate it when I get like this. I just don't want to see you get hurt, Moll."

I softened. "I know, and it's very sweet of you. But...you can't always protect me. Yeah, I might get hurt, but I might not. You never know unless you take a chance, right?"

Tanner winced a little. "What happened to the girl who thought dating was a serious deal? The girl who declared she wouldn't date just anyone, who wanted to wait for a boyfriend until she was ready to get married to him?"

I sighed. He was right; I had told him all that. But that was only because I never thought anyone would ask me out in high school. I was tired of watching my friends pair off while I got left behind time and time again. So out of frustration I had vented to Tanner and told him that I was going to be smarter than those girls and wait for my prince to come around.

But it wasn't like I was "in a relationship" with Jason. Just because we were going out to dinner did not mean we were dating or even a couple.

"Tanner. It's just dinner! We're not dating, he's not my boyfriend. He just wants to treat me to dinner. So, please, relax. You're making me want to punch you in the face."

That got him. He cracked his signature smile and huffed again. "Okay, okay. Just dinner. Got it."

We headed off to calculus, which after my amazing morning felt a lot less like torture. My whole mood had changed, thanks to Jason. At lunch, I gushed to Kristina about my dinner plans.

"Get out!" she bubbled. "Gosh, you are so lucky. What are you going to wear? Want me to come over and help you get ready?"

I laughed. "Yeah, that would be great. I don't want to overdo it, you know? We're just going to Emma's."

"Hmmm. True. Well, we'll see what we can do. Gosh, I can't believe it! So exciting."

Kristina come over that night, as promised, to help me get ready for my first ever date. "You look cute! Perfect for a dinner date," she said as she put the finishing touches on my hair. We decided to curl it just a little and pin my bangs out of my face.

I've never really thought of myself as a pretty girl. I'm only five foot three inches with feet too big for my body, which causes me to trip a lot, most of the time on flat surfaces. It takes great skill to do that, but I'm the master. My eyes are big and brown, and although I would prefer blue eyes, I think my eyes are my best feature. Tanner tells me that my eyes dance when I laugh, which must look cute. I hoped Jason thought so.

My long brown hair fails to cooperate with me most of the time, so I end up throwing my hair into a ponytail on most mornings. It's just too much of a hassle to straighten it or curl it, and it takes way too much time. I like my beauty sleep way more than I like my hair looking good for school. And at the end of the day, no one remembers what my hair looks like anyway.

Tonight was different though. Tonight, it mattered what my hair looked like, because Jason and I might look back on this night, our first date, and he might remember how my hair had curled just right and how pretty I looked in the dimmed lighting at Emma's. We would smile and laugh, remembering the slight awkwardness of our first date. But this was only if we actually started dating.

I wondered what that would do to my plans for next year. I had no idea what Jason wanted to do after graduation. Tanner would be heartbroken if I decided not to go to Iowa State with him, but what if Jason and I *did* become serious? What if Jason wanted to go to a different school? Would I be prepared for a long-distance relationship, or would I want to follow him to the school he would go to?

I shook those thoughts out of my head. This was just a casual dinner date after all!

Kristina wished me luck and took off. I still had a good twenty minutes to kill before Jason would show up. I hated waiting around, especially since I was already dressed, makeup on, and hair done. I felt like I couldn't move because I didn't want to mess anything up.

Tanner suddenly appeared at his bedroom window and motioned for me to slide mine up so we could chat. I rolled my eyes because Tanner still wasn't thrilled with the whole dinner date thing. It was almost amusing because Tanner was more worried about it than my own parents.

I had stopped by my dad's office after school to let him know I wouldn't be home for supper because I had a date. He raised his eyebrows a bit and asked who was taking me out. I told him all about Jason and how this was just a casual, nothing serious kind of deal. All he said was, "Well, you're eighteen now so you get to make your own choices. Just be careful. And have fun."

My mom would be working late tonight, but I would try to tell her about the date the next day if I got the chance. We didn't always have the time to chat and spend time together, which bothered me. I saw other girls out shopping or eating with their moms, chatting away as if they were best friends. I wished me and my mom were closer, but both of us were so busy and never seemed to put forth the effort to change that.

I opened my window and leaned out. "What's up, Tanner?"

"Nothing." He looked embarrassed and extremely awkward.

I couldn't help smiling. He was so worried about this. "Tanner, it's fine. I'll be careful, and if I find out he's a jerk, I'll forget all about him and you can say 'I told you so.'"

He laughed. "I don't get to say that very often. And I really hope I don't have to. Because seriously, if I find out he was a jerk to you, he's got it coming." He smacked a fist into his hand a few times and winked at me.

"Good to know. Glad you have my back." And I really was. Not everyone had someone like Tanner in their lives, someone who worried about them and would be willing to beat up someone way stronger and capable of kicking their butt.

Tanner softened a little. "Never forget that, Molly. I always have your back."

My heart melted a little bit. Tanner was so good to me. "I'll remember."

Later on, Tanner would tell me he regretted letting me go out with Jason. Something about this whole deal made his stomach tighten in fear. He regretted not telling me earlier that he loved me, not just a best friend kind of love, but a real, honest to goodness love. He didn't want me going out with Jason because he wanted more than friendship with me, but I was too blind to see how he really felt, plus I was too scared for a potential breakup that would ruin our lifelong friendship. Staying friends felt safer; I couldn't risk losing Tanner's friendship.

Instead, Tanner told me to be careful for the millionth time and to enjoy dinner. When Jason's car pulled up into the driveway, he closed his window and waved good-bye.

Jason came to the door, and I introduced him to my dad. They shook hands, and then, we all stood awkwardly in the living room, the ticking of the clock bouncing off the walls. He looked so handsome tonight in his blue-and-white-striped collared shirt. A brown pullover sweater completed the look, which looked totally casual with a nice pair of jeans.

I noticed also that he had shaved and the smell of his aftershave was tickling my nose. It was spicy and intoxicating, a smell I would never forget. I think it's so funny how smells stay with you forever. One smell can bring back so many memories. I wanted to capture this smell and remember the thrill of my first date and how amazing and exciting this was for me.

"Well," Jason turned to me and said in an attempt to break the awkwardness, "shall we go?"

I agreed, and we set off. Jason's car was much nicer than Tanner's, and I was instantly curious about what his dad did because he must have money. Not too many teenagers drive cars this nice. I'm terrible with car stuff, so I had no idea what kind of car it was. All I knew was that it was black and shiny and had leather seats. It smelled fresh and was surprisingly clean for a teenager's car.

I had thought this ride might be slightly awkward because the only time we ever talked was in government class. But Jason was as smooth as ever and kept the flow of conversation steady the entire drive. Some people are just born with the ability to talk, and Jason was definitely one of them, which I really appreciated. When I get nervous, it's really obvious because my voice quavers. But without the stress of trying to make small talk, I was able to make myself seem a lot less awkward than I really am.

Jason continued to impress as he opened the diner door for me and took my coat to hang up. I've heard countless girls complain that boys are rude and inconsiderate, but Jason seemed to be proving them wrong. The world still had good guys to offer! Our waitress showed us to a booth and left us with our menus. This was the easiest part of the night because, once again, I didn't have to worry about making small talk because I was busy looking the menu over. I didn't want to order something too expensive, even though Jason told me to order whatever I wanted. The service at Emma's has always been amazing, we had our drinks in no time, and our food came shortly after.

I was probably overthinking this whole dinner date, but I was really trying to impress Jason. I tried to wrack my brain for every piece of dating advice I had ever read in Kristina's ridiculous teen magazines. According to them, I could either play it cool by letting him steer the conversation, or I could take a risk and start asking questions. I really didn't know anything about Jason's life, and I was curious. I decided to take the risk and just ask him about himself.

I leaned forward, my clasped hands resting under my chin, "So, Jason, what's your story? I don't know anything about you." Immediately, when I said this, I wondered if I was being too forward.

He shook his head and smiled a little. "Well, I could say the same for you," he said.

I smiled, knowing he was trying to avoid telling me anything, so I kept my story short and sweet. "Not much to tell. I moved here when I was five, and I've lived here ever since. My dad works at an insurance company, and my mom is a receptionist at Uptown Dental and works three times a week at a late-night daycare center. I have one little brother, Josh, and one little sister, Savannah. Uh…let's see, what else…I'm thinking about going to Iowa State next year, but I don't know what I want to major in yet. And that about covers it. Pretty boring."

"No, it's your life. It's not boring." He took a sip of his drink and asked me how my meal had been.

"It was good." Once again, I was faced with playing it safe or taking a risk and pressing him to tell me about himself. I figured that if he never opened up to me, I could no longer even consider having any more of a relationship with him. He seemed great, but in the back of my head, I kept thinking about Tanner and his worries that Jason was a bad guy. Even though I didn't believe him, I wasn't going to be naive about this, so I wanted to know more about Jason's life.

"So… I told you about my life, let's hear about you now." I raised my eyebrows expectantly and swirled my straw around in my glass, trying to play it cool again. He sighed again but gave in.

"Well, my dad got a job in New Jersey when I was in second grade. He's a computer specialist, and this huge company hired him. I don't even remember what it was called. All I know is that the pay was amazing, and for the first time ever, my parents had plenty of money, and we were really happy. We moved into this amazing house in the rich part of town, and because my dad had money, people wanted to be my friend."

I smirked a little because it was happening again here. People knew he had money. Pair that with his good looks and amazing personality, and Jason was instantly popular.

"What?" he asked with a laugh in his voice.

"Nothing. So you were in the popular group at your old school?"

"Yeah, I got into a pretty rough crowd of kids who didn't really care about me at all. You know, parties every Friday and Saturday night, hangover Sunday. But I got tired of that and was actually glad when my dad decided to move back. It's just nice to start over, you know?"

I nodded. "Yeah, definitely. So your family moved back here because of your dad's job again or what?"

"No. It's actually a long and horrible story."

"Well, you don't have to tell me. It's really none of my business." I really didn't want to seem like I was prying. I wanted Jason to trust me to and feel comfortable.

"No, it's okay. Uh, well, I was out of town one weekend for a basketball tournament, and my dad decided to come up and watch. But he got caught in a freak blizzard and didn't want to chance it, so he turned around and went home. He tried to reach my mom on her cell to let her know he was okay and that he was coming back home, but her phone was off. He started to worry because she always has her phone with her. Anyway, he pulls in at about nine thirty and all the lights are off in the house, and there's a car parked in the driveway."

Jason stopped here and looked out the window. I could tell that this was a hard story for him to tell. I didn't know what to say, so I just nodded. I wanted to reach out and grab his hand, but I chickened out. He took a deep breath and continued on.

"My dad walks in and sees the table all set up for two, food all left out, candles still burning. Long story short, my dad caught my mom in the middle of a pretty steamy affair. She packed that night and left. Anyway, word eventually got out, and my dad's reputation was ruined. My mom did a lot of lying and scheming, and somehow, my dad became the bad guy. You know how shallow people can be—people that had been friends with us forever turned on my dad and rallied around my mom. We tried to stick it out there so I could finish my senior year with my team, but life in Jersey became a living hell, so my dad and I decided to come back here."

And cue the awkward silence. What do you say after a story like that? I couldn't relate at all. "I'm so sorry, Jason. I shouldn't have pried."

"No, actually it feels good to get that out. You're the first person I've told. We're working through it, mostly just trying to put it behind us and move on. I can't trust her anymore, and our relationship is nonexistent, which sucks. She's gonna miss out on so much in my life, but she doesn't seem to care. But her new little bundle of joy is due in a few weeks. A boy."

"Gosh, Jason, that's rough."

"Yeah, just feels like she's replacing me. But what can you do? Just gotta keep moving on."

Jason's story pretty much sealed the deal for me. I totally fell for the whole "I'm just a poor little wounded boy" scenario. I wanted to ease his pain, to show him that the world had so much more to offer than cheating, scheming mothers. I wanted to hold his hand and make him laugh.

And this is how I got caught in Jason's trap. Of course, at the time it didn't feel like a trap because that night felt so magical and surreal. My first real date! It was like a dream come true. How was I to know it was actually the beginning of a nightmare that would be almost impossible to wake up from?

Five

Tanner

October

Something didn't feel right about this whole situation. The minute I closed my window after talking to Molly, my stomach tied up in knots, and I felt like sliding the window back up, crawling into her room, and begging her not to go out with Jason.

She had tried to tell me that this dinner thing wasn't a big deal, but Molly was forgetting that I knew her better than anyone else in the entire world. I knew that when she was excited about something, she had a certain look in her eye. Almost like an excited five-year-old whose mom just put a giant ice cream sundae in front of her, but told her she had to wait to eat it. She had the same look of anticipation and excitement that I imagine that five-year-old would have. Molly couldn't hide her excitement over this date with Jason from me, no matter how cool she played it. She was ecstatic.

Maybe I was jealous. Once Jason came into the picture, she had taken this strange interest in him. *Fascination* was a better word though. Never before had a boy taken her interest in this way. Never before had a boy taken her focus off me before. Maybe that's why it was bothering me.

But there had to be more. I could work through jealousy. I could get over the fact that Molly didn't feel the same way I felt about her because, in time, she might. I was still clinging to the hope that she'd wake up one day and realize that no one in the world would love her the way I loved her. No one else could understand her the way I did, be able to read her every thought and emotion. No one was better for Molly than me.

But I couldn't work through this nagging feeling. It gnawed away at me day and night. Whenever I saw Molly smiling and talking with Jason, I'd first feel the jealousy. And then, I'd feel the other feeling. Because while Molly was being charmed and swept away, I saw the look in Jason's eyes that she couldn't see. I saw how he looked at her not as a person, but as a project. I knew guys like Jason wanted something more than just the kind of relationship Molly wanted. They wanted so much more than I hoped Molly was willing to give.

It was like in the movies when you're watching it and you know something bad is about to happen. The music gets scary, the lighting gets dark, and you can feel the tension thick in the air. You know the character is about to walk into trouble; it's just a matter of time before the whole mood of the movie changes. That's how I felt about Jason. There was no scary music or dark lighting of course, but I felt that same tension. I had this horrible feeling that Molly was about to walk into trouble. Maybe it wouldn't change our lives, but it would cause damage, and I didn't want my Molly getting hurt.

It had surprised me that Molly couldn't remember Jason. We both hadn't recognized him that day Patches attacked him while he was running, but later I pulled out our old class pictures and found his face, which brought all the awful memories flooding back. Meanwhile, Molly was too busy checking out his six-pack to remember how mean he had been to us.

After Molly moved next door to me that summer, we'd been inseparable. We'd figured out that our first floor bedroom windows faced each other, close enough that late at night, we could open them and talk and laugh in the cold night air. When we got tired of kneeling at our windows, Molly would usually creep out of her window and camp out in my bedroom. Sometimes, she'd fall asleep, and we'd have to sneak her back into her own room in the morning so Molly's mom wouldn't find out. She'd sort of freaked out the first morning she found Molly missing from her bed. So we shared this little secret between us, careful never to let her mom find out again.

When you have that deep of a bond with someone, people notice. Kids used to tease us, wondering if we were "boyfriend and girlfriend." No one really meant it, except for Jason. Usually, kids would tease all in good fun, and Molly and I didn't care. But Molly cared when Jason teased us. She'd get so worked up when he wouldn't leave us alone at recess; she cried. She'd been so relieved when he moved away one school year. How come she couldn't remember that boy?

It was unrealistic for me to expect Molly not to have crushes on people, and I always had a little jealousy when she and Kristina talked about which boys they thought were cute. But by the way Molly had always talked about dating, how she wanted to wait and be smart about it, I didn't think she'd be wasting her time on a guy like Jason.

Molly and I had talked about dating a lot over the years. We both agreed that there was nothing wrong with dating; you had to find out what you did and didn't like in a person. We thought too many Christians just condemned dating, saying it was better to focus on your relationship with God and wait for him to bring the right person into your life. Like there was only one person out there for you, and you either had to wait for them to waltz into your life or go out and find them in the midst of all the people in the world.

We didn't buy that. Of course, God knew the person you would end up with, but we didn't believe God was holding that one person out there in the world and expecting us to somehow end up with them. So we didn't have a problem with the idea of dating, but we'd simply never came across people we wanted to give our precious time to.

I guess Molly thought Jason was deserving of her precious time though, which I thought was ridiculous. Sure, we had no problem with dating, but we had a problem with dating the wrong people, people who would weigh our lives down and leave us with baggage. Jason seemed like the type of person to leave Molly with a ton of baggage, and I struggled watching her just inviting that into her life. To me, this was a stupid move, and it was frustrating that Molly couldn't see that.

But if I ever wanted a chance with Molly, I knew I couldn't push my opinions on her. She seemed to really be enjoying Jason's attention, and I guess, this was normal. No one had ever really shown her this much attention before. It probably felt really nice to like someone and have them like you back. Who wouldn't want that? *I* wanted it with her, after all.

So for the time being, I would sit back and watch. I would let her make her own decisions, even if I didn't agree with them. I had to believe that if Molly did find out that Jason was a bad guy, she'd get out. And who knows? Maybe the date would be a flop, and Molly would shrug her shoulders and return to her normal self, giving up on the idea of Jason altogether.

I clung to that hope all night, up until the time I saw Jason's headlights flash into my room. I flipped off all the lights so Molly wouldn't see me and peeked out the window. I saw Jason's car in Molly's driveway, dropping her off from their date.

My heart was pounding as I waited to see what Jason would do. Would he lean in and kiss her? I would be furious. Molly always talked about how special her first kiss was to her, and I didn't want it to be with Jason. He didn't deserve Molly's first kiss, especially not after just one date.

He got out of his car and opened Molly's door for her, his hand on the small of her back as he led her up the driveway to the door. They lingered on the front step for a few moments, chatting and laughing. Darn. It looked like they'd had a pretty good time on their date. Molly wouldn't come back talking about how the date was a flop and how she was over her fascination with him. To me, it looked like the start of a long, exhausting journey that would end with a horrible, awkward breakup. Great.

Instead of leaning in to kiss her good night though, he lifted her hand to his lips and gently kissed it. *Well played*, I thought. Now, Molly would never give him up.

She was falling right into his little trap.

Six

Molly

October

The night of my first date, I just laid in my bed thinking about Jason. The rest of the date went fine; it ended on a light note when he spilled his milkshake all over the floor as we were leaving. It got us laughing, and it broke the heaviness that the story of his mom's affair had cloaked over the night. He dropped me off, and I was even more convinced that he was a perfect gentleman when he didn't lean in to kiss me, instead, lightly kissing my hand. I kept stroking the spot his lips had touched my skin, remembering the shiver that had tickled my spine because of it.

As we walked to my door, I noticed that Tanner's light was off in his bedroom. If he'd wanted to talk to me about the date, he would have left the lights on and curtains open—that was our signal. I really appreciated that he was letting me have this night. His overprotectiveness would have spoiled my mood.

Jason seemed to have really enjoyed the night, which made me beyond excited. I loved that I was the only person he trusted with his mom's story. That must be a good sign; it meant that he thought I was different than the other girls he'd been hanging around lately. I may not have the bodies, complexions, and hair that those other girls had, but I definitely had trust on my side. To me, that seemed more important. Maybe I could be Jason's first real and honest relationship! Wouldn't that be a great story to retell someday?

After that night, Jason took things nice and slow. He texted me later that night to tell me that he'd had a really great time and to say good night. I was still trying to figure out how to not come on really strong, and I didn't want to sound desperate, so I just told him I had fun too and that I'd see him Monday. I was bored on Saturday night, so I was wasting time on Facebook, and Jason and I ended up chatting until late that night. I was sleepy in church the next day, and Tanner noticed.

He poked me during the sermon. "Why're you so tired today?"

I shrugged. "Facebook chat," I said through a yawn.

I could tell that Tanner wasn't happy about this at all by his dramatic eye roll. I'd have to fill him in later about my date and Jason's story. Jason wasn't a bad guy, he was just hurting. People tried to fill themselves with the wrong stuff when they were hurting. Maybe I could change that in him, help him to see a better side of life. Tanner would understand; he was a pretty sensitive guy.

Tanner was just looking at me with a blank look in his face. He was not taking this news well, and I was beginning to feel awkward.

"So he wants you to be his girlfriend?" It wasn't a question really, just a flat statement. Now he wouldn't even look at me. I tried explaining to him that he had it all wrong, that Jason hadn't really asked me to be his girlfriend, but that he wanted to hang out more and see what happened.

"You should be happy that Jason is taking it slowly, Tanner," I said. "You think he's this horrible guy who only wants to take advantage of me, but you're wrong! You've never spent any time with him. He's been nothing but nice to me. A gentlemen." I could feel my face heating up in anger.

Tanner snorted and shook his head. "Just because someone kisses your hand and opens doors for you doesn't make him a gentleman, Molly."

This made me even madder because it meant Tanner had been spying on me when I came back from Emma's with Jason. He must have been hiding out somewhere. I hated how Tanner was turning something I felt was magical into something that made me feel silly. When Jason had kissed my hand, it sent shivers down my spine, and now, Tanner was ruining it for me. I was so sick of this; Tanner was destroying our friendship because of his stupid jealousy.

"Come on, Molly. You always told me you were saving yourself for a good guy, someone who had been saving himself for you too! How many girls do you think Jason has been with? Huh? You deserve someone better! Any guy can open a door and kiss you on the hand. You deserve someone who can't live without you. Someone who thinks you are the world and who will cherish you forever."

Neither of us said anything, but I felt the weight of Tanner's lasts words, how "someone like me" was just hanging at the end of those thoughts. I waited for him to say it, to actually tell me that he loved me like everyone else said he did.

But he didn't. He just stood up and mumbled "I'll see ya later" and left. I sat there in stunned silence for a bit. Did he want to say it? Did he think that he was the person that I should be waiting for? Did he actually believe that he was better than Jason? Did he think I was the world to him?

I shook my head and tried to clear these confusing thoughts from my head. If Tanner thought all this about me and him, why wasn't he telling me? He kept saying that Jason wasn't a real man, that he would never treat me the way I deserved to be treated. But if Tanner thought he was more of a man, he should step up and tell me how he felt. He was no more of a man than Jason was if he couldn't do that simple thing.

I stood up quickly, stalked out of the little prayer room where we had been talking, and went out to find him. He was scanning through his phone by the coat racks. I yanked him around the corner and looked him straight in the face.

"It's hard to wait for the right guys," I said as I made little quotes with my fingers, "when none of those guys have stepped up and said anything to me. Jason is the first one to pay me any attention. How am I supposed to feel? He makes me feel special, and I like being with him."

Tanner let out a little laugh and rubbed his arm, thinking. He returned my steady gaze and said, "Sometimes, the right guys aren't ready for that yet. Maybe they want to wait until God tells them they're ready."

I wasn't prepared for that. So maybe Tanner *did* like me, but he felt the timing wasn't right. But I was too mad to admit that this logic actually did make sense. Hadn't I felt the same way two months ago when Jason wasn't a part of my life? But instead, I just made excuses because having Jason in my life was fun and exciting, and I wanted to know what it felt like to date someone. I was more than old enough to make this decision on my own. I wasn't going to let Tanner or anyone else take this away from me.

"Well, I've waited long enough. And you're not God, Tanner. Who are you to say that Jason isn't the right guy for me? Yeah, he has problems, but maybe God put him in my life so that I could help him see the right side of life."

I could see the pain welling up again in Tanner's eyes. "Well, good luck with that then," he said with defeat in his voice. "Because changing someone is harder than you think, and most people don't want to be changed. But you let me know how it turns out for you, Moll." With that, he zipped up his coat and walked out the door.

Things were tense between Tanner and me after he walked out of the church that Sunday. At the same time, though, I felt like I was living out my craziest dream with Jason. He took me walking on an adorable gravel trail along the little lake a ways out of town later that week where he gently took my hand and weaved our fingers together and I felt that little thrill zing up my spine again. I was beginning to love this feeling; it was exciting and new and fun.

We walked along the trail on one of the last glorious days of fall. Once November hit, it would get chilly; we would probably have snow before Thanksgiving. Jason smiled at me and asked, "You ever hold hands with someone before, Moll?"

The way he used my old nickname gave it a new sparkle. I could feel my cheeks heating up at his question, though. "Is it that obvious? How can you tell?"

Jason laughed, and I relished the sound of it bubbling out across the lake. "Because you're grinning like a little girl. I can tell you always try to play it cool with me, but you don't have to. Girls always think guys love being with 'experienced girls,'" he said, letting go of my hand for a moment to make quotations with his hands. "But that's not true." He took my hand again. "I think you are adorable, and I'm honored to be the first guy you've held hands with."

I felt a lot of pressure fall off my shoulders after Jason said that. He was spot on; I always thought guys wanted experience, which I had none of. Little by little, I felt my guard slipping away, and I began to open up to Jason more and more. While I still had anxiety about doing everything right, I knew now that Jason wasn't judging me for not having experience.

We continued walking and holding hands, but the sun was slipping down behind the trees, and I was feeling a little chilly. Jason must have felt me shiver because he took his jacket off and draped it around my shoulders. I smiled up at him, and he winked back. I closed my eyes and breathed in the delicious scent of his cologne. Jason laughed.

"There's something about smells," I said. "I'll remember this smell forever. If I ever bump into somebody wearing this same scent, I'm going to remember this exact moment."

He cocked his head. "Really? That powerful?"

"Definitely. It'll never leave me." I took another appreciative sniff and smiled. We decided to head back to his car even though I was sad to see this time end. The plan was to go back to my house and hang out with my family. My parents were making homemade pizza tonight—something we hadn't done in forever.

Having Jason around was changing my family. Josh was in his "I'm a moody teenage boy who never comes out of his room" stage, but when Jason came over, Josh was immediately out of his room and talking sports with Jason. Tanner and Josh couldn't connect in that way because Tanner wasn't much of a sports fan. Tanner mentored Josh, and I knew Josh admired him greatly, but there was something about Jason that pulled Josh out of his shell. Savannah, my sweet little thirteen-year-old sister, was developing a little crush on him as well. That's just how Jason was. He was a charmer. She'd talk to him about how stupid the boys in her grade were and how lucky I was to have such a nice boyfriend who didn't try to steal food off my tray at lunch or crumple up my math homework.

"Yeah, your sister, she's pretty lucky to have me," Jason would reply, sending a wink my way. I'd giggle and give him a playful shove.

Tonight, my family felt normal. I had told Jason that my parents didn't really get along anymore and that their marriage was struggling, but all of a sudden, things started getting a little better. Tonight, everyone was together, laughing and enjoying life. My mom was telling funny stories about work to my dad, and he was actually listening, laughing, and participating in the conversation. My dad started teasing Savannah, something she pretended to hate but really loved. The mood hadn't felt this light in a long time.

We enjoyed our pizza and then sat down with ice cream to play Apples to Apples, one of our favorite games. I couldn't remember when we had actually sat down to play a game as a family. I looked around at the smiling faces of my family and couldn't believe that all it had taken to bring them together was one charming boy.

Later that night, after my siblings went to bed and my parents finally left us alone, I told Jason how much I appreciated him bringing joy back to my family. We sat on the couch, him on one end and I on the other, our legs tangled together in the middle. The house settled around us. I could hear every little creak as night overtook.

Jason shrugged. "I didn't really do anything. No big deal."

"No, it's a huge deal. My parents are never like that. Tonight, they looked happy. My siblings adore you. Josh came out of his room! That's a big deal, Jason."

"I do what I can," he said with a smile and a shrug.

We talked for a while about how much we had enjoyed our day together, just aimlessly walking around the lake and the time spent with my family. Jason got really serious, saying he'd never enjoyed a date so much in his life.

"I don't have to pretend with you, Molly. You know the whole story of my mom, so I don't feel like I have to hide. You know I'm broken, I don't have to pretend I'm just some tough basketball player, ya know?"

"Yeah, and I don't have to pretend I've held hands and done all this stuff before," I said giggling.

Jason laughed too. "I'm serious though, Molly. This is different. *You're* different. I like that. I like it a lot."

Suddenly, he was leaning in, taking my face in his hands. He stroked my cheek gently and asked if he could kiss me. I could only nod, the words stuck in my throat. My heart started racing, and I was glad that the room was dimmed because I was positive that my heart was beating so hard my shirt was moving.

Every girl has anxiety about her first kiss, but I probably had twice the anxiety. Most girls got their first kiss way before they were eighteen years old, and Jason had probably kissed dozens of way more experienced, confident girls. How was I supposed to know which way to turn my head? Would my nose get in the way? What do I do with my tongue? Did my breath smell?

Jason took the lead, though, tilting my head back and guiding my lips to his. I just let him continue to lead me, but I found that kissing wasn't hard. It came naturally. His lips were soft and warm, and the kiss was gentle and sweet. It didn't last as long as I would have hoped, but I didn't want to pull him back to me and ruin the sweetness of the moment. Instead, I just ran my tongue over my bottom lip, savoring the taste of Jason's kiss that was still burning my lips. There had never been a more perfect first kiss, I was sure of it.

Seven

It was cold and windy, but I didn't care. I was driving to the lake on this horrible day because I couldn't stand to be around anyone right now. Driving was one of the only things that calmed me down when I was feeling anxious like this. Usually, I crank the music up and drown out whatever is bothering me, but today, I turned the music off and just drove. It was a Monday afternoon, and things had not gone well at school.

Friday night had been the last home football game for our high school, and Jason and I went together. The student section was filled, and I saw Tanner and Kristina sitting together near the front. I pointed to them and suggested we sit with them, but Jason said he wasn't feeling up to squeezing into the crazy student section. He wanted to actually watch the game, not sit there where thousands of conversations flowed all around and drowned out the announcer's voice. I didn't really care about football and thought it would be fun to sit with Tanner and Kristina who I hadn't really been spending much time with recently. Jason drove me to school now, and I ate lunch with him too, which left me zero time to be with either of them.

We walked past them, and I let go of Jason's hand for a second to wave hello. Tanner's face lit up as he asked if we were going to sit with them. Jason was halfway up the bleachers by now, though, and was hollering at me to follow him. Kristina gave me a weak smile and Tanner's face fell.

"Sorry, guys," I said with a shrug. "Jason wants to focus on the game. I'll catch you later, though, I miss you two!" And with that, I turned around and flounced up the stairs, my ponytail bouncing with each step.

What I missed when I turned away from my two best friends, the people who had seen me through every trial and triumph in my life, was the absolute look of betrayal and rejection. As I bounced up the stairs to sit by my "charming" boyfriend, I was losing my two best allies. And I was breaking their hearts.

At half-time, the dance team and marching band performed, and we stood to stretch our legs and sneak a few kisses. I was all snuggly in Jason's jacket, loving the feeling of being completely and only his. I always dreamed about how I would feel if a boy let me wear his jacket around, so I was totally loving this. Tanner and Kristina had been sending me hurtful, angry looks all night, which I tried to ignore as they began to annoy me more and more. Why were they so angry seeing me so happy? Would it kill them to be excited for me?

Kristina had been ecstatic at first, helping me curl my hair for those first dates and gushing with me about how adorable he was, about how strangely wonderful it was to feel his firm six-pack against my stomach when he hugged me. But as time went on, she didn't want to talk about Jason anymore, so I stopped. The more I hung out with Jason, the less time I spent with her, and this was hurting her. I was blind to this, of course, because I was caught up in falling for Jason. She started texting me less and had more or less given up on inviting me to hang out anymore.

Recently, I'd seen her eating lunch with Leah, a nice girl from our youth group and all her little church friends. I felt a little twinge of jealousy when I saw her laughing with Leah, but then, I remembered that I was sitting with the hottest guy in school, and she was probably just trying to pretend she was happy to hide her jealousy.

As for Tanner, we never talked anymore. One night, he texted me to sneak over to his room because he wanted to tell me something important. I peeled of Jason's jacket that I had stolen for the night to sleep with and pulled on an old sweatshirt and crawled out my window and into Tanner's bedroom.

"What's up?" I asked, scared that Tanner was going to chew me out again.

Instead, he just sat on his bed, playing with his phone, trying to work up the courage to tell me whatever it is he needed to say.

"I can't do this anymore, Molly. I can't." I was confused and Tanner could tell. He sighed, patted the bed, and I tucked my legs underneath me and plopped down.

"I don't like Jason, Molly. I don't know why exactly, I just don't."

"That's not fair, Tanner. You can't just—"

But he cut me off. "Let me talk, okay, Molly?" I nodded, and he continued.

"I've tried to change my mind—I really have. I don't want to be one of those jealous guys who hates someone just because they stole the girl, okay? It's hard for me to see you with him because I want it to be me. We used to hang out all the time, you know, and now it's like I don't exist."

We sat in silence for a bit, and I realized this was Tanner's way of letting me know how he felt about me. Kind of. He hadn't really said he loved me, but he at least cared and wished he could be in Jason's spot.

He took a deep breath and continued. "But I can't tell you what to do. You have to decide on your own if Jason is worth your time, which you clearly think he is, even if I disagree. I don't want to push you away—it would kill me to lose you. So I'm done giving you my opinion. You know what I think, and I'm going to stop telling you."

I was feeling awkward but relieved at the same time. I didn't really know what to say, so I just thanked him. We chatted for a bit, hugged, and I left.

Now, at the game, I could tell Tanner was still thinking about how much he disliked Jason but that he was trying to change that. While Kristina was shooting me angry looks every few minutes, Tanner was, at least, trying. When he'd look back, it would be to see how I was doing, if I looked happy, if Jason was treating me right. He didn't look angry, just hurt and concerned. I showed him a big smile and thumbs-up, and he turned around.

Not even five minutes into the third quarter, something strange happened. Some kids I hadn't seen before, probably public school kids, started shouting at Jason to get his attention. He took his arm off my shoulders to wave back, and I could see them motioning for him to join them.

"Who are those people, Jason?"

"Just some kids from the public school. I used to go to daycare with them in elementary school. We hang out on Sundays while you're at church and with your family."

I was still a little bothered that Jason refused to come to church with me because it was ruining my plan of "fixing" him. I felt a little weird bringing up God and healing from the pain his mom had caused him, and I had hoped taking him to church would open up the chance for me to do that. And here I find out, he's been spending Sundays with a bunch of strange kids I didn't know?

"Be right back, Moll. I'm just gonna go hang out for a bit. They're nice guys." He lightly ran down the bleachers, catching Kristina and Tanner's eyes. They looked back at me with questioning eyes, and I just shrugged. I could hear the boys high-fiving each other, their laughter echoing under the bleachers. They started walking away and out of the fence, which I thought was strange. But Jason said he would be back soon, so I didn't worry about it.

After fifteen minutes though, I was getting worried. There was no sign of them, and the game was getting good. I was also getting really cold up in the bleachers by myself. The minutes ticked by, and I was getting mad. This was the first time I'd been mad at Jason, a feeling I didn't particularly enjoy. I stomped down the bleachers and plopped myself by Tanner.

"Hey, stranger," he said cheerily. "Where'd Jason go?"

"No idea," I said in the most positive voice I could muster. "He saw some friends and wanted to go hang with them for a bit, but he said he'd only be gone for a few minutes. But it's been like twenty, and its cold up there."

I sat with them for the rest of the game, and with five minutes left on the clock, I decided to go after Jason. I waved good-bye to my friends and took off in search of my missing boyfriend who was in a lot of trouble with me. I walked out of the fence and took off down the road where I had seen them go, and it didn't take me long to find them. I heard them before I actually saw them. They were laughing loudly, and one of them was telling a story in which every other word was a swear word. I'm sensitive to that because I didn't grow up hearing it, and it just sounded harsh and stupid. I followed the noise behind a dumpster where I found all of them, each holding a beer. It fell silent when I turned the corner.

Jason lurched forward. "Molly. Hey. I was just coming back to watch the fourth quarter." he slurred.

"Game's over, Jason." I turned around and started walking away, furious that he would leave me alone during a game he had dragged me to in the first place so he could drink with his disgusting friends.

"Wait, Molly. I'm sorry," he said as he pulled my arm.

I yanked it free and spun around, ready to rip into him. But then, I looked into his sad eyes, and I could see how sorry he was. Those darn eyes always did me in, and I felt myself melting.

"I didn't mean for it to get out of hand. I was just hanging out, and the next thing I know, they hand me a beer. It was only supposed to be one, but time got away from us."

He looked genuinely sorry. I let all my air out, and I could feel the fight escaping too. No use lecturing him when he already knew he had done something wrong. "Just please don't let it happen again, okay? I'm so not into guys who drink."

"Promise," he said, hiccupping. The next thing I know, Kristina is running over to me to make sure I'm okay.

"Everything all right? Tanner and I were—" She stopped in the middle of her sentence and took a big sniff. She immediately smelled the alcohol, and I watched the disappointment flood into her eyes. Tanner joined our little party at just the right time—he watched as Kristina yanked me away, leaving Jason and Tanner awkwardly standing there as the rowdy public school boys fell silent.

"What the heck are you thinking, Molly? He's obviously an idiot! Drinking at a football game? At a Christian high school with a bunch of kids you've never met?"

"It just got out of hand, okay?" I retorted harshly. "Seriously, it's not a big deal. He saw some of his friends, and he went to chat, and they kinda just expected him to drink. I don't think he really wanted to—he didn't want to be rude."

Even I could hear how ridiculous that sounded. If he really hadn't wanted to drink, he wouldn't have, even if it seemed rude. But there was no way I was going to admit that to Kristina.

"That is crap and you know it, Molly. Absolute crap. He snuck out to drink with his friends! And he's cutting you off from everybody who cares about you!"

Now, I was just mad because that was not true. Kristina had never dated either; she didn't know how hard it was to juggle family, friends, and a relationship. Jason and I were just getting to know each other, and we just wanted to spend all the time we could together to speed up that process.

I know I shouldn't have said this, but out of anger it just kind of flew out. "You're just jealous!"

Kristina laughed and shook her head. "He's changing you, Molly. I am not jealous. I'm going to wait for someone better than Jason. But Tanner and I are worried about you! We never see you anymore because Jason is always hiding you away somewhere. It's like he's trying to keep you all to himself and cut you off from the rest of the world. That's dangerous, Molly. Can't you see that?"

"No, I don't see that. We *like* each other, Kristina. When you like someone, you spend time with them. That's all."

"Whatever, Molly. But if you get in the car with him, you're the stupidest person I've ever met."

Kristina's words cut me deep. It was the first hurtful thing she'd ever said to me, and I felt like I had been slapped. It's funny how even though I could agree with some of what she was saying, I just wanted to stay with Jason to make her mad. The more she and Tanner chewed me out, the more I just wanted to be with Jason. I wanted to make my own decisions, live my own life. If they couldn't be happy for me, fine. I'd be happy with Jason.

"I'll drive then," I said saucily, walking away and leaving her speechless in the road. I took Jason's keys and motioned for him to follow. He was a bit unsteady, so I let him put his arms around my shoulders to steady him a bit. And we just walked away, leaving Tanner and Kristina behind again.

At school, word had gotten around that Jason and some other kids had been drinking at the game, but once everyone had talked about it enough, they dropped it. Everyone, except Kristina and Tanner. They wouldn't look at me. I approached Kristina about it, and she pretty much said the same thing Tanner had said to me. That she was done worrying about me if I wasn't going to listen. She thought I was stupid to stay with him, and that if he hurt me, I wasn't to come crying to her. She said she was done trying to convince me that I was wrong and that it was stressful for her to be around me. So we parted on that note. We'd stay away from each other for a while.

Tanner was a bit gentler. "It hurts me to see you make what I think is the wrong choice. I'm trying to respect your decision, let you live your own life. But—" He sighed and rubbed his neck. "If he hurts you, Molly, you know I'll kill him. You can come to me if he does. I'll always be here. Kristina and I are overwhelmed right now. We're just gonna take a break from you, just for a while, okay? It's just a lot for us to swallow." He looked so sad, telling me that he needed to stay away from me when only a few weeks before, we had been inseparable. I felt this intense twinge of sadness tighten in my stomach. I was truly hurting them, these two people who meant so much to me.

I nodded and Tanner walked away. I had driven my own car to school today because Jason was staying after school to work on a project, and I was glad because I needed to escape. And that's how I found myself driving to the lake on this cold, windy, miserable day. I felt alone, but at the same time, I didn't want to be around anyone. I just needed some time to think. I blinked back tears the entire drive and choked on the marble-sized lump that kept rising in my throat. No matter how many times I swallowed, the tightness never left. I felt like I was on the verge of a panic attack. I took a deep breath, squeezed my eyes shut, and tried to calm down.

I parked in a free day-use area parking lot and just sat there watching the wind whipping the gray water around. Usually, the water looks kind of greenish brown, but in the winter, it looks dark gray. Cold. I pulled my hood onto my head and stepped out into the wind, heading for my spot. My spot was where I loved coming to in the summer to read, pray, and write. I hadn't been here since early September, and it felt strange to return in the cold when I was used to being here in the sunshine and warmth. It didn't feel the same. The magic was gone, and I felt lonely.

My little spot was just an old bench tucked in some trees. Tanner brought me here to fish once, but I'm not patient enough for fishing, and I hated getting worm guts on my hands. So I adopted the little fishing spot as my own personal escape. The bench was old and probably about ready to fall apart, but that was part of the charm. If they ever replaced this wooden bench with a plastic one, it would ruin it for me. I made my way to the bench and sat down on the damp wood. I hadn't brought my Bible or anything to write with, and God felt distant lately. In all my excitement with Jason, my prayer life had begun to suffer. So there I sat, cold and lonely and not really sure why I had even come out here in the first place.

I felt so torn because even though Jason was flawed and far from perfect, I still cared for him. And even though it seemed that my plan to show Jason a happier side of life, to change him into someone more like Tanner, was failing, I wasn't ready to admit defeat. When I was with him, I felt like a different person. All my life, people had been telling me what to do and what to believe, but with Jason, it felt like I finally had a choice. I wanted to give it a little more time, see if there was still hope in changing Jason's perspective.

On the other hand, I hated that I was hurting Tanner and Kristina. Was my relationship with Jason really worth losing the two people who meant the most to me? Was I ready to give up all that I had before for one person? Deep down, I could see that they were right that Jason wasn't really the one for me, and I was probably walking into trouble, so why was it so hard for me to walk in the other direction? Away from him and back to the safety of their friendship?

I knew it was partly because it just felt good. It felt good to do something other people didn't approve of. My whole life had been about following the rules! Eating my vegetables because it was good for me even though I hated them. Going to bed exactly when my parents told me to so I could get a full night's sleep even when I wasn't tired. Besides sneaking out with Tanner a few times, which was harmless because it was just Tanner, I had never done anything rebellious. For some reason, this was thrilling for me. I knew it was probably bad for me, but for once, I really didn't care. I wanted to do this, simply because it was a thrill, and I liked the way it made me feel grown up and capable of making my own choices.

So I would give Jason another chance. He had made a mistake, a big one, but we all do at some point. Hadn't I been taught since I was old enough to think that forgiveness was important and that everyone deserves a second chance? My whole faith was based on a God of second chances, so I would do the same for Jason.

Eight

November

In the two months that we'd been together, Jason had never taken me over to his house to meet his dad. I wanted so badly to see the inside of his huge house, but Jason's dad was out of town a lot on business trips, and I told him I refused to spend time at his house alone. I still had standards; I was not going to put myself in a position to fall into temptation. So we spent most of our time together at my house, hanging out with my family.

It was the last Saturday of November, and we were on Thanksgiving break. Jason had spent the day with my family because his dad was away again on business, and he seemed distant. It must have hurt him to have to spend this first Thanksgiving back in Oak Ridge without his family. He was probably lonely and wishing his family was whole again back in New Jersey. So I treated him to milkshakes at Emma's that night to try and cheer him up.

We climbed into his car around ten o'clock that night after a cheerful, laughter-filled evening at Emma's to go back to my house, but instead of turning the keys and driving away, Jason just let them dangle in the ignition. He was silent, and he had that distant look in his eyes again. I sighed. No matter how much fun we'd just had, no matter how much he laughed and seemed to be doing better, it still wasn't enough. Trying to change his outlook on life was harder than I ever anticipated.

"What's wrong? You okay?" I asked quietly, stretching out and gently touching his arm—he was so tense. He continued to stare silently ahead, and I could tell that he was really upset.

"I just…I just really want you to meet my dad. It feels weird, going out for this long and not introducing you, ya know? Why don't we head back to my place, and we can hang out with him for a bit?"

My heart tightened in nervousness. He'd been bothering me to go over to his house a lot more lately, but I was trying desperately to stick to my morals. I didn't want to go to his house alone. "I thought your dad was out of town again," I pointed out.

"I'm sure he's back by now," he argued. "It was supposed to be a short trip. Can we just check at least?" He was getting angry. Actually, he seemed to be angry a lot of the time lately. He'd get mad when I suggest we try and spend time with Tanner and Kristina or even some of his friends. We never did anything with anyone. It was always just the two of us. Was Kristina right? Was he trying to distance me from everyone?

No, I reasoned. He wouldn't do that. He just liked spending time alone; I was sure of it. And that was flattering. Although I did miss being with people, it was nice to be alone. Until recently of course, with Jason all moody and clingy. He'd text me every ten minutes when we weren't together, wondering what I was doing and who I was with. On Saturday mornings, he'd text me and plan out our whole day out together, making sure I didn't make plans with Tanner or Kristina.

And now, the thing with meeting his dad, of trying to get me over to his house. Something didn't feel right about this, but maybe, I was just overreacting. Tanner had more influence on me than I liked, so this was probably just a product of his worry about Jason. So far, Jason had proved to be trustworthy—minus the incident with the drinking—so I really had no reason to believe he was up to something now. Right?

"All right." I consented begrudgingly. "But if he's not home, let's go back to my place, okay? It's late." I shivered in the cold because Jason still hadn't started the car yet.

He smiled. "Perfect. You're the best."

"I do what I can," I teased.

And with that, he started the car and we drove off. Light rain was falling, and I hoped that the temperature would drop enough to bring some snow. There was something absolutely magical about the first snow of the year. Wouldn't it be great to wake up to that in the morning? Everything all clean and fresh and white, like a new beginning.

We turned the corner onto his street, and everything was dark. Not a light on in any of the huge houses, and no car in Jason's driveway. There was no sign of life in his big house either. But Jason pulled in anyway, stopped the car, and looked at me like I was a crazy person as I just sat there.

"What?" he asked cruelly. I winced at his sharp tone.

"No one's here. You said we'd leave if he wasn't here." Instead of nodding his head and agreeing that it probably wasn't the best idea to be at his house alone so late at night like Tanner would have done, he reached over and gave me a light kiss on the cheek, unbuckling my seatbelt as his lips brushed across my face. He stroked my cheek lightly and ran his finger over my lips.

"Sometimes, he pulls in late. Let's wait up for a bit. Please?" he begged, kissing my ear and tickling me with his soft breath. I felt my guard slipping down, and I caved.

"Yeah, okay," I heard myself agreeing. We got out of the car, and he led me up the front porch, his hand on the small of my back. He unlocked the door, and it creaked as it opened. It was dark in the house, with only a soft light glowing from one of the rooms down the hall. I saw hardwood floors covering the gigantic living room. Where I had grown up in a house with secondhand furniture and antiques serving as decorations, Jason's place was as modern as ever. It looked like a house straight out of a home and garden magazine, all sleek black leather couches and glass-end tables. A flat screen TV hung from the unpainted wall, and the curtains were dark. It certainly didn't feel very welcoming, and I assumed Jason's dad had simply hired someone to come in and decorate for them.

Jason pulled me into the house, which felt empty and cold. My heart was pounding because even though I promised myself I would never be here alone with Jason, I had to admit it was a bit of a thrill. My parents would not approve of this, but technically, I was eighteen years old, and there was nothing they could do about it. I could be here in Jason's house alone if I wanted to. I was an adult, after all, fully capable of deciding where and with whom I should hang out with.

"Sorry, it's so cold in here," Jason apologized. "I turned it down because I knew I'd be spending most of the weekend with you. No sense wasting money heating an empty house, right? Let me just turn the heat up a few notches." He padded across the room and clicked the up button on the thermostat while I made my way to the couch. On his way back to me, Jason flipped on a lamp and settled on the couch as well, stretching his arm across my shoulder.

I tried to make small talk and hint to Jason that my being here alone with him did not mean I desired any kind of sexual activities to take place. But It was only a matter of time before Jason was kissing me, one hand around my neck and the other up the back of my shirt, searching. His hand was cold on my bare skin, and a shiver ran up my spine. I pulled back, uncomfortable.

"Jason, what if your dad walks in. Awkward." I wiped my mouth and sat up a bit, but he pushed me back down.

"Aw, he probably won't be in tonight. He never really comes back this late anyway," he said with a grin—a grin that looked mischievous, evil, almost, as opposed to his normal charming one.

"But you said—" I was confused. Why would he lie to me? He just chuckled when he saw the confusion in my eyes.

"I had to get you home with me somehow," Jason explained between laughter. "Usually, it's easy—girls want to come over right away when they learn I have a huge house all to myself every weekend. But you've put up a nice little fight. That's okay though. It's like a game," he said as he covered my lips with his again, his hand sliding up my shirt again, still searching.

Suddenly, I was terrified because I knew Kristina was right. He'd cut me off from everyone I cared about and made me depend on him. I was just a piece in his little game to get as many girls as he could home with him. He'd seen how vulnerable I was, how naive and trusting I was. He'd molded me into someone I wasn't, and now, here I was alone with him in this big empty house, far away from all the people who tried to protect me.

I sat up and pushed him away. "I need some water," I said, and I got up to walk to the kitchen. But his hand grabbed my arm, hard, and pulled me back down roughly.

"But we're just starting to have fun," he whispered in his charming little voice. He pressed his lips against mine harshly, his hand forcing my head to stay locked with his. I struggled to get away, which was useless because Jason was bigger and stronger. The more I panicked and struggled, the harder he kissed me and pulled me closer. I felt my heart trying to beat out of my chest. This was not happening. No way.

But suddenly, he was on top of me, ripping away our layers of clothing. I pushed against his chest, but his weight was crushing; and suddenly, my arms were trapped between my body and his. After a while, I stopped trying to get away because it wasn't going to happen. He was too strong. The only thing I could do was squeeze my eyes shut and wait for it to be over. I couldn't scream because his lips never stopped crushing mine, and who would hear me anyway? So I bit down on my tongue until I tasted blood as he violated me over and over again. After what seemed like hours, his body relaxed, and he looked into my eyes, a sick smile on his face.

"How was that, darling? Isn't this great?" he said as he twirled a piece of my hair in his fingers. "I was the first to hold your hand, to kiss you, and now we've come full circle. First one to make love to you."

I shut my eyes again, trying to block out the image of his body pressing down on mine. He pushed a lock of sweaty hair out of my face, and I swatted his hand away angrily. "That was not making love, Jason," I croaked. "Get off. Now."

He laughed. What I once thought charming sounded cruel and harsh after what had just happened to me. "Oh yeah? Well, what was it then?" I didn't answer, and he snorted. "That's what I thought." he sneered, kissing me roughly again. "You try to tell anyone I forced this on you, and they'll laugh in your face. There's a whole school full of girls that would love to sleep with me…so good luck getting anyone to believe this wasn't consensual."

My heart sunk. He was right. I couldn't tell anyone because no one would believe me. Besides, I had walked right into this! Who could I blame besides myself? I couldn't stop the tears that sprung into my eyes, and I began to sob.

"Give me a break, Molly." He cried, rolling his eyes at me like I was some pathetic little girl crying over a little paper cut. "Quit crying. It's just sex."

He heaved himself off the couch and threw my clothes at me, which I clutched in an attempt to cover myself. Though he'd seen it all in the thirty minutes of hell he'd inflicted upon me, I didn't want him to see any more of my body. He pulled on his boxers and walked to the kitchen where I could hear him opening a cupboard and then running the faucet. He poked his head into the living room where I was shoving my arms into my shirt and pulling on my jeans.

"Want some water?" he sneered. I got up, ran to the door, and slammed it as I left, the sound of his laugher echoing through the big house.

The tears that were streaming down my face as I ran down the street mixed with the pelting rain, making my skin feel raw. My hair stuck to me, and though I should have been freezing in that awful rain, my whole body felt like it was on fire. Every step I took was beyond painful, and my lungs were burning, screaming for me to stop running. I kept pushing until my body simply couldn't go another step, and I fell to my knees right there in the middle of the road. In the dark houses that lined the street, I knew everyone was dreaming peacefully, completely unaware that my life had been ruined in one short night.

I clutched my stomach and dry heaved for what seemed like an eternity until my body purged everything out of my stomach. I wiped my mouth on my sleeve and collapsed again in the street, still heaving and sobbing. I let the rain fall on me. I wanted to die.

Somehow, I managed to pull myself up and make my way home. I don't remember reading street signs or keeping track of where I was; I just let my brain lead me home. Tanner's light was on in his bedroom, and I suddenly realized that I hadn't told my parents when I would be home, and by now, it was midnight. The house was dark, but I snuck in through my window as quietly as I could to avoid waking anyone up.

I was never more grateful for my own bathroom. I stripped my filthy clothes off me, and it was then I saw the blood running down my leg. I choked, horrified. I needed to destroy all of this later, but for now, I threw the soiled clothes behind my bathroom door. I caught a glimpse of my face in the mirror and wanted to break the glass when I saw the dirty, worthless girl staring back at me—my hair was soaking wet and tangled, my lips swollen from the crushing force of Jason's kisses, and my eyes red from crying. Hollow eyes. Dead eyes.

I turned away and pulled back the shower curtain, then turned the water on as hot as I could stand and let the warmth run over my tender body. I washed the blood away and scrubbed down every inch on my body, every spot Jason had touched and violated. I winced from the pain. Being a virgin certainly hadn't helped me tonight, and I felt broken from the force Jason had used.

When the water started running cold, I still stood there. My body wash was half gone from the dozens of times I scrubbed my body, and yet, I felt as dirty as ever. I grabbed a towel and wrapped it around me; its fuzzy warmth offering me no solace. I rubbed my body and hair as dry as I could and pulled on the warmest, most cozy pajamas I owned. A pair Tanner had given me last Christmas.

I stood in the middle of my room, unsure what to do next. I was exhausted and wanted to curl up into my bed and sleep this nightmare away, but I longed for company. I wanted my mom, but there was no way I was going to wake her because I couldn't tell her what happened. No one could ever know. I glanced out the window and saw that Tanner's night was now off. It was just after 1:00 a.m. But his words came ringing back to me. "If he hurts you, Molly, you know I'll kill him. You can come to me if he does. I'll always be here." Before I knew what was happening, I was out of my window and sliding his open.

I stood awkwardly beside his bed and looked down at his sleeping form. His tousled blond hair was splayed out on the pillow, and he looked so peaceful. I sniffed and turned around, painfully aware of how bad an idea this was. Tanner had tried so hard to prevent this type of thing from happening. I had no right to come crying back to him.

"Molly?" he called out sleepily. He sat up and rubbed his eyes. "What are you—are you okay?" Instantly awake after sensing I was in trouble, he threw the covers back and padded over to me. He was just wearing shorts, and I was feeling awkward, but he didn't care. He pulled me into his arms, and I let the tears fall.

"Can I spend the night?" I hiccupped.

"Sure, Moll," he said without question and led me to his bed where I snuggled up against his warm, broad chest. He wiped the tears from my eyes and waited for me to explain myself. When I didn't, he gently asked me what happened.

I almost told him. But just as I opened my mouth, I remembered Jason's words. No one would believe me. Especially not Tanner who saw right through me and knew that I was just playing this little game with Jason because I got some weird thrill out of going against his and Kristina's wishes.

"Jason broke up with me," I lied. "Told me he wasn't ready for commitment." I sniffed, tears coursing down my face. Tanner stroked my damp hair, but he didn't say anything. I knew he was probably feeling relief because I was free from Jason's clutches. He didn't know, however, that Jason was now holding me hostage inside myself. I couldn't escape from what he had done; I couldn't tell anyone. He had me completely trapped.

After a few minutes of silence, Tanner tilted my head up to his and looked me straight in the eye. "He doesn't know what he's giving up," he said simply. No "I told you so" or "you're better off without him." He lightly kissed my hair and continued stroking.

I felt my eyelids getting heavy, recognizing that sleep was about to claim me. I thought I heard him whisper "I love you," but sleep was dragging me down, and I didn't know if I'd actually heard it.

I woke up countless times that night in extreme panic. Each time Tanner shushed me until the visions of Jason's cruel eyes disappeared from view. I would snap out of it, see Tanner's concerned face searching my eyes, and I would relax into his strong arms again. He'd kiss my head and settle me back against his body.

In the morning, I awoke with my cheek pressed against his bare chest, my arm flung across his body. His arms held me safe and warm, but I still felt alone and empty. I felt the tears coming back, but I squeezed them away. I didn't want Tanner to see me crying and think I was upset over losing Jason. I wanted him to think I had finally seen his point of view that Jason wasn't worth my time, and I was better off without him.

Tanner's eyes fluttered open and he gave me a little smile. His hair stuck out in all different directions, looking as adorable as ever. Too bad I hadn't realized what a catch Tanner was before; I could have avoided this whole mess if Tanner and I were together. But I was so incredibly grateful that I had come over last night. It would have been absolute torture to endure that night without his quiet strength to calm me.

"Morning," he said as he pushed the hair out of my eyes. I winced a little because that's what Jason had done to me the night before.

"Morning," I said back and sat up. Suddenly, I was painfully aware of the fact that I was only wearing a T-shirt and pajama pants. I hugged my arms around my chest. "I should get back," I said softly. "My parents will think I was out all night with Jason if they find me gone from my room."

"Yeah, okay," Tanner said. "You gonna be all right? Need me to come over later?" The tightness returned to my throat as I looked into the eyes of my best friend. He had just watched me waltz around for the past two months with a guy he didn't like, rejecting his feelings for me as if they didn't matter at all. He'd seen me at my lowest point ever and held me as nightmares terrorized me the whole night through. He saw me crying about this guy he thought I still liked, and yet, he still wanted to be with me. To make sure I was all right.

I did not deserve this boy. Not after last night. Not after how I let some jerk dupe me and steal my most precious gift—my virginity. I was dirty and unworthy of Tanner.

"I'll text you if I need you," I said, offering him the best smile I could muster.

"All right," he said. I started to walk away, but Tanner called out, "Wait."

I turned around, and he walked after me, pulling me into another hug, and kissing my head over and over again. "It'll be all right, Moll. Today's a new day. We'll get through this. Promise."

I knew it wouldn't be that easy, that I was never going to get over this. But I'd have to somehow make him believe in a few days though that I was fine. That I was over Jason and moving on with my life.

"Hey look," he said and pointed outside. "Snow."

How ironic, I thought. Last night, I had wished for snow, for the fresh new promise that seemed to come with snow. As if the world were covered in purity and goodness. A promise of a new beginning, a fresh start.

Today didn't feel like a fresh start though. It felt like the beginning of a prison that was just starting to close in on me. It was a deep pit, something I'd struggle to climb out of for years to come. There was no new beginning for me in this snowfall. This was an ending.

Nine

December

December was torture for me, because everyone was so focused on trying to make me feel better. I guess in their minds the best thing was to occupy all my time—leaving me alone was the worst thing to do, it seemed. But the one thing I *wanted* was to be left alone, but Tanner and my family knew I was hurting from what they thought was a breakup with Jason. And every day I wasn't back to my normal, peppy self, the harder they tried to bring me back.

In the first week after the rape, I would catch Tanner watching me with deep concern in his eyes. I knew he was wondering why I was hurting so much, why I even still cared about Jason at all. I tried my hardest to return to normal, but I felt dead. Life seemed to lose its meaning after that night; I couldn't just turn a switch back to normal and transform back into my happy, care-free self. I had been replaced with a robot that could only drag itself through one day at a time.

The first Monday after Thanksgiving, I walked back into school absolutely shaking. Tanner grabbed my hand and walked me to the guidance counselor to see if I could switch government classes. I told Tanner I couldn't stand to be in the same room as Jason. When he pressed me for details about the breakup, asking if he had hurt me physically in anyway, I just shook my head. "We just broke up. I don't want to talk about it. But you were right. He's a jerk, and I don't want to see his face."

The receptionist didn't press me for details, which I was thankful for. She just typed my information into the computer and scrolled down to see if I could switch any classes around. "We can swap honors biology and government around, so you'd go to biology during second period and government during sixth. Does that work, Molly?" she asked kindly, a helpful smile lighting up her face.

"Yes!" I said gratefully. I felt a huge weight fall off my shoulders. I could now avoid seeing Jason's face the entire day.

"Good. We'll get that set up for next week, okay? It takes a while to talk to the teachers and change it in the computer. I'll print off your new schedule, and you can start that next Monday."

"I can't start today?" I asked nervously.

"Well, it just takes a while for it to switch on the teacher's grade book. Plus, we just got back from a break, and it's too late to start today. We'd like you to start a full week with your new class, so it's just easier if you wait till next Monday."

I whipped around and looked at Tanner with panic in my eyes. He stepped forward and put his arm around me protectively. "It's gonna be okay. It's just one week. You can do it, just ask Mr. Johns if you can move to the back of the room."

I tried to take a few deep breaths to calm myself, but I was on the verge of hyperventilating. Tanner would never understand. It didn't matter if I moved myself away from him because I would still have to see him. I would still have to hear his voice and his laugh. I would see how this had not affected him at all when it was causing my entire life to crumble down around me. But I nodded and smiled to show Tanner I was fine. He walked me to government and dropped me off, waving good-bye as he disappeared down the hall.

For some reason, I thought everyone would know Jason and I had broken up and would be talking about it, but no one seemed to care. A few girls cast me sympathetic looks and offered apologies about Jason, but they looked slightly pleased that he was free for the taking. *Go ahead, be my guest,* I thought cynically.

I asked Mr. Johns if I could move to the back of the room because of personal issues. He agreed easily, and my love for this teacher tripled. One week. I could do one week. I slid into my desk and pulled my book out of my bag, and when I looked up, I saw Jason twisted around in his desk. He looked confused, and he jerked his thumb at my old spot as if to ask, "Why aren't you sitting here?" I just stared at him until that awful, cruel smile returned to his face. He shook his head and smirked, thinking I was the most pathetic creature on the face of this earth. I dropped my head and squeezed my eyes shut. I would not cry here. I had cried enough in the past week to last three lifetimes.

Class crawled by as Mr. Johns droned on and on about the presidency, all the requirements and perks and whatnot. I checked the clock every five minutes, which of course made class drag by even slower. Finally, the bell rang, and I wasted time shuffling papers and putting my books away slowly until I was the last one in the room. Mr. Johns smiled at me and told me to have a nice day as I left. *I wish,* I thought.

Suddenly, Jason was beside me, and I immediately tensed and moved away.

"Hey, now," he said, feigning hurt. "Why are you acting like this?"

I tried to walk away, but he pulled me into an empty classroom and shut the door behind us. My heart was pounding; being in this room alone with him was terrifying. I was aware of how much taller he was than me, how I could see the lining of his muscles through his shirt without him even flexing.

"Jason, please," I pleaded, sounding like a terrified third grader being bullied at recess. "Just leave me alone. I haven't told anyone."

"What, that we had sex?" he sneered. "Look, Molly. You led me on the whole time. Don't pretend you didn't want to do it with me." He raised his eyebrows and smiled. "I know you did."

I was crying. "No, I didn't. I didn't. I told you to take me home if your dad wasn't home." My voice was getting all high and squeaky, and Jason was laughing. But he got really serious all of a sudden, his voice low and threatening.

"Let me straighten this out for you, Molly, so you understand *perfectly* what happened last week." He put so much emphasis on the word *perfectly* and leaned in, pushing me against the wall and trapping me there under his outstretched arms. "I did not force that on you, I was simply taking control, giving you what I know you wanted. *Did* you want to sleep with me, Molly?"

I shook my head no, the tears slipping down my cheeks and on to the floor.

"Let me ask you again, Molly," he demanded, leaning so close that I could feel his breath on my face. "Did you want to sleep with me?" He enunciated each word, as if speaking to a preschooler who didn't know anything.

"Yes," I said so quietly he could barely hear me.

"What? Can't hear you, Molly!" He was enjoying this entirely way to much.

"Yes!" I said louder.

He smiled and leaned back, satisfied that he had successfully turned the rape back on me. "And who wouldn't want to sleep with me?" he asked as he splayed his hand over his chest, "So stop acting like I attacked you because I didn't. Now, I've been telling people we broke up, so work on getting over me. Got it?"

I swallowed the huge marble in my throat and nodded.

"Good." He let his arms drop to his side, freeing me from his prison. He tweaked my nose, and I winced. "Now get out," he commanded, and I walked as fast as I could out of there. I was late for calculus, and I was blinking back tears as Mrs. Leeson chewed me out, telling the whole class how important it was to be on time in the real world. Tanner smiled encouragingly at me from across the room, and I was so grateful he was helping me through this.

And so began my week of torture.

Tanner drove me to school every day, ate lunch with me, drove me home again, and then, spent the afternoon doing homework with me or watching ridiculous TV shows. That's one thing we've always loved doing—watching stupid reality TV shows together. We used to laugh out loud and crack jokes throughout the entire shows, but now, we just sat there and watched. Tanner tried to crack some jokes and coax me to laugh or even smile, and I tried, I really tried. But I was still in robot mode. I couldn't force myself to laugh at these shows when I felt dead inside. I just couldn't.

I could see that Tanner was getting disappointed. I still caught him looking at me with deep concern, wondering why I wasn't recovering from a breakup with some jerk boy I had only dated for two months. I was going to have to become a better actress because Tanner wasn't buying it.

Time was now separated into two periods: before the rape and after the rape. Now, after Tanner would leave, I'd retreat to my room. Before the rape, I would sit around in the living room working on homework, reading, or watching TV, but after that night, I needed solitude, I needed people to leave me alone. I took this for granted before because now when I wanted to be alone everyone wanted to check on me and make sure I was okay. My mom would sneak into my room, crawl into bed beside me as I just lay there trying not to think, and start stroking my hair. So many times I wanted to spill everything to her, but I didn't. What would it accomplish anyway?

I had no proof anymore! I had pretty much done everything a rape victim isn't supposed to do. I'd showered and scrubbed away all evidence that Jason had raped me, and I'd tied up every article of clothing from that night in a black garbage bag and thrown them away. If I told my mom, she would tell my dad, and for some reason, that embarrassed me to no end. I didn't want him knowing I wasn't a virgin anymore. They'd want to charge Jason with rape, but we were both eighteen, it wasn't like I was a minor and Jason had broken that law. Of course, rape is still rape, it didn't matter in that sense that I wasn't a minor—it was still a crime. But because I wasn't a minor, it would be so easy for Jason's dad to just hire some fancy lawyer to convince everyone I was just making it up to get him in trouble, that it was consensual sex, but I had been angry over the breakup and used rape as payback. Then, word would spread through the school and people would think I was some attention-starved diva who had cried rape to get Jason in trouble.

So there was no way I was going to tell my mom about this. No matter how fast my guard slipped down in those moments she stroked my hair, I refused to give in. It was just extremely hard, having these horrible conflicting feelings: I loved that she was there trying to ease my pain, and yet, I hated how she made me want to spill everything when I knew I couldn't. The best solution would be for her to just leave me alone, but I couldn't tell her that either. So to get Tanner and my mom off my back, I needed to step it up, to convince them I was fine.

Slowly, I tried to return to normal for them. I tried cracking a few jokes when Tanner and I watched our shows, and even though they fell flat, Tanner laughed anyway. I would try and stay out in the living room for as long as I could stand it, just to show my parents I was recovering. Though I was a lot more serious and reserved now, they bought my act slowly but surely. Tanner would tousle my hair and hug me before he left, saying how grateful he was that I was feeling better. I would give him my best smile and nod in agreement.

My family started to return to normal as well. Josh was usually in his room at night, and Savannah and I would work on homework and watch TV in the living room together. My mom still worked three times a week, and my dad just relaxed at night. The worry was gone from their eyes; they truly thought I was getting better.

So I found myself even more trapped. I had successfully convinced everyone I was fine, but in reality, I was locked in a prison of silence, and there seemed to be no hope of escape. At night, I lay in bed terrified of falling asleep because I knew without a doubt that awful nightmares would wake me up, cold sweat pouring off my body and soaking the bed. So I became a bit of an insomniac. At first, I would just lay there, but my brain would go back to that night, and I'd get angry at myself all over again.

I was stupid not listen to Tanner and Kristina. For a while, it had been fun to like Jason simply because they didn't like him, and I enjoyed the little thrill of rebelling against them. It had been fun to like someone and to be liked back. To have someone hold my hand and kiss me and take me out on dates. It felt nice. But the rebellion and all those nice feelings were hardly worth it now. Look where it had gotten me! If I had stuck to my morals of waiting for a guy to cherish and love me, if I had waited until I was ready to face any possible feelings for Tanner, I wouldn't be in this situation. I'd be living my carefree life with my best friend, completing my senior year and looking forward to the future.

I hadn't thought about college in a long time, but Tanner and I had sent in our applications to Iowa State long ago and had both gotten accepted. We used to talk excitedly about college all the time, but Tanner had dropped it for a little bit to focus on helping me feel better. I'd have to bring it up sometime soon, try to make it seem that I was still moving on and excited about life.

Clearly, I wasn't excited about life though. The rape seemed to rob me of my self-worth, of my entire identity really. I just felt dirty and cheap. I used to think God had plans for my life, but now, I was seriously doubting that. How would I ever help people or make a difference in the world when I couldn't even help myself?

So I tried not to think about God anymore. I pushed my Bible as far back as I could underneath my bed so I wouldn't have to look at it. That book was filled with verses that talked about a loving, compassionate God who had my good in mind, that he had plans to prosper me and not harm me. So where had God been when I needed him most? Yeah, I had been tempted and sort of walked into this situation on my own, but he could have stopped Jason from raping me. He could have done something, but he didn't. To me, that was not loving, compassionate, and it certainly wasn't for my good. It wasn't a plan to prosper me, and it seemed like all it was doing was harming me. So I was done with God. I'd sit through Sunday services to play the part, but I was done following God.

When I couldn't stand these thoughts swirling around in my head any longer, I turned to books. I checked out stacks of books from the library to keep my mind occupied. I would read until my eyes would droop closed, and I would let sleep claim me. Hours later though, I always woke up from yet another nightmare, my clothes sticking to me and my heart pounding.

My grades started to slip because I was so tired in class. School was a bit better once I finally got my government and honors biology classes switched, but I still felt that I was dragging myself through each day, days that seemed to have no point or purpose. And I would occasionally bump into Jason. It was a small school, it happened every few days. He would either completely ignore me on good days, and on bad days, he'd give me that cruel smile that I was having trouble erasing from my mind. I would shudder and look away quickly, grateful I no longer had to deal with him in class.

Every day, I would cross off the date on my calendar just to reassure myself that the days were actually passing. The weeks crawled by, and then, there was the flurry of final papers and tests to keep me busy for a while. I was able to shake myself out of my little funk just enough to pull straight Bs in all my classes. Barely. In calculus, I was one percentage point away from a C. Grades used to be a huge deal to me; I'd gotten high As in all of my classes before the rape. Where I once would have been disappointed to pull a B as a final grade, I let out a sigh of relief that I hadn't gotten any Cs and just told my parents it had been a tough semester for me. I was already accepted to Iowa State anyway, so obviously, my grades were good enough already.

I walked out of school with Tanner after finals were over and heaved a huge sigh of relief. We had three weeks of Christmas vacation to not think about school at all. Three weeks of not having to worry about running into Jason in the hallways. Maybe, I'd have some miraculous healing and come back second semester ready to face Jason and put this nightmare behind me. Christmas used to be a magical time for me.

Maybe God would pull through and grant me one more miracle.

Ten

January 2008

I don't know how long I sat on the cold tile of my bathroom, staring at the two pink lines down in my hands. Two pink lines. These three words had never meant anything to me until now. Now, they were more than just words; they had the power to change my life forever. My life had already changed forever when Jason had raped me. How much could one person take before they exploded from all the pressure?

I let my head fall back against the wall with a *thunk*. I already had a headache, and that hadn't helped. The tears started flowing down my cheeks again. After the rape, crying was the only thing I could seem to do anymore. I hated crying, I was so sick of it. But I felt such deep desperation, it was the only thing I could do in this situation.

This is not how this was supposed to happen. I was supposed to go away to college where I would meet the boy of my dreams. He would be charming, and I'd fall hopelessly in love with him. We'd date, and eventually, he would get down on one knee when he knew the time was right and ask me to be his wife. We would get married in my home church, surrounded by our friends and family. My parents would cry and send us off on our honeymoon, and then, we'd start our life together, learning how to cook and living in a tiny little apartment. We were supposed to enjoy sex within the bounds of marriage and share in the moment of discovering I was pregnant for the first time—together.

I wanted the moment I learned I was pregnant for the first time to be happy. I wanted to come running out of the bathroom waving the pregnancy test in my beaming husband's face. I wanted his arms to circle around me and pick me up, swinging me around. I wanted to look into his smiling face and see tears of joy running down his cheeks.

We would call our parents and tell them the good news, and everyone would cry. My mom would go shopping with me, and we'd "ooh" and "ahh" over all the cute baby clothes, wanting to buy every onesie and pair of booties we saw.

My husband and I would sit up at night with our hands on my belly, talking to our baby and arguing over names. We would delight in the first kick and laugh when my belly bounced from the baby's hiccups. We'd make late-night fast-food runs when I would get cravings. It would be a crazy, wonderful, immensely enjoyable time in our lives.

That's how I had always pictured my first pregnancy to be. That's how it *should* be. Not just a product of a night I had no control over and hadn't wanted. It's one thing to get pregnant in high school because you were willingly having sex. It was a completely different thing to get pregnant because you were date-raped.

I know in normal high schools teenage pregnancy was getting to be a pretty common thing. A girl in my Sunday school class went to the public high school, and she mentioned once that there are at least three or four pregnancies a year. In my school, though, teenage pregnancy is rare. Most of the kids there are strong Christians and come from strong Christian families. While this doesn't make them perfect, they do stay away from sex more than public school kids do. In the four years that I've gone to my high school, I can remember only one girl getting pregnant two years ago. She and her boyfriend got married before the baby was born, and they were expecting another baby soon.

If I came to school pregnant, I would be the talk of the school for years. I'd never been the topic of gossip before, let alone this level of gossip. Rumors would spread like wildfire, and no one would ever know the real truth behind how I had gotten pregnant. Jason's face flashed in my mind, and I shuddered. What would he do when he found out?

If I had learned anything in the past few months, it was that life is full of curveballs, but I was seriously sick of them. One stupid decision had catapulted me down a path of destruction, and I knew I would feel the repercussions for years. If *only* I hadn't let Jason suck me in that night at Emma's, charming me with his big blue eyes and sad sob story, my life would be completely different. Yet here I was, spiraling out of control and so dizzy I couldn't see straight anymore.

Christmas break had been the healing balm for my aching heart. It was wonderful not to have to see Jason at all, to spend time with my family and Tanner. Laughter had slowly starting returning to my life, real laughter that made my face light up and helped me forget about the pain and emptiness, if only for a night. I had even started journaling. I still wasn't able to communicate with God because I was still struggling to trust him. But journaling felt close to praying, and I would vent all my pent up emotions through writing until my hand cramped up and forced me to stop. The nightmares still visited me every night, but they became less vivid, and I could usually work through the terror and calm down enough to return to sleep.

This time with my family and Tanner over Christmas break was really like putting a Band-Aid over a gaping wound though. It had covered up the rawness for a while, letting it scab over. But I should have known it was just a matter of time until the Band-Aid was ripped off and the scab cut open, the blood flowing once more.

When my period was late, I panicked of course. But I chalked it up to the stress of the rape. The constant fear and worry could have caused it to be late; I rationalized. But the nervousness never quite left me; I had a constant nagging fear the rest of December. The weeks slipped into January, and I prayed it would return. But that week passed by as well, and it never came. I laid awake at night in pure terror—two missed periods was a big deal for someone who had never missed or even been late. I needed to know.

I took my car out early one Saturday morning and drove to a gas station on the very edge of town. I couldn't risk going to the drugstore because in a small town everyone knows everyone. The cashier would know me, and there would be people shopping there who would know me, and if they saw me buying a pregnancy test, the news would spread quickly.

Tanner and I used to stop at this gas station on our way out to the lake to pick up snacks and pops for a day at the beach. If you could call it a beach though. It was more of a little patch of scratchy sand that the parks and recreation people brought in and dumped on the edge of the lake. But we'd spend hours laying out on that sand or playing catch in the water with our siblings.

The gas station was always packed with stuff because campers and fishers used this gas station the most. It was like a mini grocery store, and I knew that there was a section that held the drug store essentials, including pregnancy tests. I always thought that was a little strange because who would want to take a pregnancy test while they were out camping? I was of course grateful that they were there though. Now, I didn't have to risk running into someone I knew in town.

There wasn't a soul in the parking lot because it was the off season. I could see the cashier leaning up against the register, bored out of his mind. The only reason this place was still open in the winter is because of ice fishers and snow-mobilers.

When I walked in a little bell sounded, and the man looked up and smiled half-heartedly. I gave him a small smile back and headed to the back of the store. There were a couple different brands to choose from, and I had no idea what was the difference between any of them, so I just grabbed the cheapest one I could find and headed back up to the front of the store.

As I set it on the counter, I could feel my cheeks burning. I was eighteen, but I looked sixteen, and I was clearly not married. One glance at my left hand confirmed it to the man, and I could see the judgment in his eyes. I was just another statistic to him, one more messed up teenager who had found herself pregnant in high school.

He rang it up for me, and I paid him as quickly as I could and made a mad dash for the door. I was glad I didn't know him, and he'd forget about me by the end of the day anyway. He'd go back to his wife and kids and forget about me and my messed up life completely.

I drove home slowly in complete silence. Music was not a part of my life anymore because music has so much power. If I listened to any music in this part of my life where everything was crazy and messed up, I'd hear it later and be instantly brought back to this place. I didn't want any connections to this time in my life, so I cut music out. I drove slowly because even though I was anxious to know if I was pregnant; I didn't want to do this. I didn't want to be in this situation. I wanted to throw the test out of the window and not have to live in constant fear and worry.

By the time I got home, I was shaking. The house was still quiet; everyone was still sleeping because it was still so early. I crept down the hallway to my bedroom and closed the door as quietly as I could, then followed the directions on the test and waited. My stomach tightened in fear, and I could hardly breathe because I already knew what the outcome was going to be—I could feel it in my gut.

I gripped the edge of my sink and looked in the mirror where I could see the terror in my eyes. My face was pale and thin, my hair limp and messy because I hadn't showered this morning. Taking in as much air as I could fit in my lungs, I lifted the test up to see the results that would change everything for me. The nice little plans I'd been formulating for myself went sailing out the window and swirled away in the howling winds outside.

Pink. Two pinks lines.

And that's when I leaned against the wall and slid all the way down to the cold tile floor. My legs were shaking violently, unable to hold me up anymore. I stared at the test for what seemed like hours, willing it to be negative when it was clearly positive. I cried until the tears ran out, and then, I just sat their hiccupping and racking my hands through my hair, trying to run through all the possible solutions I had.

Who would I tell first? *How* would I tell them? I had no clue how to go about bringing it up to anyone because I would be hurting so many people.

One thing I knew instantly though was that there was no way I could tell anyone I had gotten pregnant through rape because they'd want to press charges, and we had no proof. I'd destroyed it all. We'd lose that battle, and it was a battle I didn't really want to face anyway. I wanted nothing to do with Jason. I didn't want to see his face in a courtroom trying to convince people I was just some snake trying to make him look bad.

But even if I told my parents I had slept with Jason willfully and gotten pregnant, they'd want me tell Jason so I could get child support. They would fight that for sure. No one was going to get their daughter pregnant and then not take responsibility for it. Jason would be furious! Maybe he'd deny that it was his baby, and then, what would I do? I hadn't been with anyone else. The rumors would really start to fly then.

I was stuck. Of course I didn't want anyone to find out, but pregnancy is pretty hard to hide. I didn't want to face the look of disappointment on my parent's faces when they learned I was pregnant. I was eighteen, and they had clearly trusted me with Jason, and I had strong opinions on waiting till marriage—opinions that my parents, and most of the kids in my school, knew about because I was so passionate about them. But they wouldn't know I hadn't been sleeping around, that I'd been attacked and had gotten pregnant because of it. They'd never know that side of the story. They'd just think I had thrown my morals out of the window and given Jason that precious gift.

I knew that they would get past that anger and disappointment and help me out eventually, but I didn't want to be dependent on them, not in this stage of my life where I was so close to independence. And then suddenly, it hit me that if I was pregnant, Iowa State was no longer an option. There was no way I could have a baby and go to college at the same time. I would have to stay here in my parent's house with a baby I didn't want and watch all my friends leave for college.

I closed my eyes in disgust. The baby would look like Jason. It would come out with his dark, dark hair and those deep-blue eyes. Every time I looked into my baby's eyes, I would see Jason. Every time I combed through my baby's hair, I would think of how I used to slide my fingers up the base of Jason's neck and into his thick hair while he kissed me. When my baby laughed, I would be reminded of the night I ran out into the rain and Jason's laugh echoed out after me. I would think of the rape every time I saw Jason's child.

With a baby, I could never escape from Jason. And I could never really love that baby either because I didn't want it. It was just a product of one horrible night with Jason. Not a mistake but an attack. If the baby *had* been a mistake out of one night with Jason, one night of me letting my guard down and sleeping with him, it might feel different. But this wasn't a mistake; it had been Jason taking advantage of me. I didn't want this baby, and Jason certainly didn't want it either. And I'd be hurting everyone I loved—everyone who had trusted me not to make the same mistake so many teenagers today were making.

Tanner would probably be hurt the most though. He had tried to keep me away from Jason. He had warned me that Jason was a bad guy, but I had ignored him and chased after Jason anyway. I had played right into Jason's little game, walked right into his little trap. I really had no one to blame but myself, and when Tanner found out, I wouldn't expect his sympathy. He had put up with so much already. If I was in his shoes I would have given up long ago, and yet, Tanner stayed with me. Probably not after he found out about the baby, and who could blame him? After twelve years of devoted, loyal friendship, Tanner would only be able to handle so much.

I pushed myself up off the floor and stuffed the test as far down in the garbage as I could. I felt sick to my stomach and my face was raw and chapped from crying. I peeled off my clothes and stood in the shower for forever, letting the hot water soothe away the ache in my shoulders. I felt so tense lately, and the hot water seemed to help a little.

I wrapped myself in a towel and flopped down onto my bed. I was exhausted and had no motivation to do anything. It was still only nine in the morning, and I usually sleep in until ten thirty or eleven on Saturday mornings anyway, so if I went back to bed, my parents would think I had never gotten up. I let sleep claim me then.

When I woke up two hours later, I didn't feel any better. My stomach was still in knots, and my head was pounding. I hadn't combed my hair after I got out of the shower, and it had turned into a huge tangly mess. But that's how I was feeling right now. My life was just one huge tangly mess.

I managed to open my bedroom door and venture down the hallway around twelve-thirty. The house was quiet; everyone was in their own little world.

I wandered into the living room and shook my head in disbelief when I looked out the big picture window and saw snow falling gently from the sky. How fitting. The snow was once again falling on a day my life was spinning wildly out of control.

My head hurt from battling so many emotions. On one hand, I hated the thing growing inside of me just for existing. Because of it, I'd never escape from Jason. Ever. If I kept it, I would see Jason every day of my life in my child. And I didn't t know if it would be possible for me to love a child conceived out of rape.

On the other hand, the pregnancy was the one positive result of Jason. I had wasted so much time with him, and he had basically stolen my entire life on that one night, but now, there was a baby. A perfect, helpless tiny baby. Jason would never love me, but the baby would love me forever. I'd always wanted to be a mom, and now, it was happening. Maybe a little sooner than planned and not at all in the way I pictured it, but that's what life had handed me. Maybe I could just make the best of a bad situation.

I still had options though. I could certainly keep the baby and forfeit college. It would be hard to walk into school with a pregnancy and face my classmates and teachers, especially when none of them knew the truth. And I'd have to face Jason, and who knew how he would respond? I would have to tell him at some point, and I hoped he would just leave me alone and let me figure it out. He could go on with his life and forget about me and the baby forever.

Then, there was adoption. I'd still have to walk into school with a pregnancy and face my classmates and teachers, but I could put the baby in loving arms and carry on with my life. I could pack up my things and head off to college like everyone else. But I guessed I would carry the baby around with me forever. The emotional connection I'd make with the baby would be strong; it would be hard to give it up. But I reminded myself that I'd be looking into Jason's eyes every single day of my life if I kept the baby. I didn't want that. I wanted to forget about Jason forever.

So it just came full circle. I'd hate the baby for existing, try to reason my way through my options, and get discouraged by them all. There was no winning. I was the loser in every option. I'd face judgment and scrutiny for nine months, be stuck at home with a baby I didn't want while my classmates left in the fall, or live my life wondering about the baby I'd given up. I'd always be worried that the baby would know I didn't want it, that it would know its daddy didn't love or want it either. That its daddy was a monster. I didn't want the baby to ever find out.

These emotions were making it so much harder to keep faking happiness around my family and Tanner. When my alarm would go off in the morning, I'd snooze so long that I would eventually fly out of bed in a panic, trying to get ready to hop in Tanner's car ten minutes later. I hardly ever got up in time to shower anymore, I barely had time to pull on some sweats and throw my hair in a ponytail. I'd given up on makeup weeks ago. There was no way to hide the deep circles under my eyes anyway, even with all the makeup in the world.

I managed to keep fooling everybody, telling them I was up late studying or couldn't sleep. That I'd developed a severe case of "senioritis," and that's why I was wearing sweats to school so often. That I was too lazy to get up in the morning to shower. It worked for a while.

Until morning sickness hit.

I was definitely not prepared for morning sickness. As I walked down the hallway one Tuesday morning, the smell of frying bacon hit me like a ton of bricks. I turned around and bolted down the hall, rounding the corner into my bathroom in just the nick of time.

It reminded me of getting the stomach flu as a little kid and how my mom used to hold my hair out of my face and rub my back, then, help me back into bed and bring me juice boxes and crackers. But no one was here to hold my hair back now and a juice box and crackers wouldn't make me feel better. This wouldn't go away in a few days.

Usually on bad mornings, I could just rinse my mouth out, brush my teeth, and climb into Tanner's car without him noticing anything was wrong. But one day had been particularly bad. I'd been over the toilet for almost a half an hour, thinking I was about to die. When I finally felt like it was over, I looked at the clock and knew Tanner was in the driveway waiting for me. It was the first time I'd ever been late.

He looked at me with deep concern when I finally slid into my seat. "Are you okay?" he asked. "You don't look good. Are you sick?"

I shook my head. "No. A little queasy. Thought I might throw up, but it never came. Sorry I'm late." I scrunched my nose up—something didn't smell quite right in here, but I couldn't place what it was. I prayed to a God I was beginning to believe got some sick enjoyment out of watching me suffer to please not let the morning sickness return now, not here, not in Tanner's car.

His hand hesitated on the gearshift like he didn't quite believe me and was about to make me go back inside. But he decided against it and backed out of the driveway. As he started to tell me about the movie he and Ellen had watched last night, he pulled a microwavable breakfast sandwich up from his lap and ripped it out of its plastic. Suddenly, the car was filled with the smell of eggs, cheese, and sausage, and I knew that's what I had smelled earlier. It was too much. My stomach started to roil and I blurted, "Pull over!"

Tanner looked confused but quickly swerved to the side of the road. I opened the door and lurched to the grass in just enough time to expel whatever was left in my stomach. I couldn't believe there was still something in there to throw up!

I kneeled there in the grass clutching my stomach, the melting snow soaking through my jeans. Tanner was out of the car in a flash, rushing to my side to make sure I was okay.

"Molly! Molly, you okay?" He rubbed my back, trying to comfort me. I squeezed my eyes shut. It was getting harder and harder to keep the pregnancy a secret from him.

I took a few deep breaths. "Yeah. I'm…fine. Let's go." I pulled myself up and looked into Tanner's stunned eyes.

"I'm taking you home, Molly. You threw up!" He looked at me like I was a crazy person.

"No, really. I'm fine." I tried to reassure him. "I feel completely better now."

"Molly…"

I held my hands up, cutting him off. "I feel better. I don't want to miss school this close to midterms. Really. I feel fine. Can we please just go?" I pleaded, looking at him with the saddest eyes I could muster. Tanner was a softie, I knew I had him. He sighed but helped me up the rest of the way. But he was silent the rest of the drive to school, and when we pulled into the parking lot, he just sat in his seat and looked at me, that awful look of deep concern in his eyes again.

That was when I cracked. His level of concern for me ripped my heart in two—I had to let him in, to ease his worry a little bit. Maybe once he knew, it would all be better. Maybe then, the worry in his eyes would be replaced with compassion—a compassion that would once again pull me out of this awful darkness I was in.

So I let out a deep breath and said simply, "Tanner, we need to talk about something soon. Okay?"

Panic crossed his eyes. I had a feeling he knew what was coming. He dropped his eyes and fiddled with his hands. "Okay. Let me know when."

I nodded and we both headed for the door, each going our separate ways. I had a sinking feeling in my stomach all day because I knew what I was facing.

Another ending.

Eleven

Tanner

February

You didn't have to be a psychologist to know something was seriously wrong with Molly. She had broken up with Jason at the end of November, and since then, she seemed to have fallen into a weird "funk." Molly's pretty emotional and would fall into these moods once in a while, but she'd always snap out of it in a few days, returning to her normal, cheerful self. I'd counted on her snapping out of it just as quickly this time, but it still hadn't happened.

She'd really freaked me out last week when she puked on the side of the road on the way to school. She hadn't looked sick, just incredibly exhausted, and I believed her when she said she wasn't. It was almost like she was just so worked up and stressed out that she'd made herself sick. Finals were coming up, and she was taking hard classes, but she'd never been this worked up before. Something else was going on, something she wasn't telling me. It'd been a week since she told me she needed to talk about something, and it was killing me. But I didn't want to chase her away. She'd come to me and tell me whatever it was that was bothering her when she was good and ready.

My chemistry book lay open on my bed, taunting me with the seven problems I still needed to do for tomorrow's homework. But I just couldn't focus. Suddenly, my phone vibrated in my pocket. I flipped it open with shaking hands and read the text message from Molly.

Come over and talk?

My heart lurched inside me, and I ordered myself to calm down. Molly finally wanted to talk to me, but suddenly, I was terrified. Somehow I knew this was connected to Jason. I had worried about her the entire time she was with him, worried that he was treating her poorly or hurting her. Was she still hurting from something he had said or done to her? What lies had he told her that she had believed and was still suffering from?

But maybe I was overreacting. Maybe this wasn't about Jason at all. Sure, she'd been acting extremely weird and not herself since the breakup, but maybe, it was just a coincidence. Maybe she'd changed her mind about college but didn't know how to tell me she had found another place to go. Molly had always been concerned about making me happy, about making sure I was okay. Maybe that's why she was acting so strange now. We'd planned on doing Iowa State for a few years now, so if she had decided to go somewhere else, she'd probably be feeling a lot of anxiety. That's just how it is with people pleasers—they freak out when their decisions hurt other people. I'd had to deal with this countless times over the years with Molly.

I slid my window open and slipped out then crawled into Molly's room. I hadn't done this in months because I'd been giving Molly her space, and I struggled. She sat on her bed with her hair in a ponytail, wearing sweats and a T-shirt. She looked tired. And scared. Obviously, whatever she was going to tell me was serious. My stomach sank, but at the same time, I couldn't help thinking how adorable she looked. Even in this stressful, scary time. She was beautiful.

She turned and offered me a weak smile as I struggled to get through the window. It was hard to fold myself down to fit into Molly's tiny window, and she teased me about how ridiculous I looked when I tried to maneuver my way in. It was good to hear her teasing me, but I also knew she was still just putting on a show.

Molly thought she had been doing such a good job fooling everyone into thinking she was fine. It might have worked on her family, but it hadn't worked on me. I saw her watching me. She knew I could see the difference in her. So she'd tried to put on this big show, cracking lame jokes when we watched TV, and giving me the fakest smiles and laughs I'd ever seen and heard. When Molly *really* smiled, her eyes sparkled. When she *really* laughed, her whole face lit up. She didn't think I noticed the difference in her speech, smiles, or laughter, but I did. I knew her better than anyone else in the world.

I plopped down on the bed next to her, trying to lighten the mood. Both of us could feel the tension in the air, like a thick blanket settling over both of us, making it hard to breath. She began fiddling with the ring on her hand, something she only did when she was really nervous. I figured it was best to let her control the conversation. So I waited.

I scanned the room and remembered back to all the conversations we'd had in this place, in this very same spot. Molly would sit propped up against her pillows, her legs tucked up underneath her, and I'd sit down at the end, leaning up against the bed frame. We talked our way through every trial and triumph in our lives. Molly was always the first person I wanted to discuss things with, and it was the same for her. I felt bad for people who didn't have someone like that in their lives, someone who would pour their very heart out and listen as you did the same.

This time was different though; I could feel it. This trial would probably be the biggest one we had faced yet. But whatever it was that Molly was going to share with me tonight, I was prepared to deal with it and help her conquer it.

She took a deep breath and closed her eyes briefly, then, focused intently on me. "Okay. I figure there's no easy way to tell you this at all. I've agonized over how I would tell you…but I can't think of the right words." She was talking so fast, like she only did when she is really nervous. I leaned forward and took her hand gently in mine, encouraging her to keep going.

"Go on. I'm listening. Whatever it is, we'll get through it like always."

She shook her head and let out a little laugh. "I'm not sure we can get through this one," she said desperately. "So I'll understand if….if…" She trailed off and looked away.

"If what?" I asked gently. My heart was pounding now; I was so scared. Why couldn't she just spit it out so we could start dealing with it? I kept my cool though, ordering myself to stay calm and supportive.

"I'll understand if you leave." She ducked her head, and I knew she was crying. She sniffed, looked up, and wiped her eyes. When had she started looking so old? Had the stress of this situation aged her in this short of time?

She was still clutching onto my hand, wanting me to stay with her, but thinking that I would bolt the very second she told me whatever it was that she needed to tell me. I could feel her slender hand shaking, but even in the stress of the situation, I loved the feeling of it wrapped securely in mine. This was the way it was supposed to be. I was always the one who was supposed to hold her hand.

"Just tell me. I'm not going anywhere. I promise," I whispered, brushing her hand gently against my lips, trying to let her know that I was serious about staying through whatever crisis she was in. From how she was acting I knew it was big. But I could handle it...I could.

She started pulling my hand, then, leading it to her stomach. I began to feel incredibly awkward when she lifted her shirt up and placed my hand on her bare belly. I looked into her eyes in confusion. *What in the world...*

And then, it clicked. I wouldn't have noticed the tiny little bump if I hadn't been looking for it. I could barely feel it under my hand.

My mind began to race. She'd broken up with Jason at the end of November. She'd come into my room crying that night, and I'd held her until the morning. But she'd had a strange look in her eyes that night, something I couldn't place then. Had it been guilt? Had she slept with Jason that night, felt guilty, and broken up with him and then come crying to me about it?

The timeline made sense. She'd acted weird clear up till Christmas, though she tried as hard as she could to mask it. Had guilt been eating her up inside? She must have finally gotten over it around the New Year, though, because she had honestly been almost normal for those first few weeks in January. There was that one Saturday, though, where she had ignored me the whole day and acted strange the next Monday on the way to school. She must have found out about the pregnancy that weekend. Now it was February, and she'd been feeling nauseous all the time. Suddenly, her puking on the side of the road made a lot more sense.

I kept my hand on her belly and tried to process all of this. All I could do was just stare at her still flat abdomen, but the tiny bump seemed to grow under my hand though. I blinked and shook my head.

"No," I whispered. "You have *got* to be kidding me." I swallowed a few times and withdrew my hand quickly, like I was reacting to touching a hot burner and pulled her shirt down.

A steady river of tears was falling off her face as I searched her eyes. My Molly. My precious, innocent Molly, not so innocent anymore. I felt betrayed. I thought maybe she'd come around and see how much I loved her once she was over Jason. I had hoped that maybe next year at Iowa State I'd have the opportunity to win her over. That dream was all but shattered now.

"I'm sorry, Tanner. I'm so sorry." She hiccuped. She could barely get the words out she was crying so hard. I understood now why she had held on to my hand so desperately. I wanted to bolt out of the room and pretend this conversation had never happened. I wanted to go back to October, before Jason had showed up and corrupted my sweet Molly girl.

We sat there in silence for a few minutes, Molly clutching her belly and me just starting at her stomach, trying to process all the information. All that time, I knew there was a reason I had such a strong dislike for Jason. I knew there was a reason my stomach tied up in knots every time I saw his arm around my girl. It wasn't just jealousy, although, that had played a major role as well, it was just a nagging feeling that never left. Like I knew all along that he would hurt her or take advantage of her.

There were so many things I wanted to say to her right then. What had he said to her to make her think it was okay to have sex with him? Had she been feeling bad when it happened, knowing that sex outside of marriage was very wrong? How could she be so stupid, so naive, to think that Jason really liked her? Guys like Jason wanted one thing, and I guess he'd gotten that one thing and moved on.

But I didn't ask her any of those questions, and I didn't lecture her about guys like Jason. She was hurting right now, clearly guilty about what had happened and scared that I was going to leave her. So once again, I kept my thoughts to myself and moved in to comfort her. I gathered her in my arms and let her sob into my shoulder.

And for a second, I relished the feeling of her in my arms. I knew that this was not the appropriate time to be having these feelings for Molly, but even now, in this moment of crisis, I couldn't help it. The girl I loved was falling through the cracks, slipping right through my fingertips. I would hold on to her for as long as I could.

She stiffened in my arms and pulled back, searching my face, confused. "Why aren't you mad?" she asked innocently.

"I am," I admitted sheepishly, and she ducked her head again. I lifted her chin with my fingers, forcing her to look me in the eye.

"But that doesn't mean I just walk out on you, Molly. I'm disappointed. I'm hurt. And yeah, I'm a little mad. But I'm still here. I'm not going anywhere, okay? I'm here." And I pulled her into my arms again and felt her relax against me.

She pulled back again after a few moments and told me I had every right to be mad, that she should have listened to me, and that she was sorry she didn't. "I know you probably have a lot of questions, and I owe you the truth. So…ask whatever," she said quietly. Her cheeks were burning; this was an awkward subject to discuss.

I rubbed my neck and sighed. "Yeah. I do have questions I guess." I thought for a moment, deciding how best to go about this without making her feel any worse than she already felt.

"Was it—" I closed my eyes. Did I really want to know the answer to these questions? Not really. I didn't want to think about Molly and Jason being together in that way. But I continued on, needing to get the details of the situation. "Was it just one night?"

"Yes," she whispered, shame coloring her voice.

I nodded and swallowed. At least she'd wised up and not let it happen more than once. That was a plus, I guessed. But it was awful that after just *one* night together—one mistake—she'd ended up pregnant. Of course.

"Okay. That night you came into my room…" I let my question trail off and watched her eyes register it, remembering that cold, rainy night I had held her.

She nodded, the tears starting again. "Yeah, it was that night." She choked on the last word like it was bringing up horrible memories.

"Did he break up with you because you…weren't…good enough? Too inexperienced? Or did you break up with him because you felt guilty?"

She paused for a second, almost like she didn't know the answer to the question.

"Well. I don't know, really. I just ran out after it happened. Neither of us really said anything, it was just assumed that we were over, I guess. He texted me the next day and asked if I was done, and I said yes."

"So you lied to me that night," I said bluntly. "You told me he said he wasn't ready for commitment."

She nodded.

"And that's why you couldn't get over it? Because you felt bad?"

She was being kind of vague. I just wanted to know what she was feeling.

She nodded again. At least she felt guilty about it.

My brain was spinning. I was beginning to feel used. That night I'd held Molly in my arms, she'd been in Jason's arms hours earlier. Her hair was damp, which meant she'd probably felt dirty and tried to shower Jason off. But then, she'd crawled over to my bedroom seeking comfort when hours earlier she'd given Jason her virginity.

I tried to put myself in the same situation, but I honestly didn't know if I would have done the same thing. Would I have sought out Molly's comfort after completely going against my morals? Would I have been able to live with what I had done?

And that's when the anger came because after that night, Molly had returned to me like a lost puppy. She spent every waking moment with me because she felt guilty and didn't want to be alone. She had lied to me for two months, putting on a show when her life was falling apart.

Part of me did want to leave her alone to deal with this. It wasn't my baby; it wasn't my mistake to live with. I'd supported Molly for twelve years, and this is how she repaid me? Did she honestly expect me to stick around?

And then, I realized that no, she didn't expect me to stay around. She told me five minutes ago that she understood if I wanted to leave. I realized that she wasn't expecting me to stay around and fix this for her. She expected me to leave. She thought it would be too much for me.

I got up and walked over to the widow, staring out of it, trying to clear my mind. Trying to process what Molly had just told me and battling the emotions warring inside me.

"It's okay if you leave, Tanner," Molly said flatly. "I know I messed up, and I'm not asking you to fix it. I just thought you deserved the truth."

I laughed a little. "It's about time, Molly," I said, turning around to face her again. "You're a terrible liar. I knew something was up with you. Guess I just didn't plan on it being this big though."

She sighed again and nodded. "Yeah. It's big. I haven't told anyone else yet. I'm still trying to figure out what to do."

I nodded. "Okay. I won't tell anyone."

She smiled and whispered, "Thanks."

It was too early to work on solutions; I figured we had plenty of time to work out those details later. Right now, I was exhausted; I felt like I had been run over by this news. A whole mix of emotions was jumbling around inside of me: betrayal, anger, confusion, disappointment, and the list went on and on. I wasn't pre-pared to deal with this right now. So before I crawled out of the window and left Molly alone for the night, I turned to comfort her again. I gathered her in my arms once more and kissed her forehead. I promised her I wouldn't leave her.

Her eyes filled with tears at my unexpected support. I tried not to feel like a superhero, but I could see it in her eyes how much she appreciated this. She hadn't expected me to stay with her, but she was my life. There was no way I could just walk away and cut her out. I was here for the long haul.

That's just what you do when you're in love.

"We'll figure it out, Moll. Tomorrow's a new day." And then, I left her sitting on that bed.

It wasn't until I got back into the solitude of my room that I let my own tears start to fall. I pushed my chemistry book off my bed, letting it fall to the floor with a satisfying *thunk*.

I'd help Molly get through this. But who was going to help *me* get through this?

Twelve

Molly

Early March

After I told Tanner the news, I was experiencing a brand-new mix of emotions. I was relieved to have told him; an enormous burden had been lifted from my shoulders that night I finally spilled the truth to him. It felt good to tell the truth for once. Seems like all I'd been doing for the past few months was lying and putting on a show for everyone. It was nice to not have to pretend with Tanner anymore, at least, to some degree. He still didn't know about the rape, and I intended to keep it that way.

So while I was relieved, I also was feeling even dirtier and more unworthy of Tanner's friendship. I had expected and planned on

Tanner freaking out. On him walking out of my life forever, sick of my little game. Why did he always have to respond in the right way? I appreciated that he chose to stick with me and support me because he was all I had, but on the other hand, I would have felt better with him walking out.

Now, as twisted as that sounds, I felt so undeserving of his friendship. I didn't deserve Tanner. I didn't deserve the way he stuck with me and loved me so unconditionally. I deserved him deserting me. So when he stayed with me, it made me feel even lower, dirtier, and undeserving than ever. Tanner walking out would have felt more appropriate to me. It would have made me feel like I was finally getting what I really deserved. But he'd stayed. And in a way, it made me feel so much worse.

It had been absolute torture to tell Tanner the news. I had to look in his eyes and see every emotion play out. Confusion. Realization. Pain. Anger. Betrayal. I'd seen it all play out right in front of me, even without Tanner saying anything. That's how close we were even after all these months of confusion and separation. I knew Tanner better than anyone in the world, and it had been just awful to see him suffering because of me.

But once all those negative emotions cleared up in his eyes, I saw the raw pain and deep sadness take over. Tanner loved me. More than on the level I loved him. His love went so much deeper than mine; it was a love that would sacrifice everything and endure anything. After all the anger and betrayal faded, I saw that deep love replace those emotions, mixed with the sadness of knowing that with Jason's baby growing inside me; any chance of me loving him back pretty much disappeared. How was I to focus on any feelings for Tanner when I was now facing this enormous mountain? I had to figure out how to climb that mountain first, which would take far longer than Tanner deserved to have to wait.

I could no longer ignore Tanner's love for me, though, because he was going to live it out for the entire time I was dealing with this. He promised he'd be there for me, and I knew he meant it. I couldn't laugh it off anymore because it was right in front of me. Only love, the deep love Tanner had for me, stuck around in this type of horrible, messed-up situation.

And this made me sad, Tanner sticking around to help me fight my way through this when I knew that even after I made it to the other side, I probably would never love him back. I couldn't. Tanner was too good, too pure. I wasn't worthy of him, not after the path I had chosen to walk down. Now, I was just an empty shell, scraped of my former self on the night Jason raped me—and I didn't know who I was anymore.

And Tanner deserved someone who was full of life and joy, someone who would take his hand and hold it all the way through life's adventures and hardships. Someone who would laugh with him, cry with him, dream with him, and support him in everything he did. I wasn't able to do that anymore because I was empty. I was too busy trying to figure out how to function, how to drag myself through each new day. I could only focus on myself and coping. A relationship had to go both ways; it would never work with Tanner pouring himself into me and me never giving anything back. He'd have to keep pouring and pouring, too, because I was *that* empty. I'd never be full again. How exhausting would that be—to expend that much energy on another, never receiving anything in return? I could never do that to Tanner.

On the other hand, I selfishly wanted him to stick around with me, to stay by my side as the pregnancy became visible and the gossip started flying. I wanted him to kiss my forehead and whisper that everything would be okay. And yet, I wanted him to leave, to make me feel like I deserved to feel: dirty, empty, and worthless. I wanted him to get over me and find someone who could love him the way he loved me. I wanted him to find that girl who could give him what I could not.

So as of right then, I wasn't really sure what was going through his brain. I gave him a few days to process the information, to make sure he knew what he was dealing with.

I gave him time to change his mind.

He didn't though. After a weekend of no texts and phone calls, he finally reappeared. Immediately, when he climbed in my window, I could see a plan churning in his mind. And when Tanner gets a plan going, it'd hard to steer him away from it.

I'd seen this play out many times in the past twelve years. Tanner would get some "brilliant" idea in his head, and he would get all excited and wouldn't stop talking about it. Sometimes, I'd humor him and play along, but other times I let him know that his idea would never work. Usually, we'd laugh about it because, after I rationalized with him, he'd see the dead end to his genius. We'd end up holding our stomachs from how hard we laughed.

When I saw the look on his face as he crawled through my window, I knew he had a plan. This is exactly what I didn't need. I couldn't make plans anymore because I lived one day at a time now. My plan was to wake up each morning and just survive, to just get through another day until I could fall back into my bed and pretend everything wasn't crumbling in around me. I was the master at blocking out thoughts now, and my bed offered the comfort of lying there, clearing my head, and just existing. So right now, as Tanner climbed in, that's all I wanted to do: lie in my bed, block it all out, and just exist. Forget everything.

"Hi," he simply said once he was finally in. He pulled down his shirt that had gotten all bunched and tangled as he wrestled his way into my room. He was breathless from the exertion, and I couldn't help smiling.

"Sorry, it's been awhile," he said with a shrug. "I needed time to…process."

"I understand," I said, nodding. "No big deal."

"Yeah. So it's been a rough few days, to say the least." He rubbed his neck, embarrassed.

"I can imagine" was all I said. I could feel the marble making its way up my throat again, choking me. Tears moistened my eyes, and I blinked them back. I tried to focus on Tanner, but the look in his eyes was almost too much for me.

He sighed. "It hurts," he said, looking away. I could see the tears in his eyes when he glanced back and made his way to sit beside me. "It hurts a lot, Molly."

I sniffed, the tears coursing down my cheeks now, falling onto the comforter on the bed. I couldn't speak; the marble made sure of that. All I could do was just nod my head. I knew it was hurting him.

He lifted my chin with his fingers, forcing me to look him straight in the face. "I need to tell you something, Molly." He paused, searching my face. I knew what was coming.

I shook my head a little and winced. "Don't, Tanner. Please don't," I whispered.

But he shook his head right back and said it anyway. "I love you, Molly."

I took a deep breath and let the sobs come rattling out of my body then. I couldn't handle this right now. Tanner deserved so much more. But I let him gather me up in his arms, pulling me close to his warm body. He stroked my hair and whispered comforting words. It was torture. I loved it, but I hated it because I couldn't love him back. Someday, he'd figure out I was too empty and broken, incapable of loving him the way he needed to be loved. But someday needed to come sooner than later, because I refused to let him waste his time on me. For the sake of his conscious I'd let him help me through this pregnancy, but I couldn't let him love me, couldn't let him hold onto the hope that maybe I'd love him back. The sooner he realized this the better. It would ease the suffering for both of us.

"Don't do this to me, Tanner," I managed to choke out through my sobs. "I'm not...good enough for you."

He pulled back, holding me at arm's length, searching my eyes. He looked so sad.

"Molly, stop. I know you don't feel the same. I just…I just wanted you to know. And don't ever say that again! You messed up, but that doesn't mean I'm better than you, that I've never messed up either." His voice took on an edge that usually wasn't there. He really meant it.

I nodded, sniffed, and wiped my eyes. An awkward silence filled the room as Tanner's declaration of love still hung in the air.

"I'm not…I'm not who you think I am anymore, Tanner. I'm so different after this whole ordeal. I'll never be the Molly you fell in love with. She's gone."

He let out a sad, frustrated laugh and rubbed his neck again. "People change, Molly, and love changes too. No one is the same person another loves at first, but that doesn't mean that those changes take away the love. I know you messed up, that you made a decision you shouldn't have made. But you're still Molly. And I still love you."

"But you shouldn't!" I said angrily. I stood up and walked to the window, staring out into the dreary, cold day outside. I twirled around and said, "I can't love you the way you deserve, Tanner. I'm so empty now. It wouldn't be fair to you, to have to take care of me all the time and never get anything back. That's just how it is now! I can't figure out how to work through this thing!"

Tanner stood and was by my side in an instant, grabbing my shoulders and turning me toward him. "I want to help you get through it," he said quietly. "I love you, Molly, and I want you to get better. I know that my Molly is still in there somewhere. I *know* she is. And I'm sticking around until she comes back."

"But you deserve—" I started to say, but he cut me off again.

"Stop thinking that way! There's no one better for me than you. We get each other! We've been through *so* much together. Good and bad. Sure, this is the worst we've dealt with, but we'll figure it out! We will. Stop thinking I deserve better. I don't *want* anything better. You're the best thing I've ever had."

We both fell silent. I wasn't sure how to respond to that, because my heart was breaking at the messed up picture Tanner had of me. How could I be the best thing he'd ever had? Hadn't I basically deserted him and brushed off his warnings of Jason? As my closest friend, he deserved better. So why in the world did he think I was the best thing he'd ever had when clearly I'd demonstrated just the opposite by treating him so badly for the last few months?

I knew he was waiting for me to crack, to give into his declaration of love. But when I remained silent he simply reached out to me, then cradled my face with his hands and began rubbing my cheeks with his thumb—slow, soothing circles that believe it or not were causing me to crack. I squeezed my eyes shut as tears continued leaking out of my cheeks and onto his thumb. All I could whisper was his name. And with that, he leaned in and gently touched his lips to mine, testing whether or not I would actually let him kiss me. My body responded and took over, and I stood on my toes, pressing my lips firmly to his. I felt him smile as he kissed me again and again like I knew he wanted to do so many times before.

His arms circled around me, and I did the same. We stood there by the window kissing for what seemed an eternity, responding to the deep, supercharged emotions that had been simmering for years.

My head spun the entire time. This caught me off guard completely, yet I responded in the complete opposite way I thought I would have. I wanted to keep kissing him forever because with Tanner, I felt safe. I felt loved. This is where I was supposed to be in October, in Tanner's arms. Not Jason's.

The internal argument I'd been having seemed to crumble to pieces after what just happened. *Did* I love Tanner? Was that even possible? Had I just been fooling myself for the past few years, convinced that if I loved Tanner it would ruin our friendship? Our relationship was so deep and special; I had worried that falling in love with Tanner would ruin everything. What if we broke up? I would be left without my alibi, my best friend, and everything in the world to me. I had been so terrified of that, that I shut down the idea of love with Tanner completely. Better to be safe than sorry.

But now I knew. I *did* love Tanner. I'd loved him for years. And we'd both danced around this fact for all this time. Suddenly, my heart was light again, glowing from finally recognizing this.

I pulled back, breathless from kissing Tanner. Kissing him was far different than kissing Jason. My mouth tingled, my heart pounded, and I knew my eyes were speaking what I was saying. With Jason, it had been more of a thrill—the excitement of my first kisses with a cute boy, the strange tingle that rushed up my back. That's what my eyes conveyed to Jason when he kissed me, but with Tanner, I knew it was different. I knew they shone with love, a love that ten minutes earlier I was convinced I couldn't have, that I didn't deserve. Why had I thought that loving Tanner wasn't an option? How had I pushed those feelings to the backburner? There was no way I could kid myself anymore; no matter what my brain tried to tell me, my heart was telling me something different. It was telling me that I *did* love Tanner.

So I looked into his eyes and whispered, "I love you too." He smiled, closed his eyes, and let out a joyous laugh, a laugh that said, "Finally!"

He kissed me again, lifting me in his arms and spinning me around. I let my heart soar in this moment, finally letting Tanner's love soak into it, opening itself up to it for the first time. And ready to give that love right back to him.

Thirteen

That first half hour after we kissed, after we both admitted to the feelings that had been simmering under the surface for years, we sat on my bed with our fingers laced together, trying to figure out what this meant now.

And I was back trying to battle all sorts of emotions. Had I just responded to Tanner's declaration of love and his kiss because it felt good to feel loved again? Did I really love him, or did I love the feeling of security his love offered me? The moment he kissed me, my selfishness reared its ugly head again, all decked out in boxing gloves and ready to come out swinging. For the past three months, I had been alone in a terrible nightmare, and now that Tanner had finally told me he loved me, selfish hope poked his head around the corner, enticing me with all its possibilities. With Tanner, I would never be alone. Perhaps that selfishness was tricking me into thinking I loved him.

After all, this felt completely different than falling in love with Jason. Granted, falling in love with someone and actually loving them are two totally different things, but I couldn't ignore the fact that with Jason—it had been more of a thrill. It had been more of how falling in love is portrayed in the movies, with all the sparks of electricity and sweaty palms. I didn't feel that same rush with Tanner that I had with Jason. Tanner's kisses had been wonderful and far more passionate than Jason's, and they certainly meant more. And I *had* felt a stirring inside of me, just different than with Jason.

And maybe it was just because with Tanner, his kisses actually meant something. Jason had kissed me because that's what he had to do to get me to follow him into his little trap. Tanner wasn't trying to trap me; his kisses told me that he loved me. Could the reason falling for Tanner felt different than falling for Jason be because this was a deeper, more mature love? A true, honest-to-goodness love?

And wasn't love much more than feelings anyway? Wasn't it much more than the tingly zap up your spine when a boy touched you and kissed you? Was it more than your heart racing when you saw him? Was it more than the warm flush on your cheeks when he whispered sweet words to you? It had to be more than those feelings.

It's not like I hadn't felt those feelings with Tanner in the last few minutes, or even years I supposed. When he kissed me I had felt a rush of excitement, and my body had responded to him; otherwise, I would have pulled away and told him no, I didn't love him. But I *had* stood on tiptoe to press my lips more firmly into his. I *had* felt the feelings stirring up inside me. If I didn't really love Tanner, I would have responded differently. I guess when your heart really knows something—something your brain is trying to convince yourself otherwise about—it wins over in the end. My heart had clearly won in this situation; there was no getting around the fact that I loved Tanner back. No matter how long I had denied this fact—ignored it when so many people tried to convince me of it, no matter how dirty, selfish, and undeserving I felt—my heart could no longer keep silent on my love for Tanner.

At the same time, I was terrified. What I had told Tanner earlier was true; I was so empty right now. How could I truly love him, give him the kind of love I honestly wanted to give him, when I was dealing with all these issues? It would be hard for me to do that because I honestly didn't know who I was anymore. I couldn't trust God to take care of me because I felt like he had failed, and my former self has been scraped out and left for dead on Jason's couch. Three months ago, Tanner and I would have been perfect for each other, but now, I wasn't so sure. Just because we loved each other didn't mean we were right for each other.

And sooner or later, I wouldn't be able to keep the truth of the rape from Tanner anymore. If we tried to plan a future together, I couldn't take one step into that future without being honest with him, and that would be the hardest thing in the world for me to do. He would be furious that I hadn't told him right away—that I hadn't trusted him enough to take care of me. He wouldn't understand the fear I still had of Jason. He wouldn't understand that I didn't want to press charges. I just wanted him to disappear from my life forever. I wasn't sure if I could stop Tanner from trying to fight Jason.

Also, who knows how many girls Jason had slept with, even in the short amount of time he had before he started dating me? All the girls he'd slept with back in his old high school? He was probably crawling in STDs or STIs, and I hadn't gotten tested after the rape. If Tanner and I were to have a future together, I'd need to get tested; and if I'd gotten something from Jason, I'd be even more ashamed.

Right now was not the time to tell him about the rape. I didn't know when I would get around to telling him, but at the time being, I could only focus on one issue at a time. The issue right now was trying to figure out what to do next. We loved each other, but what now? What to do about the pregnancy? This would probably become a major wedge in our relationship because the baby wasn't Tanner's. When it was born, what would Tanner do?

I looked down at our hands, at our fingers laced together. "What about the baby, Tanner?" I asked, the fear causing my voice to tremble.

Tanner's face lit up, which confused me. He should not be excited right now, not after he just told his best friend that he loved her, but she was pregnant with another boy's baby.

"That's why I came over, Molly. I have a plan." He was grinning, which made me smile too.

"I knew it!" I said, teasing him. "I knew the minute I saw your face today that something was going on in that brain of yours."

"Now, just hear me out, okay? Because this is kind of a crazy plan. No one knows you're pregnant yet, right?"

"Right…" I said slowly, confused.

"Okay. So no one knows about it yet, which means no one knows who the father is right now."

I scrunched my face up in confusion, unsure of where he was going with this. "Right," I said again.

"No one has to know it was Jason, Molly. What if—" he paused, trying to pick out just the right words. "What if we don't tell people the baby is Jason's? What if we tell them—" And suddenly, it all fell into place. Tanner wanted to convince everyone that the baby was his!

"That it was *yours*?" I said, cutting him off. I pried my hand out from his. I could *not* let Tanner take the fall for my mistake. I couldn't let him trick people into thinking we had slept together and gotten pregnant. What kind of sick game was that anyway?

I stood up and began pacing, my voice picking up speed because I was getting upset. "The baby won't *look* like you, Tanner. No one will buy it! And besides, in November you were staying as far away from me as you could, and I've always told everyone that we've always been just friends! Won't it be weird to tell everyone that 'Ha-ha, just kidding, we actually love each other and look what happened?'"

Tanner stood up too and grabbed my arm. "Hey, calm down. Molly, *calm down.* Yes, you were with Jason at the time, but you *did* break up, remember? And you came into my room that night crying. We could just say that we both realized that night that we actually did love each other, and it had spun out of control from there. You *did* spend the night with me in my bed, remember?"

My face started burning then, and I shook my arm out of his grasp. He let his arm fall limp to his side, discouragement flooding his face. "It would be a lie, Tanner. I've been doing enough lying and hiding for the past few months. I wouldn't be able to lie for the rest of the pregnancy and then for the rest of the baby's life, telling it you're the dad when you're not."

He grew silent after that, and I could see the logic lining up in his face. He let out a huge sigh and flopped back down on the bed, sprawling out. I crept to his side and snuggled up to him, relishing the feeling of his arms around me. He kissed my head and starting stroking my hair. I knew he was thinking of how unfair this whole situation was. We both finally own up to our feelings, and yet, my wrong decision was keeping us apart.

"All right, so maybe we can't convince people the baby's mine, but…that doesn't mean I still can't be the dad, right? I mean, Jason probably won't want to be a part of the baby's life, and it needs a daddy. And I love you. I can learn to love the baby too."

I felt my already abused heart break a little bit more, because Tanner didn't deserve this. We should have done this earlier. If we'd stopped dancing around the truth of our feelings months ago, we wouldn't be dealing with an unplanned pregnancy, and we could be planning for college and a future together.

"But what about college, Tanner? If you stick around with me after the baby comes, where does that leave college?"

"Well. We could still go after the first semester. Find a babysitter and do college in the daytime. I'd get a part-time job at night. We'd make it work, Molly."

"I can't ask you to do that for me, Tanner. You're so excited for college. Waiting around for me and a baby that isn't even yours isn't the smartest thing or the best thing for you."

He lifted my chin up again so I was looking right into his eyes. "*You're* the best thing for me, Molly. If I can't have you, I don't want anything else. College can wait because I don't want you to do this alone."

Once Tanner sets his mind on something, it's really hard to change it. I could tell that his mind and heart were set on this plan.

"So we just tell people it's Jason's baby but that you're the dad?" It sounded weird to me.

"Well, maybe the baby will come out looking more like you. Who knows? Maybe no one will ask. I think your parents need to know it was Jason, and mine certainly will too. They probably won't be too keen on the idea of me claiming his baby, but who cares? They know I love you, and they love you too. And it's our decision. If I want to be the daddy, I'm gonna. And if people ask who the real dad is, it's really none of their business anyway. Jason may have fathered the baby, but that doesn't make him the daddy."

"True," I said slowly. It did make sense. If Jason didn't want to be the dad, then, who was to stop Tanner from being the dad?

So for the first time since that cold, rainy November night, I felt true hope. I didn't feel like I was climbing a mountain anymore, not with Tanner by my side now. I didn't feel like I was marching toward another dead end, another ending. I felt like I was turning a corner, one that shone brightly with hope and the promise of a new beginning.

Fourteen

Mid-March

I was now fourteen weeks pregnant, and no one besides Tanner knew anything about it, which was soon becoming a stumbling block in our blossoming relationship. I agreed that it was probably time to tell my parents, but I disagreed about telling Jason. I already knew he'd be furious about it, that he wouldn't want anything to do with it. Tanner had already agreed to stay with me, so why did I have to face Jason's anger? He didn't need to know.

"Molly, it's *his* baby," Tanner argued, getting more and more frustrated. "He needs to know! He *deserves* to know! We'll tell him he doesn't have to stick around, but you never know if he'll take some responsibility for it. You know, child support? He's a horrible guy, but maybe, he has a soft side. Maybe once he finds out, he'll feel guilty. Child support would really help us out," he pointed out, trying everything to get me to grasp this idea. I didn't want to hear it though.

I looked up from the poem I was trying to dissect and interpret. Tanner and I were in his basement working on homework, which was quickly becoming impossible because Tanner wouldn't drop this. I put my pencil down and sighed. My head was pounding, so I started rubbing my temples. I didn't want to deal with this today.

"I don't want child support from him. I don't want *anything* from him, Tanner. I want him to go away forever."

"We need to do the right thing here. It would be wrong to keep someone's baby from them."

I gave him a dumbfounded look. "Wow, seriously?" I said sarcastically. "A few days ago, you wanted to convince everyone that *you* were the father? And now, you're saying we need to do the right thing? Don't lecture me, Tanner. It's *my* baby. Mine. If I don't want Jason to know, I shouldn't have to tell him, okay?"

Tanner shut his chemistry book and turned to look at me. "Yeah, well that was a bad plan anyway. Wouldn't be able to pull it off, and it was only in my mind for like half a day. So technically, it doesn't count. But keeping this from Jason is totally different. He needs to own up to what he did to you. Why should you be the only one to deal with what happened? That's not fair. Don't you think we should give him the chance to do the right thing?"

No, I thought. I didn't think we should give him the chance to do the right thing, because he *wouldn't* do the right thing. Tanner would never understand this unless I told him about the rape, and I didn't want to do that either. Not yet. I'd tell him after Jason was long gone. So I somehow had to convince him to drop this altogether.

I ran my fingers through my hair and huffed. "Look, he's not gonna do the right thing! He's not that kind of person. I just want to forget about him. If I tell him about the baby, and by some miracle, he does decide to do the right thing, we'll never get rid of him! What if he wants visitation rights, Tanner? Could you handle him coming around at holidays and birthdays, taking the baby away from us for weeks in the summer because some judge said he could?"

For a minute, Tanner was silent as that sunk in. Of course, Jason would never want anything to do with the baby. He was three months from graduating, then, off to some fancy college on a basketball scholarship. He wouldn't want a baby to slow him down and take money from him, but I was getting desperate. Anything to convince Tanner that telling Jason was a bad idea.

"True," he said slowly. "That would be hard. But I couldn't live with myself if we kept this from him. If we get married and I raise that baby, Molly, I'd spend the rest of my life feeling guilty knowing that the real dad was out there somewhere, never knowing that he had a kid. I'd feel like a thief!"

I sighed and racked my fingers through my hair. He wasn't going to give this up. It was a legitimate reason though. It would be unfair to the baby, at least, to keep the truth about Jason from it. This whole situation was just a mess. Deep down I knew that Jason needed to know, I was just being selfish again. But was it really too much to ask after what he did to me for him to just leave me alone?

"Let me think about it for a while, okay? Let's just get through telling our parents first."

Tanner agreed, but I knew that after we hurdled that obstacle, he'd be right at it again.

We decided to tell my parents the next night. My mom didn't have to work and Tanner was getting antsy. So the next night, we sat around my kitchen table, my parent's hands wrapped around steaming mugs of coffee, deep looks of concern in their eyes. Our family wasn't one to just sit around the table for a nice chat. They knew there was a reason to this talk, and they knew it wasn't good news.

We just sat there for a while making awkward small talk until conversation stalled, and the room grew silent. Savannah was over at a friend's house doing homework, and Josh was in the basement watching a movie. It was so quiet; the clock's ticking bounced off the kitchen walls. My parents were waiting for us to take charge, but my mouth dried up and I panicked; my heart raced wildly out of control. I looked to Tanner with wild eyes, telling him I needed him to take charge because I couldn't.

He took my hand in his and dove right in. "Well, I guess we first need to tell you two that Molly and I...uh. We...sorta like each other." He looked over at me and cracked a big smile; he couldn't help it. I smiled back. Even in the midst of this awful mess, we couldn't help but be happy about the fact that this was finally out in the open.

My dad looked at my mom and shook his head, a smile slowly stretching across his face. He hit her lightly on the arm. "See, told ya. Always knew these two would end up together."

My mom laughed. "Okay, you win. I never thought Molly would own up to her feelings," she said smartly, raising her eyebrows at me. My mom used to badger me all the time about Tanner. She was one of those people who, for years, tried to get me to see that Tanner was hopelessly in love with me, but I had ignored her.

So for a few minutes, we sat around the table laughing about how for years I had kept Tanner at my fingertips. My dad was surprised and impressed at the same time that Tanner has stuck around waiting for me for so long.

"So have you come to ask permission to date my daughter then?" he asked teasingly, but at the same time probably meant it too. My dad was old-fashioned in that way, so it had been surprising that he had accepted Jason for the short time we were together.

"Well, of course we are," Tanner replied. He knew my parents loved him and would approve of us, but my dad loved teasing Tanner.

"We're very happy for you two," my mom said, swatting my dad on the arm.

I fell silent, though, because after this good news I had to dump the bad news on them, dampening this happy occasion. My stomach was roiling. I didn't want to do this. I didn't want to face the looks of disappointment of their faces. Thank goodness Tanner was here beside me though. It would have been a million times harder doing this by myself. Tanner squeezed my hand gently, encouraging me to go on.

"There's something else I need to tell you guys though, and… please don't be mad at me." I ducked my hand and felt the tears squeezing out of my eyes. Everyone was silent, waiting for me to go on. When I looked up my parents had fear in their eyes.

"I'm…" I took a deep breath. "I'm…pregnant." I whispered.

More silence. My dad closed his eyes and turned away, my mom's eyes got as wide as saucers. Tanner squeezed my hand again. "Well, that was fast, you two," my dad said, a hint of annoyance in his eyes. I hated that they jumped to that conclusion so fast. It wasn't fair to jumble Tanner up in this mess.

"It's not Tanner's baby, Dad," I said sadly. I kind of wished it was his baby at this point.

"What?" my dad said loudly.

"Whose is it?" My mom looked incredibly confused, but then, it clicked in her mind. She knew. And the last few months were suddenly making sense to her. My sad mood, withdrawal, and excuses.

"Jason's." I explained. "It was just one night, and I broke up with him after it happened. I didn't mean for it to happen…" Sobs were making talking impossible right now.

We sat around the table in silence for a few minutes, my parents soaking in the information. Tanner jumped in then, telling them that he loved me and wanted to help me through this. He explained that we didn't really have a plan at this point. We didn't know if we would go to college in the fall or wait till the baby was older and go the following year. We didn't know if we would get married; it was too soon to jump into that.

My dad was immediately against the plan, which was making my blood boil and my anxiety level climb higher and higher. This hadn't been my idea anyway! It's what Tanner wanted. We had finally realized that we couldn't live without each other, and we'd be together with this plan. We weren't giving up on the idea of college altogether; we would postpone it. Iowa State was probably out of the question, but there were smaller colleges close to home where we could go to during the day while the baby was at daycare. My dad was just concerned that Tanner was throwing his life away for me.

"It's not your baby, son. We couldn't ask you to stick around and help Molly through it. Not your responsibility."

"I know it's not," Tanner argued. "And Molly didn't ask me. It was my idea." Tanner looked at me tenderly and gently took my hand in his. I gave him a weak smile. It was clear to everyone in the room that no matter what, Tanner was here to stay.

My dad sighed and ran his fingers through his thinning hair. We talked about setting up a doctor's appointment soon, but we'd figure out what to do later. My parents still thought it was unfair for Tanner to take on the burden of a child that wasn't even his. I assumed they'd push me toward adoption, which I would look into but probably never do. Not with Tanner in the picture now. The baby was still Jason's, but Tanner wanted it. Maybe I *could* love this baby if Tanner loved it. If he wanted to keep it, I would do everything in my power to do just that.

I went in for an appointment the next Monday; I was right at fifteen weeks. Tanner was by my side the whole time; the ultrasound technician just assumed he was the daddy. And even though my mom still wasn't thrilled, she came too. The technician squirted that cold jelly on my still tiny baby bump, and when the sound of the baby's heartbeat echoed across the room, my mom melted. The ultrasound was cool, but it was hard to see clear details. The 3D ultrasound, however, was breathtaking. We could see the perfect tiny features of my baby clearly on the screen, the little legs and feet, the tiny head. She looked like she was sucking her thumb!

This was the first time I had thought about the sex of the baby. I'd been trying to think of the baby as an "it," not a he or a she. But I was so relieved that Tanner and my parents knew now, that it was easier to deal with the pregnancy. Could I actually get excited about the arrival of this little one?

It would be rough, having to deal with a newborn just out of high school. The baby was due August 18, three months after graduation. I, for sure, would not be going to college this fall. Tanner could still go to the community college a few towns down the road, live at home, and commute. If we didn't get married for a while, he'd still just be next door.

His parents were more okay with the idea than mine were. Brian and Evelyn knew that Tanner was smitten with me and that he would never let anyone convince him to leave me. And they loved me too; they were excited that I would be taken care of. Ellen was ecstatic; she had wanted to skip school that day and come to my appointment. She was obsessed with babies and always wanted to see and feel my belly, even though there still wasn't much there. I hoped my baby bump would stay fairly small so that I could disguise it for a few more months. Some women hardly gained weight or grew at all. Maybe that would be the case for me.

Tanner held my hand and smiled as the technician moved the wand over my belly and pointed out the baby's delicate features. She explained some of the symptoms I'd probably be feeling, like some weight gain and a stuffy nose. Something about the combined effect of hormonal changes and increased blood flow to my mucous membranes. Tanner laughed at how the technician turned a simple stuffy nose into something that sounded a lot fancier.

My parents' attitude about the baby softened a little after that appointment. My mom put the ultrasound pictures up on the fridge and spent time explaining all the details the technician had told us to my dad, Josh, and Savannah. Josh was the only one having a hard time with it still; I think he just felt extremely awkward. And he thought Tanner was stupid to stick around and raise another man's baby.

Tanner was thrilled though. You'd never know that it wasn't his baby. He talked about how he wanted a girl too, and he was always shouting out names. His favorite was Eden, which made sense because his family had a thing for *e*'s with his mom being an Evelyn and his sister an Ellen. I thought it was a beautiful name.

We figured it was probably time to let Kristina in on the whole situation after the appointment. It'd been torture seeing her in the lunch room every day sitting across from Leah and the rest of the girls from youth group, laughing and smiling like she didn't have a care in the world. I envied her because she was living the life I was supposed to be living, finishing out her senior year surrounded by friends and with a bright, promising future ahead of her.

So we took her out to Emma's after school that Wednesday after the appointment so we could tell her the news. She wasn't surprised when we told her we were together now, and she actually looked happy about that. We hadn't spoken since that night at the football game where Jason had been drunk, and since then, she had kept me at a safe distance, ignoring me and basically replacing me with Leah. So this conversation was awkward, it felt stiff and forced. It was only after we told her about us that she started warming up to me again, looking somewhat pleased that I was finally making good life choices. Things would probably never be the same between us again; we could never go back to how it was before Jason. He'd inflicted damage deeper than he would ever realize. She'd never trust me again, and we'd been apart for so long now—it was impossible to reverse the damage.

Her good feelings about me quickly vanished when I broke the news about the pregnancy. Her face drained of all blood, and she clenched her fists together in anger and disappointment. I just sat there and had to watch all the same emotions that Tanner had felt play out right in front of me again. I explained that it had been only once, that I'd broken it off right after it happened. Tanner tried to explain that he was going to stick around and help me out, but she responded just like my parents and Josh responded. She thought it was a horrible idea for Tanner not to go off to Iowa State like planned and move on. Why should he suffer from my mistake?

"I'm not going to suffer," Tanner argued. "It was *my* idea, and it's the plan we're going with. Our parents finally agreed to it, and I'll still be going to college, just not at Iowa State. But I want to be where Molly is, and if Molly has a baby, then that's what we'll deal with. If you disagree, that's fine. We're not asking for your approval, we just thought you needed to know."

She shook her head and stared out the window, discouraged. I knew she was probably thinking that it was a good thing she had dumped me when she had, that she wasn't tangled up in this sticky mess too.

"No one knows yet. Jason doesn't know yet. So please don't say anything," I pleaded.

"Yeah, okay. I won't tell." She swirled her straw around in her drink, clearly uninterested in the chocolate pie that lay half-eaten in front of her. I understood, of course. News this big tends to steal your appetite.

I knew that this was the end of Kristina and me for good. After our little meeting she hugged Tanner, then, hugged me out of obligation and wished us luck. After an awkward goodbye and a half-hearted wave, she hopped in her car, slid her sunglasses onto her face, and drove away. She never looked back once, and I knew I'd never hear from her again. We were over.

I turned to Tanner and fell into him, letting him fold me into his arms, my tears soaking through his flannel shirt, though he really should have been in a coat. It was still early in March, much too early for spring in Iowa. Snow was still melting on the grass, the sun was shining, but a biting wind cut through us, leaving me chilled and miserable.

When I saw Kristina in school the next day and caught her eye across the lunchroom, she instantly looked away. I did notice that she glanced back at my belly, but it was still too early for me to be showing, and I'd gone out that weekend and bought a whole new wardrobe of loose fitting shirts to disguise any evidence. I guessed I better get ready for people to stop looking me in the eye and start starting at my belly.

So now we'd told everybody that mattered about the pregnancy. Everybody except Jason, that is. It was Thursday and Tanner hadn't brought up the subject for a few days, and I was getting hopeful that he had just dropped it, finally understanding that it would be best for me to keep him in the dark. Little did I know that Tanner was about to take matters into his own hands, destroying my life forever.

Fifteen

I had a project to work on Friday afternoon after school, so instead of carpooling with Tanner like normal, I drove myself, so he didn't have to wait around for me. He was in the process of looking for a part-time job anyway, so he was planning to do some scoping while I finished up my midterm literature paper. I was in the library researching *The Grapes of Wrath* when I got that creepy feeling that someone was watching me. The hair on the base of my neck stood on end as I slowly turned around in my seat and scanned the library. Only a few other poor souls, mostly literature students, occupied the library on this gorgeous March day, and the tired-looking old librarian. She was counting the minutes till four forty-five when she could usher everybody out and close the library up for the weekend.

And suddenly, I saw him out of the corner of my eye. Jason, leaning against the back wall of the library with his hands folded across his chest and a scowl on his face. My heart leaped inside of my chest. Why did he still have to be *so* attractive? I hated that I was still drawn to his looks after what he had done to me.

I twirled back around in my chair and tried to calm down, tried to focus on the computer screen. It was four fifteen, but suddenly, I didn't want to be here anymore. I couldn't focus on research with Jason looming in the background, watching me. What was he doing here anyway? He clearly knew that just seeing him in the hallway made me want to throw up. Why did he have to come here and give me an anxiety attack? I hoped he would just go away and leave me alone. I didn't want to deal with him anymore.

No such luck. As I tried to search through some journal articles to support my research topic, Jason sauntered up and took a seat in the empty computer station next to me. He didn't say anything; he just logged on and checked his e-mail. I felt myself start to shake. I hadn't been this close to him since that day he trapped me in the empty classroom and turned the rape back on me, convincing me that I had lead him on, that I had wanted to sleep with him. In his mind, he hadn't raped me; he had just given me what I wanted. What a snake.

After a few minutes of silence he casually said, "So you and Tanner, huh?"

I nodded my head and mumbled, "Mmmhmm."

"Nice," he responded.

"Yeah," I said sharply, hoping he would get the hint that I didn't want to talk to him and to leave me alone. Forever.

"And what a nice guy he is, hmm? So friendly. So honest. So truthful." He looked over at me and cocked his head, his eyes narrowing. "So, so truthful." I was confused. And then, I saw his eyes scan my body and stop at my midsection. My growing midsection. At our baby.

My heart was slamming against my chest now, and my eyes darted from his face to my screen and back to his cruel face. He knew. My hands went instinctively to my belly, protecting the baby from this monster.

He chuckled. "Come on, Molly. Let's you and me go have ourselves a little chat."

"No. Way," I said through clenched teeth. I was not going anywhere with him. I'd made the mistake of being alone with him once, I wasn't going to do it again. "I'm not going anywhere with you," I said defiantly.

But he just chuckled again and reached over to my computer, logging me off with the click of a few buttons. "Oh, yes, you are," he demanded, pulling me out of my chair and then dragging me away. He hoisted my bag onto his shoulder and continued dragging me out of the library and down the hall to the janitor's closet. I stumbled the whole way because of the fast, angry steps he took, but he continued yanking me along, his grip tightening around my arm, digging into my bare skin.

He shut the door and turned to face me as I backed up against the farthest wall of the closet. The small space was forcing us to be face-to-face, something I did not want to be doing with Jason. He let my bag fall to the floor, then leaned in and put his arms out, pinning me against a wall like he had done last time we talked. I was trapped under his arms one again.

I looked down but he grabbed my chin and forced me to look him in the eye. I struggled to get away but he held it hard. "Get rid of it, Molly."

"I don't know what you're talking about," I lied.

"Don't even try," he retorted nastily. "I know you're pregnant. I should have *known* you'd get pregnant and ruin everything!"

"Um, hello!" I said furiously. "You did this to me! It's not my fault!"

He brought his face inches away from mine, his warm breath hot on my already flushed face. "We went over this months ago didn't we, Molly? You made me do it. Don't you blame this on me. *You're* the one who got pregnant, okay. And I don't want it. So get rid of it."

"No," I spat. "I don't want anything from you, Jason. No child support, no visitations. I'd never let my baby be with you anyway. Just leave us alone."

"Oh, that's sweet, Molly. Real sweet. That baby would be lucky to have me in its life. Not that I'd want to be in its life. But I'm not going to have some snotty teenager searching for their real father in sixteen years, demanding to know where I was for their whole life. Wondering where I was and why I didn't want them. And I'm not going to risk you finding me in five years when you're on welfare, living in some nasty little apartment, demanding child support."

"I won't," I sobbed. "Tanner wants to raise the baby with me. He already loves it. He has names picked out. There's nothing to worry about."

"Oh yeah, Tanner mentioned that he was planning to stick around. But no one in their right mind sticks around to raise another man's kid. He won't love that thing, Molly. Minute it comes out he'll see it looks like me and he'll go running."

My heart skipped a beat because something Jason just said wasn't lining up. *Tanner* mentioned that he was planning to stick around? Had Tanner gone against my deepest wish, gone behind my back and told Jason about the baby without my permission?

Jason saw me panicking, saw my eyes darting back and forth as I tried to piece this all together. He laughed a slow, cruel laugh. "Ohh. Your boyfriend didn't tell you he talked to me. What a winner." He pushed off the wall and clapped his hands, amused at the sick game Tanner was playing with me.

I was breathless. This realization had knocked all the wind out of me. "Tanner…Tanner…told you?" I stammered in utter and complete disbelief.

He laughed again, obviously thinking I was pathetic. "You catch on quick, Molly. Good job. Yes, Tanner told me today. And I wasn't too happy about it either. But I'm glad we had the chance to chat about it, clear any confusion up. First of all, I don't want it. Second of all, I don't want you to have it. I'm not risking you chasing after me and hounding me for money when Tanner deserts you in the hospital room. And I'm certainly not risking you giving it up and then having it come searching for me when it's some lonely, messed-up teenager. I've been through that, Molly. It sucks to have a parent not want you anymore. I'm not doing that to some kid. So the best thing would be to just get rid of it." He pulled out his wallet and handed me some bills.

Money to kill my baby.

When I wouldn't take it, he pried my fingers open, pressed the bills firmly into my hands, and closed my fingers around them, his larger hands crushing mine. I shook my head.

"No. I'm not killing this baby. It's not yours anymore. It never was yours. I promise you with all I am that I will never come looking for money, even if Tanner leaves me. I never wanted to drag you into this mess! I *told* Tanner it was a bad idea to tell you, that it was better for you to never know. Please, Jason," I was begging now, fully aware of how pathetic I must sound to him. "Just please leave me alone. I don't want anything from you. We're going to raise the baby as Tanner's. She never has to know about you, and I won't let her search for you."

"So it's a girl then?" he asked, disgusted.

"I don't know. That's what we want, but it's too early to tell yet. We'll know by the next ultrasound appointment."

Jason huffed in frustration and pinned me against the wall once more, where I cowered in fear. His face was beat red, the veins sticking out of his neck in sheer anger. "What appointment? Cancel it, Molly. Do not get attached to this thing. Just get rid of it!"

"No," I said again.

He leaned in close to my face, his teeth clenched, anger seething from his eyes. "If you don't take care of this, I will," he said slowly, the words so cruel and calculated. "I'll make sure Tanner can never be with you. Or maybe, I'll go after your family—whatever it takes to get it through your thick skull to get rid of this pregnancy. Don't underestimate me, Molly. Now it's up to you. Either you take care of it, or I will."

I didn't even want to know what Jason would do to take Tanner or my family away from me. I didn't want to know what he would do to me, to force me to get rid of our baby. But I knew that he was serious. If I didn't promise to do something, he'd do something horrible to me, to Tanner, my family. My whole life— as if he hadn't stolen enough of it already.

So I nodded my head, and with that, he spun around and shut the closet door on me. I let out a huge breath; I was shaking so hard from being so close to him. I couldn't hold myself up any- more, so I let myself slide to the floor, and I buried my face in my hands and let the tears flow freely.

If the situation had been different, I would have had more options. I would have been able to go home to my parents and tell them all about Jason's threat, and they'd take care of me. They'd make sure that Jason stayed far away from me, far away from the baby. And Tanner and I could start our life together with the baby.

But my situation was unique. I wasn't just pregnant with Jason's child. I had been abused, raped. I'd been violated and left to deal with the consequences by myself. I didn't have any other options because I was terrified of Jason, of what he would do to me and to Tanner and my family if I didn't listen to him.

When I saw him, my heart started pounding and my palms started sweating. Being in this small space with him had been horrifying; all the memories of that night came flooding back. I couldn't handle seeing him or being near him, and if I didn't listen to him, I'd never escape him. He'd never leave me alone. What other choice did I have? I didn't want to face him or what he could do to me if I told people about how he was manipulat- ing me, so I had no other choice than to listen to him.

Maybe I could just leave though. I wouldn't ask Tanner to come with me; that would be asking too much. And I was pretty mad at him right now anyway. He'd deliberately gone against my wishes and gone behind my back with Jason. I wasn't sure I wanted him to follow me if I decided to run. Would Jason really know if I just took off and raised the baby by myself? I'd raise her to know that her daddy was out there somewhere, but that he hadn't been ready for her and he didn't want her to come looking for him. She'd grow up learning that her daddy never really grew up. He'd never owned up to what he had done to me.

As I drove home, I was still shaking, shaking out of fear and out of anger. I kept running different scenarios through my head—things that Jason could do to Tanner to keep him away from me. Horrible things he could do to Savannah or Josh. Did he mean he would somehow convince Tanner that I was the bad guy in this situation and drive him away from me that way, or did he mean he would physically harm him? And would he really go after sweet little Savannah? I didn't know to what extent Jason would go to force me to kill our baby just so his life would be easier.

When I got home, I didn't text or call Tanner. I didn't want to see him. I ate dinner with my family who were now all concerned with what I was eating, how much I was eating, and if I was drinking enough milk. Usually, I didn't mind their concerns, but after my conversation with Jason, I didn't want to think about the baby right now. I didn't know what I was going to do with it anymore.

I retreated to my room as soon as possible, claiming that I was exhausted and needed to rest alone for a bit. My mom waved me off and told me to get as much rest as I could.

It was a Friday night, three months before graduation, and I was sitting alone in my room, pregnant and scared out of my mind. Plan A had seemed to be going so well! Tanner was with me, my parents were with me, I would have the baby, get my degree when she was old enough, and life would keep moving forward. But now, it seemed like Jason was ripping away that plan, and I didn't know what plan B would be yet. It would probably include a lot less baby and a lot less Tanner.

And as if right on cue, Tanner knocked on my door and let himself in.

"Hey, your mom said it was okay for me to come up. You all right? I've been texting you all night!" He settled at the foot of my bed and looked at me as if he'd done nothing wrong at all.

"No, Tanner. I'm not all right." I folded my hands in front of me and narrowed my eyes at him, but he looked dumbfounded.

"What's wrong? Are you okay?" he asked again. "Is the baby okay?"

I stared at him.

"How *could* you, Tanner? I told you it was a bad idea to tell him! He hates me! And he's furious!" I said as loudly as I could without yelling and catching everyone's attention. I threw the thing nearest to me, which happened to be a pillow, straight into his still dumbfounded face.

"Whoa, wait! How does he know?"

I just looked at him. Was he seriously pulling this on me right now? Did he think he could lie about this? Jason *told* me that Tanner had let him in on the secret. He wasn't going to get out of this one.

"Don't play dumb with me! He caught me after school today, and he's absolutely furious, just like I knew he would be. What gives you the right to make decisions for me, Tanner? I said I would deal with it, but you went behind my back and ruined everything!"

"Molly, I—" But I cut him off.

"No! Don't lie! How could you do this to me? Obviously, you don't trust me, and if you can't trust me to make the right decisions, maybe we shouldn't be together!"

"For crying out loud, Molly! You weren't going to make the right decision! Somebody had to tell him! You're not the only teenage girl who's gotten pregnant, okay, so it's hard for me to feel sorry for you. *You* made the wrong choice before, and now you're dealing with the consequences of that. You need to grow up and start facing the music. You're having a baby, and the father deserved to know. He knows now. Let's move on." Though his words rang with truth, his harsh tone cut into my already battered heart. Tanner had never spoken to me that way before. It felt like I had been slapped across the face. I needed to grow up and face the music? I'd been facing it since November! He'd never understand all the trauma I'd been through.

"It's not that simple! He doesn't want the baby. He doesn't even want the baby to exist!" I argued, desperately trying to get him to understand the gravity of what he'd done.

"So what?" Tanner said loudly. We were trying not to yell because my bedroom was on the first floor. "It's not his baby anyway. He doesn't have to deal with her."

"You don't understand," I replied with a quaver in my voice. "He wants the baby gone no matter what. Who knows what he'll do to accomplish that. It doesn't matter if you want to raise her. He still wants her gone. And because of you, because you told him, I'll never escape him!"

"Molly, stop it. I didn't—" I cut him off again.

"Who else would have told, Tanner? Who?"

"I don't know, but does it really matter? He can't force you to get an abortion! I won't let him. And he'll leave soon and forget about us."

I shook my head. No, he wouldn't just leave. He'd know I'd kept the baby, and he'd always be on the lookout for me. He'd always fear that I'd come looking for money or that the baby would grow up and want to find him. And when she was grown, I couldn't stop her from looking for him if she really wanted to. If she found him, he'd be furious all over again and extract his revenge then, possibly on her. So the way I saw it, if I ignored his threats now, he would do something to me, my family, or Tanner, or later in life he would do something to my baby. Either way, he'd come after somebody I loved. And I would be the loser. Again.

I gave up, defeated. Tanner didn't get it. He'd never get it. And how could he sit here and lecture me about facing what I had done when he was blatantly denying the fact that he'd talked to Jason and spilled the news of the pregnancy? He was a hypocrite.

We sat in silence for a while before Tanner couldn't handle it anymore. "Talk to me," he asked softly.

"I have nothing to say to you, Tanner," I spit out at him. "I feel like I can't trust you anymore."

He looked at me with pleading eyes. "Don't do this to me. Don't believe the lies he's telling you. I would never do anything to hurt you!"

I made a choice right then. I needed to leave, and I wanted to leave alone. I couldn't trust anyone anymore. I was hurt, angry, and scared, and I needed out. Enough was enough. But Tanner would never let me leave without him. The only way was to escalate this fight even higher, make him so mad that he never wanted to see me again.

"It's too late for that. You hurt me even worse than Jason did. Jason used me and lied to me, but you went behind my back and lied to me too. And coming from you, it hurts a million times worse than when Jason did. I can't raise my baby with someone who sneaks around and doesn't trust me."

He was getting mad, his face turning red. "Oh, so you think you can do this alone? Without me?" he challenged sarcastically.

I nodded. "Yes. I do. I never said I needed you." And that did it. Immediately, Tanner's eyes flooded with pain, and he gulped. It took him a minute to formulate an answer, but it was just the one I needed in order to make my getaway.

"Well, good luck with that then. The world's a cruel place, but if you think you can do this alone, fine. I'm probably better off without you anyway since you don't believe me and refuse to trust me." And with that he shoved himself off my bed, slammed the window open, and left. I got up and closed the window, then, watched him close his blinds and walk away, never looking back.

It was the last time I talked to Tanner before I ran. My plan had worked; I'd gotten him worked up and just angry enough at me that he had left. But it still hurt. He thought he would be better off without me—I let out a shaky sigh, closed my eyes, and hung my head. *There goes my last alibi,* I thought sadly.

We'd probably both be better off without each other. Our emotions got in the way too often; it would be difficult to ever have a functioning relationship. And today, I had seen a side of Tanner I'd never known before. A side that was capable of going behind my back and sneaking around.

A side that lied. Tanner had never lied to me before today. Combined with how he had lectured me about owning up to my mistake and facing the music and then his comment about not needing me, I was furious. I was hurting and felt rejected, totally alone. Jason hated me and the baby. Tanner didn't want me anymore. My parents had no idea what was going on, and they didn't deserve me messing up their carefully manicured lives. I was just a horrible black smudge on their picture-perfect life. With me, people would look at our lives and see all our broken-ness. It wasn't fair of me to ruin everything for them.

And so I packed. I needed to get out before my parents came to check up on me or Tanner tried to come back. So I quickly gathered up clothes and toiletries, stuffing them in a duffel bag. I grabbed a box and filled it with a few keepsakes and knick-knacks. As I reached under my bed to see if anything worthwhile lay under there, my hand bumped into my Bible. I shoved it away again.

But something compelled me to reach back under and grab it anyway. I sighed as I sat on the floor holding the book that had once meant so much to me. I wasn't going to be opening this up anytime soon because God felt so distant, and I was angry at him. So I shoved it to the very bottom of the box. Maybe someday, when I'd worked through this whole mess, I'd consider opening it once again. Maybe.

On the nightstand stood the three hundred dollars that Jason had pressed into my hands for an abortion. I considered leaving it, but it was money, and I'd need it anyway. So I stuffed it into my purse and convinced myself I'd use it for food or other expenses—not for the abortion it was meant for. I'd have to figure out how to get the rest of my money later. For now, I had this money and a couple hundred dollars in my checking account.

I scanned the room one final time with a heavy heart. I'd occupied this room since I was five years old. It held a thousand memories, most of them happy up until this past year. I always assumed I would pack up this room one day, but I figured I'd be excited and leaving for college. Right now, I was angry and terri-fied, left with no other choice but to flee. Not the way I wanted to leave, but what choice did I have? With a heavy heart I flipped the light off and slipped out into the darkness, ready to leave it all behind and sort this mess out somewhere far away, where I couldn't hurt any more of the people I loved.

It was about eight forty-five, and the night was chilly and damp. Tanner's blinds were still closed, and I peeked around the corner at my family's big picture window. The blinds were down on it too, and the lights were off. My family must be watching a movie. Still, I tiptoed across the lawn with my bag and box to my car, fumbling to open the door with my full hands. There I deposited everything I had in the world into my car and slipped into the front seat. I started the car, and just like Tanner had done that night, I left and never looked back.

Part Two

Into the Desert

For everything there is a season,
a time for everything under the sun....
A time to search and a time to quit searching.

—Ecclesiastes 3:6

Sixteen

It was dark. I hated driving in the dark, not being able to clearly see what lay ahead. I was limited to how far my headlights shone onto the road. That's how my life was like right now though. It was dark. I couldn't see what was ahead of me because I had no plan anymore. I was just blindly wandering down a path to who knows where. Anywhere but here though.

The weight of the past few months was crushing down on me—like there was some gigantic boulder strapped to my shoulders, and no matter what I did, I couldn't shake it off. All my planning had failed me, and the future was so unclear. Being in the car didn't help either; the small space was closing in on me, suffocating me. For the first full hour of the drive, I sobbed uncontrollably, loud, heaving, gut-wrenching sobs from the deepest part of my heart. I hadn't allowed myself to cry like this before because I was always afraid someone would hear me and ask me what was wrong, and I knew I'd never be able to tell them the real reason why I was so broken and empty.

And so in the absolute aloneness of my car, I let myself really grieve. I grieved for my lost innocence, the innocence that Jason had come in like a thief and robbed me of. I grieved for all the months I had lost after the rape, stuck in a life-sucking coma when I should have been enjoying my last carefree year of school and looking forward to the future. I grieved for the baby inside me, the baby I had never asked for and wasn't sure I wanted anymore. I grieved for her because I knew no one really loved her or wanted her at this point. And finally, I grieved for my loss of Tanner—my rock, my ally, my best friend in the whole world. I'd lost him once, but we'd found our way together again, only to be torn apart because of my actions. All this because I had chosen to follow Jason into his trap.

Jason. I cut off my sobbing when his face popped into my mind. As a little girl, I'd been taught that Christians are never supposed to hate anyone. But surely, they didn't mean people like Jason, people who raped and lied and manipulated. How could anyone love a person like that? Right now, I wasn't sure if I still believed in Christianity, wasn't sure if I wanted to be a Christian anymore if that was what was expected of me.

And so, I let the hate boil up inside me. I thought back to the night of the rape, Jason's cruel laugh echoing out into the cold night air. I thought back to the day he pulled me into the classroom and threatened me, how he had justified his actions and turned them back on me. I thought back to all the sneers he gave me when he saw me in the hallway. And I thought back to earlier this afternoon when he had trapped me in the janitor's closet and demanded I kill our baby.

How could I not absolutely despise that snake? I hated him! I hated him with every fiber of my being. A deep, burning, life-consuming hatred, a hatred that he deserved for what he had done to me. I screamed "I hate you!" over and over into the darkness, pounding my fists on my steering wheel until I'm sure they bruised.

Finally, I stopped screaming and let all my air out, settling back into my seat. I was beyond exhausted. I'd been driving aimlessly for about two hours, not really sure where I was headed. I knew I was headed north, so I hooked up on I-90 and continued east. It was nearing midnight and my gas needle was ever so slowly creeping its way toward the red; I figured it was probably time to stop for the night, so I turned off and pulled into Fairmont, Minnesota. I found the cheapest motel room I could find and collapsed into the dirty bed, not even bothering to peel off my clothes or splash some water on my face, which was chapped and raw from crying for so long. The tears had dried up for the night though, so I curled up in a tiny ball and held my stomach. This was the first time in my life that I truly and honestly wanted to die.

I shut my phone off and planned to pick up some cheap TracFone later on, because I didn't want my parents or Tanner trying to reach me. I didn't bother to set an alarm for the next day either, and when I woke up, it was nearing two in the afternoon. How had I slept that long? I pushed the thin motel comforter away and rubbed the sleep from my eyes. I didn't feel any more rested than I had before I slept. I vaguely remembered waking up many times during the night, strange nightmares jerking me awake, then, sleep pulling me back under only to plague me with the same terrifying images. The nightmares had stopped a while ago, but I guess they were back with a vengeance. Just what I didn't need right now.

I flipped through the information booklet sitting on the tiny table in the corner of my room. The bright map of Minnesota caught my eye. I knew I was in Fairmont, and I scanned the map for a potential landing place. My eyes fell on Minneapolis. It had a population of about four hundred thousand people, and I knew there were colleges there. Maybe after I figured out what to do with the baby, I could enroll in some classes. Then, I remembered I hadn't graduated yet, so I threw that plan out the window. I'd have to figure out how to somehow get my GED in order to start classes. But I liked the fact that it had a large population; I could blend in. I could become invisible. No one would question my story or look at me like I had committed some great sin when they saw my pregnancy. They wouldn't cluck their tongues at me and lecture me about how I should have waited for God's perfect timing. Maybe, I could escape from my demons in Minneapolis. Maybe I could reinvent myself.

So I quickly showered, checked out, and settled into my car with my new plan swirling around in my head—I even let myself get a little bit excited. This was the most daring, most adventurous thing I'd ever done before. Not the kind of adventure I ever imagined myself having, but an adventure all the same. I reached down and flipped on the radio, and for the first time in months, music filled my car. I felt okay about letting music back into my life now because I was finally moving on from this horrible time in my life. Maybe now when I listened to this music later on, I'd remember that I had finally taken charge of my own life, that I had stopped letting others control me. I'd remember how much courage it had taken for me to drive away from my entire life in Oak Ridge to recreate a new one in Minneapolis.

I'd also remember that I was truly and utterly alone. I'd remember that I was pregnant and terrified and not sure what I was going to do when I reached Minneapolis. How was I supposed to get a job? Where would I live? My money would quickly run out if I didn't formulate a solid plan soon. So I reached back down and flipped the radio off. I wasn't quite ready for music, I guessed. It was easier for me to think in the silence anyway.

Minneapolis was only about two and a half hours away from Fairmont, for which I was extremely grateful because I didn't feel like driving all day. When I finally neared the cities, however, I heard a strange thumping noise. It sounded like I had a flat tire. I heaved a huge sigh and pulled over to check. Luckily for me, my dad had taught me to change a tire last summer, but I'd only practiced a few times and wasn't sure I'd remember how.

I'm sure I looked ridiculous on the side of the road, trying to figure out how to get the flat tire off my car and replace it with the spare. I had the car jacked up but was struggling; working with tools had never been my strong suit. I heard a car pull up behind me and felt a mixture of gratitude and dread. It would be great if someone could help me, but how embarrassing to be stuck on the side of the road in the middle of changing a tire but unable to complete the job.

I turned around to see a tall, thin, blond, and curly-haired young woman shut her car door and sashay over to me. That's the only way I could describe her walking; it looked like she was dancing. She snapped her gum and waved at me, a smile on her face. How was this chick going to help me? She looked like she'd be even more useless with tools than I was!

"Gotta flat?" she asked. *Clearly,* I thought saucily. I wanted to say, "Oh no, I just thought it would be fun to change my tire real quick, just because." But of course, I didn't. But really, how obvious was it that I had a flat tire?

"Um...yeah," I said. "Thought I knew how to change it, but I got stuck."

She dropped to her knees in front of the tire, ready to take over. She was wearing light-wash jeans, a pink top, and brown ballet flats. Total girl. But she dug right in and changed the tire faster than my dad when he had taught me how to do it. My eyes were as big as saucers as I watched her fingers expertly maneuver the wrench, removing the nuts, taking the old tire off, and replacing it with the new one. She tightened the nuts, checking to make sure they were all snug and tight. Then, she lowered the car back down, rechecked to make sure everything was tight enough, and replaced the hubcap.

I continued staring at her with a look of pure shock. She smiled smugly back at me and patted me on the back. "Looks can be deceiving, girl. I grew up with four brothers. There was no way they would let me go out into the real world not knowing how to do that. And one of my brothers and I liked to tinker around with old cars with our dad. So that's a piece of cake." She wiped her hands together and stood up. I got up too, and we just stood there awkwardly, the wind whipping our hair into our faces and the silence making it even more awkward.

"Well, thank you." I fumbled. "I would have been in a real jam if you hadn't come along."

She waved off my thank-you. "No big deal. Minute I saw you squatting by the tire just looking at it, I knew you were in trouble. My name's Melissa, by the way." She stuck her hand out for me to shake.

I shook it and told her my name too.

"So where ya headed?" she asked. "I just got back from a week-end at home, but I'm going in to work now, at a little diner in Minneapolis. You could come grab something to eat if you want."

I was surprised at this invitation. We had just met, and she was inviting me to eat? Granted, she'd be working, and I'd be eating alone, but still.

"Um…sure. Yeah, that sounds great actually." I didn't realize till now how hungry I was. I hadn't eaten since last night at supper with my family. Now it was getting close to five o'clock. How had I survived this long without food?

"Cool. So just follow me." And with that, she twirled around, walked back to her car in her strange dancing step, and took off.

I followed her into Minneapolis. The diner was downtown, but in all honesty, it looked like a dump. The building was dark and low to the ground, the shades pulled down on the dirty windows. A flashing neon sign declared that the diner was open, making the building look tacky and cheap. In chipped painted, the simple title "Frankie's" graced the dirty and smudged glass of the front doors. But maybe like Melissa had said earlier, looks can be deceiving. Maybe inside, it was clean and cheerful. Maybe the food was great.

Melissa ushered me in, and immediately I knew that the building's look had not been deceiving. My shoes stuck to the grease on the floor, and it was dark and hazy. Old, chipped tables with mismatched chairs pulled in around them crowded the dining floor, and the booths that lined the walls looked old and saggy. At one time, it must have been okay to smoke in here because although it didn't smell like fresh cigarette smoke, I could smell the faint traces of stale cigarette smoke—it clung to the walls, dreary dark-green curtains, and all the booths. Melissa offered me a small smile and a shrug then led me to a corner booth and plopped a menu down in front of me.

"I'm going to clock in and get my apron, but I'll be back real quick. Can I get you something to drink?" She snapped her gum, and I winced at the sharp crack. I used to yell at Tanner all the time for snapping his gum in my face.

"Uh…yeah. Coffee would be nice."

I considered asking for a Coke, but I wanted to make myself seem older than my eighteen years. Maybe I could fool her into thinking I was twenty-one or so.

"Sounds good," she said as she twirled around and disappeared into the swinging doors that led to the back room.

She came back wearing a clean black apron. *The only clean thing in the room*, I thought. She placed an empty mug on the table, poured the steaming black coffee into it, and set the pitcher down for me to refill as I pleased. Pulling a pencil from the front pocket of her apron, she took my order. When she left again to fill the order, I took a sip of the black coffee, but I wasn't in the mood for its strong bitterness. So I ripped open one of the little creamers and mixed in a couple packets of sugar to sweeten it up. I took another sip, much better. I closed my eyes and breathed in the scent of it, remembering back to how I used to wake up to that smell on lazy Saturday mornings as a kid. I'd jump out of bed knowing my dad was standing at the kitchen counter making huge fluffy Belgian waffles. My mom would be at the table in her robe, drinking coffee and reading the paper. But when all us kids wandered out of our rooms, she'd give us all a hug and a kiss, then, plop us down at the table with orange juice and milk, and we'd all stuff our faces.

Oh, to go back to those carefree days of childhood. I shook the image away though, knowing I could never go back and the memories were too painful, so I continued scanning the dirty little diner. I was surprised at how many people came in to eat at this dump. It was at least giving me hope that the food was good. Three girls were waitressing, all of them about the same age as Melissa. There was one scrawny teenage busboy scurrying around, trying to stay out of the girls' way. When they'd come in and out of those swinging doors, I could see the faded and grimy white walls of the kitchen and hear the shouts of an angry cook. I couldn't tell if he was serious or was teasing the girls as he called after them when they left with steaming plates of food. Usually, the girls would be rolling their eyes, but they never looked hurt or upset. Just slightly annoyed. The guy must be harmless, but I couldn't imagine working with such a man.

By the time Melissa brought me my food twenty minutes later, she already looked exhausted. I gave her a weak smile and asked, "How late do you have to work tonight?"

She huffed, sending her bangs flying. She'd pulled her curly mass of hair back into a ponytail, but loose tendrils had escaped and stuck to her flushed face. "Just till nine. I wasn't supposed to work but got called in for a quick shift. Usually, I work six or seven, sometimes eight-hour shifts though. They really need to hire some more help."

My spirits lifted a bit when she said this. Maybe I could get a job here! Could it really be that easy? I nodded and she twirled around. "I'll check on you later. Just holler if you need anything."

I dug into my food immediately. While it wasn't the best cheeseburger I'd ever had, it was decent. At the moment, I probably wouldn't have cared if it was cold, but the fact that it was fresh and hot made it that much more enjoyable. I was finished in a flash, so I lingered over my french fries, which were also hot and actually very good. As I popped french fries into my mouth, I watched Melissa and the other waitresses scurrying around, trying to keep up with the demands of the dinner rush. They picked on the busboy constantly, always yelling at him to hurry up and get his job done as soon as the customers left the table. He was wearing rubber gloves that were dripping wet at the moment, and his arms looked red, so I assumed he was also in charge of dishes as well. He was sweating like crazy because I imagined it was very warm in the dish room, and he winced every time one of the girls would get on his case. Poor thing. He probably hated working here, but I figured he was trying to save for college. Or maybe he was helping his family out. Whatever the reason he was working here, it must be important to him because no teenage boy in their right mind would work at a place with this much stress and demand with three young women yelling at him constantly.

I waited around for a while, but Melissa never brought the check out. As it neared seven thirty, I flagged her over, but she waved me away. "I'm going to grab some food and take a quick break with you, 'kay?"

I nodded, unsure what else to do and a little uneasy about the fact that she wanted to eat with me when we'd just met. Five minutes later though, she came bustling out of the kitchen with a cinnamon roll and a mug of coffee. I'd been here so long and drunk most of mine already. She flopped down into the seat across from me, let out a huge sigh, and dug into the delicious-looking cinnamon roll.

"So are you headed somewhere or were you planning on staying in the cities for a while?" Melissa was so forward, so unafraid to ask me personal questions.

I hesitated for a moment, unsure how to answer because I was running away. I hadn't known until this morning that I wanted to stay in Minneapolis.

"Uh…well," I stammered, caught off guard and not sure whether or not to be truthful. "I'm trying to get away from some stuff back home," I ventured. "I'm from Oak Ridge, Iowa. It's a tiny little town close to Storm Lake. I got onto I-90 and saw a map in a motel in Fairmont, and I just decided this morning that I'd come here. I don't really have any plans at the moment." I absently stirred my lukewarm coffee, feeling awkward revealing these personal details to a complete and total stranger.

Her eyes brightened like this was the best news she'd ever heard. "Really?" she said excitedly, leaning forward in her seat, frosting clinging to the corner of her full lips. "That is *so* weird! One of our roommates just flaked on us, and we're trying to find another girl to room with us. Do you wanna?"

My first thought was, *No way. I don't know these people, I can't trust them.* But then, I realized that I had nowhere else to go, no other plans. And here this girl had just handed me a new plan, a place to stay.

"Yeah, I do. That would be great."

She clapped her hands. "Yay! That was so easy! The girls will be so excited. One of them works her too." She twisted around in the booth and pointed to a girl setting drinks down at a table a young family occupied. "See that cute brunette? That's Casey. You'll probably room with her unless we do some switching up. But yeah. Cool!"

I figured since I was being bold and moving in with someone I had just met, I would keep going. She'd handed me a place to stay, maybe she could help me land a job too. "And did I hear you say that they should hire more help? Because I need a job too."

"Perfect!" she exclaimed. "Let me talk to the owner, and I'll bring him out to meet you at nine when I'm done. His name is

Frankie. That's why the diner's named Frankie's. Creative, right?"
She rolled her eyes.

I nodded and smiled, trying to force a laugh.

And just like that, I had a place to stay and a job. Frankie, a
big greasy man came lumbering out when Melissa was done with
her shift to meet me. His hair was thinning, and his big beer belly
was hanging out under his dirty, grease-stained white T-shirt. He
barely talked to me for five minutes and didn't even ask if I had
any work experience. He just said I could come back the next day
with Melissa to train. Then, he shook my hand and waddled back
to his office.

Melissa grinned at me and gave me a thumbs-up. I shrugged,
stunned that I had gotten this lucky. I'd been ticked off when I
heard my flat tire thumping on the road earlier that afternoon,
but it had turned out to work in my favor. Because I'd gotten that
flat, I'd met Melissa and secured myself a place to stay and a job.
Not too shabby.

I followed Melissa back to her apartment that night, to a
dirty little part of town. The building was five floors tall, dark,
and run-down. I winced when she pulled into the lot; I'd hoped
for a second that she'd keep driving to another building but no
such luck.

We trudged up three flights of stairs. Melissa had offered to
carry the one box full of my knick-knacks and random items from
home while I struggled with the rest of my belongings. She burst
through the door, and I could see that the apartment itself wasn't
too horribly disgusting. The lighting was bright and florescent,
making it feel sterile and cold, but the girls had done a decent
job making it feel homey. Two mismatched couches were in the
tiny living room area, which overlooked a small TV that a cheesy
sitcom blared loudly from. A frizzy-haired blonde was sprawled
out on one of the couches, eating Chinese from a takeout box. A
cheerful area rug covered the dingy carpet, but there were books

and other school supplies scattered upon it. One of the girls must be going to school.

The kitchen was small but clean. The cabinets were dark and the appliances were old, but there wasn't a huge pile of dishes in the sink, and the tile floor looked spotless. Someone was a clean freak, at least in the kitchen. The living room must have been the domain of the girl sprawled out on the couch. She looked exhausted, with deep circles under her eyes.

"Hey, Britt, this is Molly. She's moving in!"

Britt turned around, slurping a noodle. She gave a wave and a jumbled hello and then turned back around to focus on the TV show.

Melissa shrugged and jerked her thumb to Britt. "Britt's going to nursing school, so she's super stressed out all the time. On the weekends, she crashes, watching stupid TV shows all night."

"Hey, you'd do the same thing if you were taking some of the classes I'm in, *plus* juggling clinicals. I will not be mocked for lounging after a hard week," she teased, stabbing a finger in the air for emphasis.

I laughed. She seemed really nice. Stressed out, but nice.

Melissa turned back to me, rolling her eyes. "So you saw Casey at the diner, she's working late like she always does. Seriously, she's *always* working. Saving up for a new car."

I nodded, unsure what to say because I was feeling incredibly awkward. While I was thrilled with how this had all worked out, I was surprised that Melissa had invited a total stranger to live with her and her friends. I must look like a trustworthy person I guessed. And I must look older than eighteen. She'd never asked my age. She hadn't even really asked why I was in Minneapolis, what I was running away from. Melissa just knew the girls needed another person to pay rent, so even if she was suspicious of my age, she probably wouldn't ask. She needed me too much to get hung up on a little thing like that.

"So…um…I'll show you your new room, I guess. Ashley left a week ago, so this is really awesome that we found you so soon! The room's pretty small, but I guess you don't have to spend much time in here if you don't want to. We usually all hang out in the living room and just sleep in the bedrooms. Not much room for desks, except in me and Britt's room 'cause she's actually in school. But yeah. I'll let you get settled and do whatever.

"And don't ever feel like you hang here with us all the time. Just let us know if you're bringing anyone back with you. Neighbors get mad if it gets too loud, and Britt is up late studying so much, so just let us know. No boys unless your roomie is away and you warn us first. And that's about it for rules. Just cleanup after yourself, don't be too loud, and oh yeah. Don't waste the hot water. We all want hot showers, so don't just stand in there hogging it all. Do your business and get out."

I nodded again, and she left me alone. Trying to stay positive even as I felt the loneliness creep up inside me, I threw my duffle bag on the bed Melissa had plopped the box containing my last precious treasures. This was all I had left in the world. I began pulling out clothes and toiletries from the bag, spreading them onto the bed and taking inventory. In the box lay a few knick-knacks from childhood, but I didn't even know why I had bothered to bring them. I was running away from what lay back in Oak Ridge, so why had I brought these reminders? Especially the framed picture of me and Tanner.

The picture had been taken on a warm summer day from last year, both of us tanned and carefree. We sat on a blanket, me cross-legged with Tanner slightly behind me, his arm thrown casually around my shoulders. My mom had snapped the picture and printed it off for me, raising her eyebrows suggestively, trying to get me to see the love shining in Tanner's eyes—love only for me. I disagreed of course and rolled my eyes, but slapped the picture in a frame and set it on my bedside table. While I had looked at the picture every day since, I couldn't handle setting it up now. Too painful. So I buried it in the box and slid it under the bed.

I got up and sat on the bed, discouraged by how little I had left in the world. Probably for the best though. Fewer reminders of what I was running from. I didn't know what else to do, so I peeled off my clothes and curled up into the hard bed. I squeezed my eyes shut; the tears leaking out and spilling onto my cheeks. I hugged my pillow and breathed in the scent of home. Had I done the right thing by leaving? Could I have escaped from Jason some other way?

No, I couldn't have. Tanner had left me no choice by telling Jason. Perhaps if he never knew about the baby, it would have been possible for me to stay at home, but Tanner had shattered that possibility. I'd been forced to choose between fighting for my family and Tanner or fighting for the baby. And even though I was angry and hurt by Tanner, I'd still chosen to protect them. The baby simply wasn't important enough to me; I couldn't place it over those back at home. Now I just needed to figure out the next step to getting rid of it.

I woke up the next morning, and Casey was sprawled out in the bed, her arms and legs hanging off the edges. She snored softly. I was surprised that I hadn't heard her come in last night; I hardly ever slept that deeply, not since the nightmares had returned. I wandered out to the tiny kitchen where Melissa sat at the worn table, sipping coffee and reading the newspaper. She glanced up and me and said, "Our shift doesn't start until four, so you have pretty much all day to do whatever. I'm sure you have errands to run, things to settle, right?"

"Yup, I do. I'm just gonna shower quick and get going."

"Cool. Feel free to grab breakfast. I know you don't have groceries yet, so we'll share this time. But normally, everyone is in charge of their own food here. Mark it if you don't want someone to take it."

I nodded. "Sounds fair."

She nodded back and returned to her paper.

While showering, I was careful not to stand in there too long, not wanting to hog all the hot water. I didn't spend any time doing my hair or makeup because I had no one to impress here. I didn't really care how people saw me, so I quickly slapped on some foundation and mascara and called it good. I towel dried my hair and put it up in a ponytail then headed out the door.

The weather in the Midwest is so strange. Once spring hits, it can be thirty degrees and windy one day and sixty-five and sunny the next. It was only nine in the morning, yet today the sun was shining, and it was already shaping up to be a gorgeous day. I was pleasantly surprised to discover that the dark neighborhood seemed a bit friendlier in the warm sunshine. So with a bit of cheer in my heart I climbed in my car, pulled out the map of Minneapolis that I had snagged at Frankie's last night, and set out.

My first stop of the day was at the library to figure some stuff out. It was a bit of a struggle to find, but once there, I settled myself into a computer cubicle and started researching. First, and most importantly, I needed to get the rest of my money out of my bank so I could trade in my car for something cheap. I didn't want my parents tracing me out here, though. Luckily for me, my bank in Oak Ridge was a branch of a fairly large bank in Iowa, and there was a location here in Minneapolis, so I scribbled down the address. I'd ask a banker where the best place in town was to trade in my car.

The banker who helped me raised his eyebrows suspiciously when I said I wanted to withdraw all my money. But I needed a new car, and I didn't know if my parents would be able to see me depositing money from the diner into my account here. I figured it was probably wise to switch banks so my parents couldn't trace me by finding out the city this branch was located in. Better to be safe than sorry, I reasoned.

I had close to four thousand dollars in my account. My grandparents had been depositing money in there for years for college, and I had saved every other penny I got. Birthday money, Christmas money—it all went into saving. I'd also worked close to full time every summer since freshman year with a landscaping company in Oak Ridge. It was hard work but it paid well and they gave me all the hours they could. College had once been an important dream of mine, and it was too bad all my scrimping and saving wasn't being used to fulfill that dream.

I took the cash, closed my account, and headed for the used-car lot the man had directed me to. I traded in my little Honda Accord for a used Chevy Impala, leaving me with a little over two thousand dollars. I said my good-byes to my Accord and settled into the Impala. From there I headed to *Walmart* to pick up the cheapest TracFone I could find. Relief welled in my heart as I dumped my old phone—with a new number, no one back home could reach me anymore. This was the final cut to all ties back in Oak Ridge, and while that stung, I knew it was for the best. I couldn't start over if I hung onto them.

As I got used to my new car I glanced at the dashboard. It was only noon, so I swung by the grocery store for a few essentials. I was a decent cook but didn't know how to make much. I'd have to spend some time at the library researching some quick meals I could do. I got the impression from Melissa that everyone just took care of themselves. No shared meals in that apartment. That was fine with me; it would be nice to expand my cooking knowledge.

When I finished my errands, I headed back to the apartment to get ready for work. Melissa said there wasn't really a dress code; I just needed to wear jeans and a plain-colored T-shirt. Luckily for me I'd collected a mountain of plain T-shirts over the years. Living in the Midwest, I appreciated the art of layering clothing, so I'd stocked up on T-shirts and cute sweaters to layer over them.

We carpooled into the diner together—where Melissa jammed out to the local hip-hop station on the radio and jabbered the whole time about her latest romantic fallout. I sat in silence and attempted to appear interested as she filled me in on all the gory details about her recently ex-boyfriend, Kory, and I winced at the blaring music. I was still so turned off by music right now, but of course I couldn't very well ask her to turn it off after all she'd done for me yesterday. When we finally reached Frankie's, a dull pain was already thumping in my brain, and when we walked in I knew things probably wouldn't get too much better. Frankie threw me an apron and hollered in his gruff voice for Melissa to show me the ropes. But it got to be too busy for me to tag along with her, and I was on my own, left to figure it out all by myself.

I quickly found out that waitressing was by far the toughest work I'd ever done. Melissa hadn't had time to train me properly, and I panicked when I found myself taking and filling orders on my own. I was on my feet from four until close to ten thirty, and I had to deal with rude customers and meager tips. We were being paid only $2.50 an hour, so I found myself relying on customers to give good tips. Never again would I stiff a waitress on the tip. They needed them badly.

I fell into bed that night, completely and utterly exhausted. I didn't have to be in tomorrow, so I planned to sleep as late as possible. As I drifted off to sleep, I planned to ask Melissa tomorrow if she'd help me take care of the pregnancy. I'd done some research on abortion at the library earlier, and I'd need someone to drive me back after the procedure. I'd go in tomorrow to set up an appointment; and if all went according to plan, by Tuesday, it would all be over and done with, and I wouldn't have to worry about Jason going after Tanner or my family anymore. And Jason would never have to worry about me begging him for money or the baby growing up and contacting him. He was safe. And hopefully now, I'd never have to see or deal with him ever again. I was eliminating the one thing that held us together for good.

Seventeen

I woke with a start the next morning; the terrifying dream was still clinging to me. I'd been running from something, but I kept tripping over things and stumbling. Tree roots had grabbed my ankles and yanked me to the ground, and whatever had been chasing me had closed in and was about to finish me off when my body jerked itself awake, and I sat up suddenly, heaving deep raggedy breaths. I shook my head to erase the nightmare from my brain and stumbled into the kitchen. Melissa sat in what I assumed was "her" spot because that's where I found her every morning, reading the paper and sipping a steaming cup of coffee. She informed me that everyone chipped in for coffee, so it was free for the taking. I pulled out a mug, filled it up, and plopped down at the table.

Melissa never took her eyes off the paper; she just continued gobbling up whatever article she was reading. She told me yesterday that she'd always wanted to be a journalist but had dropped out of school because she couldn't pay for it. Her mom had died when she was in middle school, and her dad was a lazy drunk, unwilling to help his daughter finish school. So she'd had no other choice but to drop out and earn some money. But she seemed like the type of person who didn't give up easily, and I assumed that when she had saved up enough, she's be right back into school to finish her degree. This was merely a bump in the road for her.

I mustered up all my courage and just went for it. I had no idea what Melissa's stance on abortion was, but I forged ahead anyway. The worst she could say was no, and I'd just ask the other girls or someone at the diner to take me. But in the short amount of time I'd been here, I felt closest to Melissa and was the most comfortable with her.

I cleared my throat. "Um…hey. Can I ask a favor of you?"

She set the paper down noisily, fumbling with the creases in the large paper. "Sure. What's up?"

I swallowed. "Well, I need to have a procedure done. I don't know what your thoughts on abortion are…but…" I looked away. This was something I never thought I'd have to ask someone to help me with.

She nodded. "Thought you might be pregnant" was all she said.

I looked at her quizzically. I was still hardly showing. She smiled. "Some people can't hide it well. You walk funny. And when we rode into work the other day, you held your stomach weird, not just resting your hands on top of it, but like your hands were holding it. And I saw you gag a few times too. Like you couldn't handle all the greasy food and weird smells in the kitchen."

"I guess I didn't realize how obvious I was making it," I replied, stunned that Melissa had been so observant. She shrugged. From how she was responding, I assumed she wasn't against abortion; otherwise, she would have stiffened up or just put an end to the conversation, advising me against it. Telling me I'd regret it. Spouting off facts about how the thing inside me was a person who deserved life.

"So I'm guessing that's what you're trying to get away from back home? Is the father a jerk?" She looked at me sympathetically.

"You have *no* idea," I replied. "He was the lowest of the low. A snake."

"Trust me," she responded, putting her hand in the air stop sign style, "I've dealt with plenty of jerk guys in my life. You don't have to explain anything to me."

"Thanks. It's hard to talk about it anyway. But I just couldn't handle seeing him every day, and I don't think I can handle having this baby on my own."

"Totally understandable," she said sympathetically. "It sucks not having money!"

I nodded. Melissa had naturally assumed that the father of my baby was a jerk and that I didn't have enough money to raise the baby by myself. She had no idea how deep the complications in this situation ran. So I just went with her assumptions, but I choose my words wisely, I didn't want to get personal with this. Our relationship was only surface level, and I intended to keep it that way. I didn't want her to see that this decision was killing me.

"Again, I don't really know how you feel about abortion, and before I got pregnant, I was against it myself. But there's just no other option for me, you know? I feel…trapped." That was the best explanation I could give without getting too personal, without diving deeper than surface level.

She waved her hands at me, responding, "Molly, it's no big deal. It's *your* body. If I were in your shoes, I'd be doing the same thing for sure. How far along are you anyway?"

"Just about fifteen weeks," I replied, trying to sound as nonchalant as possible. I was in the second trimester already, so an abortion now was a much bigger deal. I saw the shock wash over her face.

"Holy cow, girl! Do they even do abortions that late?" Her eyes were wide and concerned.

I nodded. "It's a bit riskier the later you wait, and that's why I need to do it soon. I'm going in today to schedule it for tomorrow since we don't work. It only takes like twenty minutes, but recovery can be a few hours I guess. You could just drop me off, and I could call when I'm ready."

"Yeah, that'd work fine," she said casually, nodding her head and sipping her coffee. "I'd probably keep this from Britt though. She's gonna be a nurse, you know, but she's real touchy on the abortion subject. Best not to tell her." Then, she lifted her paper back up, signaling the end of the conversation.

I sat back in my chair, a little stunned at how nonchalant Melissa was on this subject. Not that I had expected her to be a big pro-lifer. She was too independent, so set on making her own way in the world, wanting nothing else but to go back to school and become a journalist. If she ever ended up with an unwanted pregnancy, she wouldn't wait as late as I had. She'd have taken care of it long ago without giving the moral complications a single consideration. That was just the type of person I could already tell she was. A real women's rights activist. A feminist.

I left and allowed myself the luxury of a bit longer shower. Melissa and I were the only ones up right now, and I figured that with Britt up late studying all week and Casey working so many hours, they'd both take advantage of sleeping in as late as possible. Besides, Britt didn't have classes until later, and Casey didn't work until tonight, so I let the hot water wash over my exhausted body. My muscles ached from holding enormous trays of food and running around all night and from simply being on my feet for so long. But even though no one needed the shower for a while, Melissa came and pounded on the door anyway, reminding me of the rule to not hog hot water. I rolled my eyes but finished up, not wanting to upset her.

After I dressed and fixed my hair, I began to feel restless—like the tiny apartment was closing in on me. I craved fresh air, so I pulled on my tennis shoes and let Melissa know I was going on a walk. She waved but didn't say anything; she was still gobbling up the paper.

Once outside, I heaved a huge sigh. My head was spinning from how fast my plans had changed. Friday morning, I had gone to school and spent the day with Tanner. My plan then had included him; I was going to keep the baby and raise it with him. I hadn't ever really let myself consider abortion. But once Tanner was out of the picture and Jason's threats entered, my whole plan had been flipped around. I had the money for it; Jason had at least made sure of that. This seemed like the only way to finally sever the tie between me and Jason. It was my final option.

I knew I needed to break all connections with the baby. I had to go back to the first moment I saw the positive pregnancy test, how I had hated the baby for existing. With Tanner, he had made it fun and exciting. He gave the situation hope. But now that the hope was gone I had to go back to hate. I had to realize that the baby was bad for me—if I kept it, I'd never escape Jason. I couldn't move forward. So for once, I had to start thinking about what was best for me, and that meant getting rid of the baby. I had to let go of all the moral arguments that were battling in my head. If I had more options, of course I would listen to what my heart was telling me. But I didn't have any other options; I'd walked right into another dead end. And so, to get around this dead end, I needed to go through with this new plan.

I found it slightly funny how I had been so passionately against abortion before I found myself pregnant. It had been all too easy to point fingers at the women who terminated their pregnancies, rationalizing that there were other options available. I had never stopped to consider how an unwanted pregnancy could destroy someone's life, how sometimes, there simply weren't any other options. I couldn't think about the baby; I needed to think about myself and what was best for me. Didn't I deserve that after all I had been through? People who ended up pregnant because of rape, like me, shouldn't have to deal with the product of an attack. It hadn't been my fault, so why should I take responsibility for Jason's actions? It was so unfair that I was the one who had to deal with what Jason had done to me. I didn't want to deal with it anymore, and I wasn't about to bring a child into a world where no one wanted it—a world where its mother hated it. I simply couldn't do that.

Right then and there, I let myself feel the satisfaction of finally making a choice for only me. I didn't think about how this would affect Tanner, my family, or anyone else. Just me. And this would be good for me, I reasoned. It would free me from Jason's bond; it would allow me to move forward with my life. And at fifteen weeks, was it even really a human yet? It didn't know what it was missing out on, and this was a horrible world anyway. I was doing the baby a favor by protecting it from this cruel world.

So really, this decision was in everyone's best interest. I could care less about what the people back home thought about this decision because I didn't plan on returning any time soon. If Jason knew, he'd be pleased. The baby would never have to suffer through this horrible world. And I'd finally be free from my demons.

But if I truly thought I was freeing myself, why did I still feel like the chains were only tightening their grip on me further?

I felt a huge cold raindrop plop on my shoulder, and it was only then that I looked up and saw the angry rain clouds gathering together. The wind picked up, whipping my hair into my face. This had sure come up suddenly, and before I could even formulate a plan, the rain was falling down in sheets, and I was soaked in a matter of seconds. I looked around, panicked, and made a run for a picnic shelter in the little park across the street from me.

I stepped into the little shelter the same time as another young man. He glanced at me and grinned, rain dripping off his shiny brown hair. His cheeks were flushed from the cold and the exertion of sprinting to the shelter as the storm blew in suddenly. Jagged lightning ripped through the sky and thunder cracked loudly, the rain continuing to fall in sheets, violently pounding the ground.

I gave a little laugh to the stranger and plopped down on the cold metal picnic bench. He sat down next to me—much too close for comfort.

"Crazy storm, huh?" he said, his voice smooth and sexy. I nodded, trying not to encourage him to keep talking to me. I simply wanted to wait out the storm and return to the apartment, change out of these wet clothes, and snuggle down, resting before the two hard days ahead of me. Clear my mind before I went into the clinic later to set up the appointment. No such luck. Apparently, this stranger was not easily discouraged.

"So what's a pretty little thing like you walking alone through this rough neighborhood? Where's your big handsome boyfriend to protect you?"

I smiled. I couldn't help it. He was a charmer, and I was a sucker for charm, even after all I'd been through with Jason. I turned and said saucily, "Don't have one, and I don't need one. I'm done being taken care of."

He raised his eyebrows and grinned again. He hadn't been expecting sass out of me I guess.

"Ooh. Well, then. Miss Independent, aren't we? Been hurt one too many times, sweet thing?"

I must have something written on my forehead that encouraged random strangers to strike up conversation with me. On Saturday, Melissa had stopped to help me, a complete and total stranger, and then offered me a job and a place to stay. And now *this* complete and total stranger was flirting with me. If I was at home caught in a storm like this, seeking shelter with a stranger,

I would have smiled politely and exchanged pleasantries, but the conversation would have ended there. No flirting, no conversation beyond what was polite and expected.

"Yes, as a matter of fact, I have. Boys are nothing but trouble. No offense."

"Oh, none taken," he said, splaying his fingers out on his chest. I could see his flannel shirt was soaked and sticking to the muscles under his fingers, and his blue eyes sparkled with mischief. "I know the male species is despicable. I'm ashamed to belong to it."

I shook my head, trying again to discourage him from talking with me. But he was persistent.

"You know," said slowly, turning to face me with a sly expression dancing in those blue eyes. "I bet I could change your mind about my despicable species. In fact, I *know* I could. What do you say? Want to grab coffee with me when this lets up?" He looked at me expectantly, but I was flabbergasted. A complete stranger had just asked me out! I think I had the right to be a little freaked out.

"No, thank you," I declined as politely as possible. I might have considered it if I wasn't planning on going into the clinic today. "I need to take care of something today. Thanks for the offer though."

He heaved a dramatic sigh. "Don't worry," he mourned. "I'm used to being turned down by beautiful women in picnic shelters. I've heard every lame excuse in the book. I'm sure you have something very important to take care of though."

I laughed. "No, really. I do have to take care of something personal."

He shook his head, convinced I was lying. "You don't have to lie to me. But…can I at lease walk you home?"

I couldn't resist his adorable blue eyes, but I was still hesitant. "Uh…" I tried to think of a good excuse but couldn't. And what harm would it do if he walked me home? I'd probably never see him again anyway. "Why not," I said with a smile.

So we sat on that hard cold bench and chatted until the rain subsided, and he walked me back to the little run-down apartment. When he turned and walked away, he said smoothly, "My name's Tyler, by the way, since you never bothered to ask."

I smirked. "Well, my name's Molly. You never bothered to ask either."

"Touché," he responded. "See you around, Molly." And then, he was gone.

I walked up the dark stairwell, confused by what had just happened. Why was my heart pounding? It was baffling to me after all I'd just been through that I had enjoyed meeting Tyler and flirting with him. That once again I was being charmed by a pair of beautiful blue eyes. I should have realized by now what trouble blue eyes caused me. Still, I was a little sad that I probably wouldn't see him again.

When I stumbled into the apartment, the room was empty. Britt must have finally left for classes, and Casey and Melissa had left for work. I was supposed to go in but Frankie saw how exhausted I had been after the shift last night and let me have the day off. I had nothing else to do except change and head down to the clinic. It was time for me to get my new plan rolling into motion. It was time to stop running away.

Time to start my new burden-free life.

Eighteen

When I walked into the clinic later that day, I realized it was nothing like I thought it would be. The lobby was simple and clean with dark-green carpeting and potted plants gracing the corners of the room. A friendly receptionist smiled and greeted me when the little bell above the door tinkled. It smelled like a dentist's office.

I was terrified, and feelings of guilt and remorse assaulted me. *Maybe I should just turn around and walk right out, try and work through my options a few more times*, I thought, panicked. The lady must have sensed my unease, though, because she immediately stood up, greeted me warmly again, and rounded the corner of the desk to usher me to a small back room.

"You look like a deer in headlights, honey. Now just calm down, and I'll get someone in here to talk to you, okay. What's your name?"

"Molly," I whispered, feeling twelve years old. My name was so young sounding. I was old enough to get an abortion without parental consent, but I certainly didn't look like it. A young woman, probably in her late twenties or early thirties, came in to talk to me. She was wearing scrubs so naturally I assumed she was a nurse.

"Hi, Molly. I'm Clarissa. Do you have some questions for me today?"

I nodded, my hands shaking out of nervousness. "Yes. And just so you know, I'm eighteen," I blurted nervously.

She smiled, trying to reassure me and calm me down. "We'll work through all those details later, sweetie. I'm just here to talk."

I continued, fidgeting. "I need an abortion."

"Okay, well, you came to the right place. We can certainly help you obtain a safe abortion here. When did you find out you were pregnant?" She smiled encouragingly at me, trying her best to put me at ease and to earn my trust. At this point I had no other option but to trust her, so I allowed myself to relax and let her take the lead.

I decided to lie about how far along I was. I wasn't showing at all, and I knew it was a bigger deal the farther along I was. I told her I was twelve weeks, not fifteen. And would it really matter anyway? What difference could three weeks make anyway?

We went back and forth discussing details, and never once did the nurse use the word *baby*. Over and over again, she used the word *fetus*, which I thought was strange, but it was helping me remove myself from this situation. It was easier to think of the baby as just something taking up residence in my body, something that could be easily and safely removed.

"So would you like to set it up for tomorrow?" she asked politely.

My head was spinning and my palms were sweating. I wasn't so sure I wanted to go through with this. And then, I remembered an important piece of information that I'd found while researching abortion clinics in Minneapolis. Some states have stricter laws regarding abortion, and I had stumbled across one particular law about abortions in Minnesota.

"Aren't I required by law to talk to a physician or something?"

She looked panicked for a second. Had she purposefully neglected to tell me this piece of information? The physician was supposed to tell me all the risks of carrying the pregnancy to full term and also the risks of getting an abortion. Did she think that talking to a physician would change my mind? I was worried about that too because I really wanted to just get the abortion and move on. And I'd have to wait a full twenty-four hours after I talked to a physician. It would be Wednesday before I could get my abortion, which wasn't exactly convenient.

"Yes, yes, of course," she agreed quickly, waving it off as nothing. "It slips our minds sometimes. The good news is that you don't have to meet in person, the lecture can be done by phone," Clarissa said. I just sat there wringing my hands, the nerves getting the best of me. "And once you get that done, you can come right back in here, and we'll deal with this together, okay? Everything will be fine. Abortions are very common and very safe. Nothing to worry about."

She gave me a number and instructed me to give the physician a call tomorrow afternoon and come back Wednesday at two o'clock for the abortion. I assured her I had a ride and a place to recover once the procedure was over. But she could still see that I was uneasy about this plan.

"Don't worry, Molly. We perform abortions every day here. It's very safe."

"I know," I said quietly. Tears sprang into my eyes. "I'm just worried…that…that I'll regret it."

She reached out and laid her hand on my shoulder, squeezing gently. "That's a normal emotion. But remember, it's just a fetus. You're young and alone. Do you really think you're ready to carry the pregnancy to full term, endure hours of hard labor, and then raise a child on your own? From my perspective, you don't seem financially or emotionally stable. If it were me, I'd go with abortion." But this wasn't her. How could she possibly say that without having waged this emotional battle inside her own mind?

I nodded. "I've counseled hundreds of young women in your situation, Molly," she continued, fully determined to not let me walk out of here without a clear decision made, "and most of the time it's a huge relief. Like a huge burden was lifted from them. You can move on with your life. You're so young! You shouldn't let a baby or anything else slow you down."

"I know. You're right." I sniffed and wiped the tears from my eyes. "I'll be back on Wednesday. You'll be here, right?" I asked, panicked.

"Of course. I'll hold your hand the entire time if you want."

"I'd like that," I said gratefully.

"Great! Let's just get through some paperwork, and I'll get you on your way, okay, sweetie? Just calm down. You're doing the right thing."

I shook the entire way back to the apartment. It had been an extremely long day, and I was grateful that everyone would be gone when I got back. I needed time to process all the nurse had told me. She made it seem like I was doing some heroic act. That I was strong to make this decision and get on with my life. She hadn't mentioned adoption at all, or pointed me to any resources that would help me raise a baby if I ended up making the decision to keep her. Granted, I didn't want to go with adoption, and I certainly didn't want to keep her, but I thought she would at least tell me all the options I had. Plus, she had neglected to tell me about the law that said I had to talk to a physician. I had chosen to go to a local women's health care center, but it made me wonder if the other big abortion clinics did this too.

Whatever. And even if I *did* have to talk to a physician, I wasn't going to change my mind. The nurse was right. I wasn't financially or emotionally ready to deal with a baby. And if I wanted to work and save up some money, a pregnancy would just slow me down. Labor sounded long and painful, and I'd be going through it all alone here. My visit to the clinic had confirmed what I had already decided. Abortion was the best way to go.

The nightmares plagued me again that night. Someone was screaming. I was in a little room with no doors, only one dirty little window let in a single shaft of light. Tanner was pounding the window, begging me to let him in. But I turned away, and suddenly, I was falling into a dark tunnel, going down and down and down until I jerked awake, cold sweat pouring off my body. The clock said it was four fifty in the morning, so I flopped back down on the bed, wide awake and terrified to go back to sleep.

I was exhausted when I finally dragged myself out of my room later that morning. Melissa sat in her spot again with the paper.

"How'd your appointment go yesterday?" she asked noncommittally. Melissa only took a genuine interest in me when it was convenient for her. Most of the time, I got the feeling that I was simply an annoyance; someone who hogged all the hot water and forgot to wash her dishes.

"Uh, it went okay. I can't go in today and get it done though. I have to talk to a physician today to learn about all the risks and stuff. Do you think Frankie would let me come in today instead so I could get it done Wednesday?"

"Probably. I'm guessing it won't be super busy on Wednesday. Just give him a call. But I work at four on Wednesday, so you'd better be done by then."

That comment stunned me a little bit. I felt bad that I was being such a burden to her, but this would be the only time I'd need a favor like this.

I called Frankie, and he grunted his approval. Then, I wasted time until I mustered up enough courage to call the physician, which was quicker and less painful than I expected. I had read most of what he told me that day in the library. I knew all the risks of carrying on with the pregnancy and the risks of abortion. I knew all about the physical side effects I would experience. And I knew adoption was an option. He steered clear of any emotional side effects I might suffer, which I was grateful for. I'd know soon enough if I had made a mistake, but at this point, I was fairly certain I was making the right choice.

Throughout the rest of the day and all through work that night, I tried to convince myself that this was best for me. If I truly wanted to get away and forget about Jason and all that lay back in Oak Ridge, I needed to do this. And the nurse had reassured me over and over that it was safe, that girls felt good about their decisions and were able to get their lives back. That's what I really wanted. My life had been stolen from me, and I just wanted to get it back.

Wednesday dawned bright and sunny, a rare beautiful March day in Minnesota. I thought this might be a good omen, a sign that I was making the right choice and everything would turn out okay. Melissa was in an extremely good mood, and she blasted some peppy song the whole way to the clinic. She pulled right up to the front door, wished me luck, and waved happily as she drove away.

The same woman sat at the front desk, and she welcomed me enthusiastically when I walked in, the little bell tinkling. I had to wait for a bit because a couple other girls were getting abortions today too. I tapped my feet nervously the entire time, trying to focus on the home and garden magazine I found lying on table.

When they finally called my name, I was ushered into a back room to fill out some medical history paperwork and take a urine test to confirm that I was actually pregnant. Then, I was given a paper gown, and the nurse I had met with the other day led me to the procedure room. The doctor, an older gentleman with salt-and-pepper hair, came in and introduced himself. Clarissa held my hand as he explained the procedure to me. They told me I could be sedated since I was so nervous, but that freaked me out even more. So they just gave me the normal pain medication and told me to relax. The doctor said that would be just fine, and there was nothing to worry about.

The only thing I really remember about the procedure was putting my legs in stirrups. I really started hyperventilating then. But Clarissa stayed with me the entire time, just like she said she would, holding my hand and smoothing my hair. I watched the doctor and other nurses hovering above me, but I blocked out whatever was happening down there. I blocked out all feeling, all noises. I tried to focus on Clarissa's gentle murmurings, but the entire time, I was just waiting for it to be over.

It only took about thirty minutes, but it was the longest thirty minutes of my life. And even though I had tried my best to block out what was happening, I could tell the doctor was struggling a bit, and that he had to change his plans. Clarissa didn't say anything, but moved in to comfort me, murmuring soothing words into me ear—I could sense something wasn't right. Suddenly, it dawned on me that lying about the fetal age had been a mistake, because three weeks made all the difference in the world, and the procedure needed to be done differently in order to remain safe. But even though he had to change his tactics, the procedure continued on. When it was over, I didn't feel anything like I thought I might. I just felt…empty. In recovery, Clarissa came to check on me.

"Was it a girl or a boy?" I asked groggily.

"Oh, honey, we don't check. You can't really tell after it's all over, you know?"

I nodded, but deep down inside, I knew it was a girl. I had aborted Tanner's little Eden. I closed my eyes, trying to erase that thought from my mind. It would destroy me if I kept thinking like that.

I lay in recovery for what seemed like an eternity until Melissa came to pick me up. I was cramping pretty badly, so she helped me into the car, and I slept the entire way home. I fell into my bed and didn't wake up until nine o'clock on Thursday morning. I was supposed to go into work, but I told Melissa I was still recovering from the abortion. She raised her eyebrows and muttered okay as she closed my bedroom door and headed to work alone.

I had always assumed that women feel intense regret and guilt after they aborted their babies, but I wasn't feeling that. And while I wasn't feeling happy about what I had done, I simply felt nothing. I simply felt like I was hovering above my body that first week after the abortion. When I returned to work, it was like I wasn't really there. Melissa was on my case all the time, telling me I was being rude to customers and that I needed to snap out of this. I tried, I really did, but I never felt the same after that warm Wednesday afternoon.

My days took on a predictable rhythm. Frankie started giving me more and more hours, and soon I was working more than Melissa, and I started driving myself to work. We just couldn't connect after the abortion, so it was for the best. She'd try to strike up conversation with me, but I'd usually answer with a simple yes or no, and then, she'd get mad and quit talking. My life consisted of working, eating, and sleeping. I wished more than anything that sleep could be my escape for it all, but the nightmares took on a new form. Usually, I'd wake up with my head spinning; I could never remember what I had dreamed, I just woke up in a panic, strange images still swirling around in my head.

One night, I dreamed of a crying baby, and I woke up, confused. I was still half-asleep as I stumbled out of bed and into the living room in search of my baby girl. I looked everywhere, but I couldn't see the cradle anywhere. When I flipped the bedroom light on, Casey groaned and pulled the blanket up over her head. It was then I realized I was only hearing things, and I quickly flipped the light off again and mumbled an apology.

I felt just like I had those first weeks after the rape. I tried to forget about what had happened, but it was impossible to flip the switch of normalcy on and off. I had been through something major, and it would probably be a few months before I finally felt somewhat normal. Or a new kind of normal. There was no way to go back to how I felt and acted before the abortion. I had to figure out how to live now, how to deal with what I had done. And this would take a very long time. I had recovered fairly quickly, or rather, I'd been able to somehow block it out and forget about the rape after it happened because Tanner had been there helping me through it, but here, I was all alone. And now, I was dealing with a rape, an unwanted pregnancy, *and* an abortion. It was all piling up on top of me, suffocating me. I had thought the abortion would free me and allow me to finally move on. But I felt even more trapped, and I didn't know how to escape this time. No one was here to help me and offer a new solution. I was completely and utterly alone. It was as if I was wandering in a desert, thirsty and disoriented and with no hope of escaping anytime soon.

My only option was to learn how to survive in the desert. I had to get used to feeling lost, thirsty, and confused. Because I knew I would be here for a long, long time.

Nineteen

May 2008

On the day I was supposed to graduate from high school, I was stuck in Frankie's working a double shift. All week, my mind had been wandering back to Oak Ridge, wondering how my classmates were feeling. Graduation week was so fun. The seniors voted on the senior polls, choosing who had best smile or who was most likely to become president. I wondered if Tanner got best smile. I thought he definitely deserved to win that. The local churches put on baccalaureate, a school church service, and I wondered who would be speaking, singing, and dancing. There were the athletic awards, the fine arts awards, and the academic awards ceremonies, and I already knew which people would get the most scholarship money. And then, there would be the chaos of final papers and tests, and on Sunday—today—my classmates would walk across the stage, shake hands with the principle, and get their diplomas. Everyone would clap, the orchestra would play "Pomp and Circumstance," and the graduates would throw their caps into the air as parents wiped their eyes and cameras flashed furiously.

And I was in a stuffy, greasy diner serving food to customers who seemed incapable of doing anything else but complain.

Casey seated a young man and asked me if I could take care of him because she was already running between a few other tables. I nodded and headed over to the booth where the young man sat scanning the menu.

"Welcome to Frankie's, can I get you something to drink while you decide what you'd like today?" I asked absently—my mind was back in Oak Ridge.

The young man glanced up, and to my surprise, I found myself looking into the blue eyes of the bold young stranger who had sought refuge with me from that sudden storm in March. He grinned.

"Well, hello, gorgeous. I didn't know you worked here!" He sounded genuinely pleased to see me, and I couldn't help smiling back at him and laughing. I hadn't let out a carefree, spontaneous laugh in so long. It felt great. Kind of odd though that this random stranger was the first to make me laugh again.

"Tyler, right?" I asked, suppressing a grin.

"Good memory. I must have made an impression on you, huh?" He was such a tease.

"It's kind of hard to forget a conversation like that, sitting in a picnic shelter in a rainstorm." I saw Casey flash me a look, wondering why I was still just standing around chatting with this guy when the diner was so busy today.

"I thought you might remember me from my rugged good looks and charm, but whatever. I remember you too, Molly."

I nodded. "Congratulations. Now, can I get you something to drink?"

He laughed. "Okay, okay. I'll have a lemonade. You sure you can't just take a break and share lunch with me? Please?"

"Sorry. We're swamped today."

"But otherwise you would, right?"

"Maybe," I teased, turning to leave. He chuckled.

Tyler continued flirting with me every time I returned to his table. Casey was getting increasingly annoyed the longer I stood there chatting with Tyler, but she was leaving soon, so I ignored her.

When I brought him his check, he asked, "So what time are you off tonight, pretty lady?"

I flirted right back, asking, "Who wants to know?"

"Well, a handsome young man who is being taken away by a lovely young lady, who looks entirely too overworked and deserves some down time. What do you say?"

I clicked my pen nervously, unsure if I really wanted to take a chance with Tyler. He was nice and cute, but he was also a mystery to me. My life had been such a whirlwind recently, and nothing good had come from me putting myself out there with boys. And when compared to Jason and Tanner, Tyler seemed more like Jason, all charm and flirt. Could he be capable of doing what Jason had done to me? I hardly knew him! It probably wasn't safe to be alone with him.

He sensed my unease. "C'mon. I'm harmless! Please?" He stuck out his lower lip for emphasis, his eyes huge and pleading. I couldn't help but smile. He was adorable.

"I'm working a double shift. I won't be done until ten tonight."

"Well, the night is young at ten! Maybe I'll come back and whisk you away. Looks like you haven't been treated in a while."

I smiled shyly, my cheeks heating up. As I watched him walk out of the diner later, he turned and gave me a wave good-bye.

Casey raised her eyebrows suspiciously, and I just shrugged. He was probably joking about tonight.

But Tyler continued to surprise me, and when I walked out of the back door of the diner that night, Tyler was there leaning up against the brick wall, waiting for me. I smiled and let out a laugh as I untied my apron.

"What are you doing here?" I asked, actually very surprised to see him.

"I'm here to treat you! What, did you think I was kidding? I don't kid about taking pretty girls out and showing them a good time. What kind of guy do you think I am?" he asked, feigning hurt.

"Well, I couldn't be sure. I don't know anything about you."

"So let me show you who I am." He held his hand out for me to take, but I hesitated. Images of that cold, rainy night with Jason flashed in my mind, paralyzing me. I was too afraid of the unknown, and I'd been through so much more than any eighteen year old should have to deal with. I was just finally starting to get over and work through this whole ordeal; I didn't know if I could risk all of that with Tyler. He could do the same thing to me and restart me on that horrible path.

"Hey," he said gently. "It's okay. You can trust me. I promise I'm not crazy. I just can't get you out of my mind."

"Yeah, right," I said skeptically, my hands on my hips.

"No, really!" he protested. "I thought about you that whole week I met you, beating myself up for not getting your phone number. I knew where you lived, but I figured it was too creepy to hang around there and wait to bump into you."

I laughed. "Yeah, that's a little creepy."

"But now we randomly meet again! Don't you think it's some sort of sign? I think about you all the time, feeling sorry for myself that I missed my chance with you. Just give me one night, and if there's no spark, I'll leave you alone for good, okay? But

I want to see if this goes anywhere, if there's a reason I can't get you out of my head."

"Well…okay. We'll see how it goes." I surprised myself with that answer. Why was I so willing to make myself vulnerable?

He jumped and pumped his fist into the air, and I laughed again. I felt more myself around him than I had in a long time. Maybe this would be good for me. Maybe for a night, Tyler could make me feel human again.

We dropped my car back at the apartment, and I considered running up to let the girls know where I'd be. But they weren't my parents; I could go out and not tell anyone where I was. Besides, Casey stayed out all night all the time. We never really knew where she was, and no one really cared either. So I figured it didn't matter, and I relished the feeling of doing something spontaneous and crazy for once.

I hopped into Tyler's car, and we were off. I didn't worry about making small talk or filling the silence in the car like I had the first time I went out with Jason. I didn't feel like I had to impress Tyler because he already so badly wanted to take me out. I figured I'd already made a good impression on him; it was time to just be myself, whoever that was now. I still wasn't really sure who I was at this point.

In the few short months I'd been living in Minneapolis, I already knew it was a pretty artsy town, but I was surprised when Tyler took me to a chic little jazz café. I thought maybe he'd take me to a bar, but this place was nothing like a bar. The entrance was in a dark alley, and we immediately went down a short flight of stairs to get in. The lighting was dark and sensual; smooth jazz music from a live band was playing. Sleek modern furniture graced the room, and it was occupied solely by young people, mostly couples clustered together throughout the room. Soft murmurs of conversation filled the dim space. It was calming and serene, and it was safe to say I was thoroughly impressed with Tyler's choice.

"Impressive, huh?" he asked, sensing my surprise.

"Yeah, it's great. I love it." I offered him a small smile—what other things would he surprise me with tonight?

"Well, just wait till you try their coffee. Best in Minneapolis, I think."

He was right—it was smooth and delicious, not too strong, but not weak either. They served their coffee in white ceramic cups with little shortbread cookies for dipping resting in the saucers. It was all so classy, I thought, and I smirked at how impressed I had been with my first date with Jason. All he'd done was take me to the local diner in Oak Ridge, nothing unique at all. But I had been so thrilled about my very first date that he could have taken me to the cheap, smelly movie theater and I would have thought it was amazing. But compared to this date, or whatever it was called that we were doing, Jason's attempt to woo me felt flat on its face.

I was a little nervous that Tyler would try to ask personal questions though, which I wouldn't be able to answer truthfully. So I figured it would be better for me to ask him about himself first.

"So, Tyler, have you lived in Minneapolis long?"

"Not really. Moved here three years ago for school. I'm studying photography."

"Wow, really?" I asked, completely surprised again. First an interest in jazz, now photography? I'd never met a guy like him before. Guys in my hometown stuck to more traditional gender roles—sports, video games, loud rock music. "Manly" stuff.

"Yeah. I've always wanted to be a photographer, but my parents didn't think I'd be able to make a career out of it," he said with a shrug. "They wanted me to be something fancy, you know? Doctor, lawyer, something that pays a lot, and something they'd be able to brag about back home."

I nodded. "And where is home?" I asked as I took a sip of my delicious mocha.

"Just a tiny little town in the middle of nowhere. Way up in northern Minnesota. You've probably never heard of it."

"Probably not. I'm from Iowa. Never really been anywhere else until I moved here." I was sheltered, and I knew it. No sense trying to play it cool with him. Never seemed to work out for me anyway.

He laughed. "It's okay. Most people who've lived in Minnesota their entire lives have never heard of it either."

"Good, I feel better." I teased. It was easy to tease Tyler. "So… were your parents mad when you left to do photography?" I asked, trying to steer back into the conversation about his life.

"A little. But they got over it. My little brother just got accepted to medical school and recently got engaged though so that's what they're focusing on now, which is fine. My parents have always smothered me, so it's nice to be here doing my own thing, becoming what I've always wanted to be. A photographer."

I admired him for following his dream, for not allowing anyone else to make choices for him or push him into something he didn't want to do. So unlike me. I'd always listened to what others thought was best for me. I was so concerned with pleasing people that I never really fought for what I wanted. Until recently, of course. I shuddered thinking about the recent choices I'd made—maybe it had been in my best interest to listen to what others thought best.

When the conversation steered to my life, I skirted around the personal details, just telling him things hadn't been working out for me back home, and I had ended up here trying to escape all the drama. I didn't tell him my age, that I'd never graduated high school. When he asked about school, I waved it off, making it seem like school had never been for me, that I couldn't imagine sitting in classrooms for another four years just to get a degree. He totally understood though because he was doing hands-on work with photography. He didn't strike me as a "sit nicely and quietly" in a classroom type of person, so he easily bought that story and thought we were that much more similar and compatible.

We sat and talked in the dim lighting of the café long after the jazz musicians left for the night. It was nearing one o'clock before we ventured out of the café and into the still warm summer air. But Tyler wasn't ready for the night to end, so he suggested we take a walk. I agreed, and as we walked side by side, we didn't say much. The night was so beautiful; we walked in silence as the sounds of the city echoed around us. When he took my hand, I relished that warm feeling that pooled in my belly. It had been so long since I felt like this, but it was a little scary. I wasn't sure if I was ready for someone to get close to me, to break down the thick brick walls I had built up around my heart.

We finally meandered back to Tyler's car, and he drove me home, soft classical music drifting out from the speakers. Tyler was so different from all the boys I'd been around my entire life. He wanted to be a photographer. He enjoyed jazz and classical music. And he didn't try to fill the silence with useless chatter. Instead, he let the silence settle in around us, but it didn't feel uncomfortable or awkward. It felt natural, and I didn't feel the need to break it either.

As I was about to open the door and get out of the car, Tyler asked, "So. Were there?"

I looked at him quizzically, my hand resting on the door handle. "Were there what?"

"Were there any sparks?" he asked, his eyes dancing.

I giggled. "Yeah, I suppose there were a few."

He settled back into his chair contentedly. "Good. And I finally have your number, so I guess I won't hang out waiting for you to come out of our apartment anymore. I'll probably just give you a call like a normal person if that's okay with you," he teased.

Laughing, I replied, "Yes, that would be great."

"Awesome." And before I could even finish opening the door, he was out in a flash and opening it for me. We stood inches apart, and I noticed for the first time how much taller he was than me. His wavy brown hair was blowing in the gentle summer wind; I could smell his cologne wafting off his body, tickling my nose.

And then, he was leaning in and gently kissing me, testing his limits. To my great surprise, I kissed him back. It didn't feel dangerous like it had been with Jason or desperate like it had been with Tanner. It was just a kiss, sweet and simple, and everything a first kiss between two people should be. I smiled, pulled back, and licked my lips, savoring the taste.

"Good night, Molly," he whispered. He tweaked my nose, got back into his car, and then, he was gone, leaving me alone in the apartment parking lot with my heart pounding and my head spinning.

That night with Tyler had been a long, refreshing drink after months in the hot desert that had become my life. I hoped he would call me back soon though because one drink was nowhere near satisfying. I wanted to gulp him in, fill myself up with how he made me feel.

And I didn't know if I would ever get enough.

Twenty

Summer 2008

For the next few months, Tyler and I fell into a whirlwind romance, or something like it. We were together all the time. He would surprise me often by waiting in the alley behind the diner, whisking me off to our little jazz café for coffee and dessert. On weekends, he took me to art galleries and taught me how to use some of his fancy cameras. I was shocked at how many he had, but he just shrugged. It was his little obsession.

Tyler made me feel human again. With him, I could smile and laugh and forget all about the past. He was restoring my faith in the male species, making me believe that not all men were manipulators, attackers, and liars. I didn't have to pretend with

Tyler or try to impress him. He got me. He didn't expect me to be perfect, to always look nice and put together.

Sometimes, he would stop in unexpectedly to the apartment on Friday nights when I was in sweats and my hair was in a messy ponytail, bringing takeout Chinese and cheesy foreign films. Casey and Melissa were always slightly annoyed when Tyler did this, but Britt adored Tyler. He even started picking Britt up her own little box of Chinese and, usually, just expected her to watch whatever movie he brought over with us, which was perfectly fine with me. And after a while, Casey and Melissa warmed up to Tyler as well. It was hard not to, he was *that* charming. They constantly reminded me, however, that he wasn't allowed to spend the night unless Casey was gone, and I warned everyone first. I reassured them, however, that Tyler was never going to spend the night with me. I wasn't about to sleep with him; I didn't want to risk another unwanted pregnancy.

Tyler wanted to move things along quickly, but I was hesitant. Things had moved much faster than I wanted with Jason; I'd trusted him prematurely and he'd swooped in and taken advantage of me, attacking me and throwing me aside like a twelve-year-old girl tosses her old childhood doll aside. And with Tanner, I'd barely had time to process what had happened. One moment, we were just friends struggling to adjust to traumatic news; the next minute, we were kissing and planning a life together. This time, with Tyler, I wanted to take it slowly, feel it out, and decide if I really wanted to let him into my world.

On a hot, sticky evening in July, Tyler took me to a little hole-in-the-wall restaurant where they only served breakfast food. My favorite. I was delighting in the menu, page after page of delicious pancake, waffle, and french toast concoctions when Tyler cleared his throat. I glanced up; he had his menu down and his hands folded in front of him. He looked much too serious, not at all the silly, flirtatious Tyler I was falling in love with.

"Can I ask you a favor?" he asked seriously.

I figured he was playing around, so I jokingly responded, "Sure. Anything for you, babe."

"My parents invited me home for the weekend for my brother's engagement party. I was hoping you'd join me. You can meet everyone, do a little schmoozing, and I can show you the town I grew up in. Sounds like fun, right?"

I closed up. Meeting his family and seeing his hometown would propel things further and faster than I was ready for. If he brought me home, it was like he was telling his family that he had found someone serious, someone he was thinking about settling down with. I'd never even considered settling down with Tyler; I simply wasn't ready for that. Right now, I was just enjoying how he made me feel. I was enjoying smiling and laughing again. I didn't want to go much deeper right now. I wasn't ready to go much deeper.

"I don't know, Tyler," I said hesitantly. "It's a long drive, and I've worked a couple double shifts already. I really just like relaxing on the weekends, you know that."

"C'mon, Molly. It's just one weekend," he argued, disappointment lacing his voice. "No big deal. And they'll be plenty of time to relax on Sunday. We'd do the party on Saturday, I could show you around town that afternoon, and then, we'd just relax. Please, pretty lady? It'd mean a lot."

I sighed. He was going to make me feel horrible if I didn't do this, but I just couldn't. But again, I was stuck in an awkward place, I couldn't tell him the real reason I didn't want to go. That would mean traveling back to a time in my life I was just now starting to untangle myself from.

"I'm sorry, Tyler. But I just can't. I'm not ready for that yet."

He looked at me quizzically. "What? To meet my family? That's not a big deal either. I know you're not in touch with your family, but mine really wants to meet you."

"But they'll think we're—" I didn't want to hurt his feelings, but I didn't want his family thinking we were serious, because we really weren't. At least, I didn't think so.

"That we're what?" He was so confused.

"That we're serious, or something," I mumbled.

He sat back in his chair, slightly taken aback.

"Aren't we…getting serious?" he asked, clearly hurt.

I sighed, swirling my straw in my orange juice. I knew this would happen. Why had I fallen for someone who actually cared, who wanted to make plans? I'd tried to tell Tanner I couldn't make plans, but he'd made them anyway, gotten excited. And then when I ran he was left to deal with what I was running away from. He was left to sort through all the confusion and anger. He had to figure out how to move on without me. And now, here was this sweet, charming young man trying to do the same thing, trying to make plans when I wasn't ready.

"I don't know, Tyler. I don't think I'm ready to be serious with anyone right now."

"Then, what are we doing?" he exploded, clearly very agitated. An older couple in the booth in front of us turned to see what was going on, why the crazy young man was yelling in this sleepy little restaurant.

"Shh. People are staring." My cheeks burned in embarrassment.

"Let them stare! I can't figure you out, Molly. You won't let me in! Whenever I press you for details about what you've left behind, what you're trying to run away from, you shut down. I *really* like you, and I want to help you through this. Why won't you let me?" he questioned with pleading eyes.

I swallowed a few times, trying to get a grip on this situation. This was embarrassing, certainly not the place to be discussing this.

"Let's talk about this later, okay? This isn't the place."

He stood up, throwing his napkin on the floor. "Fine. Shut me out. Again. One day, you're gonna have to let me in though, or this is never going to work. I'll see you when I'm back from my brother's engagement party."

And with that, he stalked out of the restaurant, leaving my mouth hanging open in shock. Every eye was locked on me, and I tried to pull myself together. I fumbled in my purse, slapped a few bills on the table, and quickly walked out, only to see him driving away, leaving me to find my own way home.

This is how I had expected Tanner to react to the news of the pregnancy. To stand up in anger, rightly accuse me of shutting him out, and leave me standing in the dust. That's how he *should* have responded; it would have made me finally feel like I was getting what I deserved. But now, it hurt. It hurt that Tyler had gotten so angry that I wasn't ready for a serious relationship. I needed a bit more time. Maybe in a few months, I'd be ready. But not now. Why was that so hard to understand?

I walked back the apartment, defeated. He'd spend all weekend angry at me. I, of course, had met a sensitive guy. Someone who felt things deeply and was capable of making me feel extremely guilty.

I usually don't work on Sundays, but with Tyler gone, I picked up an extra shift at Frankie's just to distract myself. He hadn't texted or called all weekend, proof that he was still harboring anger. When I stumbled out of the diner late that night, however, he was there in the alleyway, leaning up against the grimy brick wall, hands stuffed in his pocket.

He smiled weakly. "Hey, pretty lady."

"Hey," I said simply. I was still feeling guilty. "I'm really sorry, Tyler," I offered lamely.

He pushed off the wall and gathered me in his arms, smoothing my hair out of my face. "Hey, it's okay. I was out of line, trying to push you into something you clearly weren't ready for. And I realized immediately when I got there that it would have been a disaster. I forgot how crazy my family is! You would have been completely overwhelmed. *I* was completely overwhelmed!"

I let out a small laugh. "So you forgive me then?"

"Of course I do," he said sweetly, kissing me on the nose. "Now, it's barely nine o'clock. Want to spend some time with me after our long weekend apart, gorgeous?"

I nodded. "Sure do."

Tyler had the power to completely change my mood, to take an awful day and turn it into a great one. I'd spent all weekend worrying that he was furious at me, but as I stood wrapped in his arms, breathing in the spicy scent of his cologne, all worries blew away. I was still his.

We climbed into his car, and Tyler said, "I kinda feel like just chilling tonight. It's been a long weekend, to say the least. Want to check out my place?"

I swallowed hard, uneasy. The last time I allowed a boy to take me to his house alone, it hadn't ended well at all. It had sent me on a reckless tailspin, spiraling wildly out of control. I was still reeling from it, still feeling its effects. Every day, I lived with the fact that I was used and dirty, that I had gotten pregnant, and then disposed of it for my own good. That was difficult to live with, and I was beyond terrified that Tyler would do the same to me, even after three months of dating him. I knew he was nothing like Jason; in fact, the more time I spent with him the more he reminded me of Tanner. Totally willing to pour himself into me. But unlike Tanner, he was now expecting the same. He wasn't buying the story that I was too empty to fully love him back like Tanner had. He wanted me to return his love, he wanted me to pour my love right back into him. Was I capable of doing that? I wasn't sure.

But I figured I had already told him no enough in the past few weeks. He had been so disappointed when I didn't want to meet his family this weekend, and the guilt was really eating me away. So I found myself agreeing to go to his apartment alone just to make him happy. He grinned, and we were off.

Tyler lived in a really cool part of town. His apartment was some historic building that the city had converted into apartments to preserve the history. It was right up Tyler's ally. He loved art and history, and I knew he absolutely loved living there. He told me mostly old people lived in his apartment, but that was okay because they were quiet, and he had befriended many of them. One older lady sort of adopted him, bringing him home-baked goodies and watering his plants for him while he was out of town. Tyler always picked up her groceries for her at the neighborhood grocery store, buying her little packages of Swedish Fish or some other little candy for her as a treat. From the way it sounded, the old woman adored Tyler, and I understood why. He had a certain effect on people, drawing them in with his charm. But his charm was sincere, unlike Jason's. He genuinely liked people; he had a way of making everyone feel special when he was around.

When we walked into his tiny apartment I just stared, and I realized once again how different Tyler was from the normal guys his age. He had devoted an entire wall to his photography, various sizes of framed photos arranged artfully. I walked up to the wall and examined his beautiful work, but one picture caught my eye right away. It was a picture of me, my head thrown back in carefree laughter. I didn't remember him ever taking this picture. He saw me examining it and jumped in to explain.

"I took that a few weeks ago when we were picnicking. You were in such a silly mood that day, I couldn't resist. Luckily, I had my camera in my hand when you laughed. I think it turned out amazing."

He was right, the picture was amazing. It was a black-and-white picture, but it was crisp and clear, every detail stunning. The camera had caught every crinkle and laugh line on my face, every wisp of hair that had been dancing in the slight breeze. It was beautiful, and I was honored that a picture of me was hanging on this wall next to the rest of his stunning art.

The other pictures were just as amazing. Some were in color, others old-fashioned–looking sepia, and others black-and-white like mine. They were all framed in bold black frames, however, tying them all together. I marveled at the diversity I saw—there were landscapes, old run-down buildings, and a few portraits. My favorite was an old couple holding hands on a park bench, watching their little grandson chasing after a butterfly. I smiled and touched my finger to the glass, running it across their faces.

"I like that one too," he said, joining me at the wall. "They live downstairs. Their little grandson is the cutest little thing you ever saw, but the mom is a train wreck. He spends a lot of time with his grandma and grandpa because she's out doing God knows what. Pretty sad. But they adore him."

I smiled and nodded, unable to add to his explanation. I continued drinking in Tyler's work, thoroughly impressed. Tyler was already an amazing photographer. He'd do well in his career.

He made himself busy in the kitchen, whipping up a fresh pot of coffee while I explored the rest of his amazing little apartment. It was so charming, with old, rustic-looking hardwood flooring and its low gold-painted ceiling. His furniture was secondhand and mismatched, but it was so cozy with the fireplace and large red area rug that I hardly noticed. There was one small bedroom and a tiny little bathroom, but I suppose he lived alone and it was enough for him. It only took me a few minutes to walk through the whole place.

"Like it?" he asked.

"It's gorgeous. I can't believe you live here!"

He shrugged. "Yeah, it's something else. I'm pretty lucky I found this place."

We settled at the counter, sipping coffee and chatting quietly. He told me about his weekend, about how his mom had made such a huge deal out of this engagement party. His brother, Jacob, had pleaded with his mom to calm down, but to no avail. His fiancée, Sidney, was so stressed out by his mother's fretting she'd barely enjoyed the party, and the two snuck out early to escape her. She didn't find out until all the guests left that Jacob and Sidney had snuck away, and she flipped out even more. The weekend ended on somewhat of a sour note after that, and Tyler had been relieved to head back to Minneapolis. I chuckled, even more grateful that I'd stayed back.

When conversation lulled we snuggled down and popped in one of our favorite movies, dozing on and off. The movie ended right around midnight, and I got up to stretch my legs, stopping again to appreciate Tyler's amazing wall of photos. He snuck up behind me, wrapping his arms around my middle, and nuzzling my neck, gently kissing my ear. I smiled and turned around, folding myself into his hug. He tilted my lips up to meet his, and we stood in the hallway kissing until he lifted me up, and I wrapped my legs around his middle. Somehow, in the dark, we stumbled into his bedroom, collapsing together on the bed, still kissing. My heart pounded as I let Tyler slowly peel away layer after layer of clothing; it was the first time I was willingly letting someone undress me. Somewhere in the back of my mind, my former Christian self was yelling at me to stop, trying to convince myself that being raped didn't really count as losing my virginity, and I still had a chance to keep it if I simply told Tyler no. But this felt too good, his fingers caressing my skin, his chest pressed up against mine. And I was still feeling guilty about refusing to come home with him to meet his family, so I silenced the voice inside me and offered it all up to Tyler.

I woke sometime early that morning, Tyler's arm throw across my middle, and our bodies still spooned together. He slept peacefully, a contented look on his face. Sunlight filtered through the little window in his room, and I could see our clothes strewn about the room. I laid there absently twirling a strand of hair, not sure how I felt about what had happened last night. Sometime between kisses, Tyler had murmured, "I love you," but I had been too shocked to say anything back, which he didn't really seem to mind. He probably thought I'd say it when I was good and ready.

He woke up half an hour later and smiled, pleased to be waking up next to me. "Good morning, pretty lady," he said groggily. His hair was all smashed up, eyes still foggy with sleep. He was simply adorable. "Care for a shower?" he asked.

I nodded shyly. *Why not?* I thought to myself. I'd given it up already, no reason to tell Tyler no anymore. So we showered, made waffles and coffee, and spent the rest of the morning and a good part of the afternoon in Tyler's bed, kissing and replaying last night on and off. Sometimes, we'd just lay there, and Tyler would run his fingers through my hair, telling me how beautiful I was, how much he loved me. It really was a wonderful afternoon.

And yet, when I dressed and Tyler dropped me off at my apartment later that afternoon, the magic was wearing off and my stomach was tightening. My nineteenth birthday was a month away, and I knew that if my former bright-eyed eighteen-year-old self could see my life now, she would hardly recognize me. Last year, I had been anxiously looking forward to senior year and what lay ahead after graduation. Clearly, those plans hadn't worked out, and I was hundreds of miles away from the town I grew up in and from everyone I loved. I had no diploma, no plans beyond a few weeks at a time.

The girls gave me curious looks when I came in, their eyebrows raised in question. I just shrugged; I wasn't going to fill them in on all the details of what had happened last night. They could draw their own conclusions, and they'd most likely draw the correct ones. Tyler and I had been seeing each other for a few months; it was pretty much assumed we were sleeping together by now. It made me a little sad that society just expected couples to sleep together before marriage. I'd grown up believing that sex was sacred and only to be shared between a man and wife. My emotions were in battle again. On one hand, I had enjoyed stepping out of the boundaries that had held me so tightly for my entire life; but on the other hand, I could see how those boundaries were meant to protect me.

In the movies, they made it look so easy. Two people would have a romantic chance meeting, similar to the way Tyler and I had met at random during that March thunderstorm. They'd keep bumping into each other, unable to keep each other out of their minds. Finally, they'd start seeing each other, and then a steamy bedroom scene would ensue, much like what had happened with me and Tyler last night. But it was always a deep, satisfying experience that sealed their love forever, making it seem like sex was the magic that brought two people together and strengthened their relationship. There was never any guilt or remorse; it was always a positive experience.

I wasn't convinced yet that sleeping with Tyler had been a positive experience. Sure, it felt good, and it had been fun, but now I was feeling empty. Empty and alone. I knew that Tyler would go whistling into work later today, on cloud nine after last night. But he hadn't grown up the way I had, believing that sex was sacred and meant to be protected. He'd grown up thinking this was just the next step in the relationship. It was expected.

I got ready for work, looking hard into my eyes as I combed my hair. I didn't look the same as I had five months ago when I had fled my hometown and all that lay behind there. My eyes looked cold, empty, and dead. Void of all hope and happiness that they used to dance with back at home before my life had started crumbling. Some of that sparkle returned when Tyler came into my life, but it had dimmed again after last night. Was this all there was to my life? Just slogging through life day by day, depending on other people to fill me up, to satisfy me? Living everyday haunted by what I had done?

There had to be more. I'd walked into so many dead ends. Was there any way to turn around or climb over them now? I felt so stuck here—nineteen in a month and no diploma, no promising future ahead of me. And every day, I woke up, looked myself in the eye, and had to somehow digest that fact that four short months ago I'd been pregnant, but I'd chosen a path that was most convenient for me, a path that left me void and lifeless. A path that had disposed of the tiny life inside me without a care.

I didn't know what else to do though. I had nowhere left to run. And I was so sick of running. I just wanted to know what I was supposed to do with my life, what I was supposed to live for. I didn't want to live just to work, just to survive. I wanted to have a purpose again. I wanted to hope and dream again.

Here in Minneapolis, I felt like I was journeying farther and farther into the desert, unsure where to turn and with no hope of ever reaching the other side. I needed rest. I needed water.

I needed to get out of the desert.

Twenty-One

August 2009

Fall. Winter. Spring. Summer. It all blended together, and before I knew it, I'd been in Minneapolis for a little over a year. When the anniversary of the abortion rolled around, I slogged my way through work, turned my phone off, and then, later curled up in my bed, numb. I couldn't handle the sunny, warm weather on that day. I couldn't handle the girls' happy chatter and laughter. I wanted the whole world to mourn with me over the loss of my baby girl. Nobody besides Melissa even knew though, and she hardly remembered it. It hadn't affected her at all; she didn't have a clue when the anniversary was or how it was affecting me. She'd rolled her eyes when I finally stumbled out of the room later that night, scooping myself a bowl of ice cream and then returning to my rumbled bed and my tearstained pillow.

Tyler and I were still together, but I was getting increasingly annoyed with our relationship. He never again brought up meeting his family after that weekend, but I could tell he wanted things to move much faster than I was willing. On lazy weekends, we'd spend all our time lounging in his bed, and he'd bring up moving in with him. But I always made up some lame excuse, which would most of the time only end up frustrating him beyond belief, and we'd part angry and hurt. But he always took me back, sorry for pushing me and reassuring me he was fine with the way things were. But I knew better. He wasn't okay with the way things were, and if they didn't change soon, our relationship would come to a swift end.

I'd shut him out too on the anniversary of the abortion. He, of course, had tried calling and texting all day, but my phone was off. He'd gotten so worried that he stopped over to the apartment around one in the morning to make sure I was okay. Britt had answered the door and then snuck into my room to let me know Tyler was standing at the door wanting to see me. I waved her away, saying I wasn't up to any visitors today. She had just shrugged and closed the door and Tyler left. But he was furious the next morning when I finally answered my phone.

"What in the world is going on, Molly?" he demanded angrily. "I've been worried sick!"

I sighed, rubbing my temples. I didn't want to tell him the real reason I'd been unable to face the world yesterday. He'd never look at me the same. In fact, he'd probably break up with me right then and there. Tyler wasn't a fan of abortion. He'd only mentioned it casually a few times, telling me his distaste for women who selfishly chose abortion just to make their own lives easier. I'd shuddered inside each time he said something like that, knowing I'd never be able to tell him about the rape or abortion.

I needed an excuse, but everything fell flat. "I'm sorry, Ty. Yesterday was a really hard day. Something…" I searched for the right word. "Something…tragic happened on this day a while back. I didn't want to be around anyone or even get out of bed. I just needed to think. I should have told you."

He let out an exasperated laugh. "Um… yeah, you should have. You know you can always tell me anything. Nothing is too big for me to handle."

Yes it is, I thought sadly. This was *way* too big for him to handle.

We got through March, however, despite his frustration over my lack of zeal for anything. He tried being more spontaneous, surprising me with flowers or whisking me away to art exhibits or new little restaurants. But I was slipping further and further away from him, and he knew it. I was slowly but surely shutting him out.

It happened on a muggy August evening. We were sitting at Tyler's counter, eating ice cream in silence. The ticking of his clock bounced off the walls, and Tyler shifted anxiously in his seat, uncomfortable with this silence. He reached over to brush a lock of hair out of my eyes, but I stiffened. He dropped his hands, sighed, and pushed out of his chair, scraping it on the wood floor. He dumped his bowl in the sink and turned around, crossing his arms.

"What, Molly? What am I doing wrong? Why are you shutting me out?"

"What are you talking about?" I tried asking, denying the obvious truth that we could both see plain as day.

He shook his head. "Not gonna work this time. I'm not buying that. You can't even pretend you don't know what I'm talking about. We've been together for a year now, but the closer we've gotten, the more you've shut down. And I don't get that, Molly. I'm doing all I can to keep you, but it's getting pretty difficult with you resisting so hard."

I just sat there, my eyes downcast. He looked at me expectantly, wanting me to offer up some kind of explanation for this strange behavior. I didn't have one though, not one I could tell him. I was still afraid of the whole idea of a relationship. Jason had abused me and Tanner had tried too hard to mold the situation into a plan that perfectly fit his life. And then Tyler had come in at a time where my world was spinning off its axis, he'd brought laughter back into the picture. He made life somewhat worth living again. But he wanted too much of me, and I wasn't willing to give him all of me. I didn't want to get attached because I was afraid he'd get bored with me and cast me aside. I didn't want to meet his family or move in with him. I just wanted a simple, no-strings-attached kind of relationship. It figured that I'd found one of the only men in the entire city who wanted so much more than that.

"Well?" he asked, getting more upset by the minute. "Talk to me, Molly."

I swallowed and shook my head. "I don't know what you want me to say," I said quietly, shrugging my shoulders.

"Well, maybe just explain to me why I'm not enough? Why no matter what I do, what I say…it's never enough. It's a little hard watching you turn your back to me after every time we sleep together, like it's tearing you up inside. It's hard watching your eyes glaze over when we're out together, like your mind just goes somewhere else, and I constantly have to pull you back. And it's certainly not a walk in the park having full days where you ignore all contact, shutting off your phone so you can avoid me."

Again, I stayed silent. He was justified in being upset.

"Nothing?" he asked. I shook my head again.

"Then, what do we do now, Molly? I refuse to go on like this. I want a future with you, and I have no clue what you want."

I rubbed my temples. He deserved some sort of explanation. "I've been running away from my past for so long, Tyler. I left Oak Ridge because there was no hope of a positive future for me there." I swallowed, trying to figure out how to only skim the surface of the details behind my story. "But when I got here, it was impossible to escape from it all, and I made a big mistake, one that I can't move forward from."

He pushed off the sink and leaned across the counter, taking my hands. "Just let me in. I want to help you through it."

"I can't," I choked.

He dropped my hands and ran his hands through his hair. "Then, what am I good for, Molly? If you won't tell me what's wrong, and you won't let me help you, we can't go anywhere from here."

I chose my next words carefully. "I know this sounds horrible…but when we first started hanging out…you made me forget about it all," I said with a sheepish shrug. "You made me laugh and smile again. I didn't think you wanted this to turn into something serious."

"Who do you think I am?" he exploded. "Of *course*, I want something serious. I'm not going to play around my entire life!"

"I just…I don't know if I'm ready for something like that. I've had such bad experiences…"

"Well, if this is just another bad experience, it would have been nice to know a long time ago. At least then, it wouldn't have been so hard saying good-bye."

I looked up sharply. "You're breaking up with me?" I asked.

"I'm sorry, Molly. But I don't think you'll ever change. I've done all I can for the past few months, tried to prove to you I'm different. That I love you. But I can't handle you always shutting me out, and I honestly don't think you'll ever trust me enough to let me in all the way."

I nodded. "I see." We let silence settle over us, both of us unsure what to say. The clock continued ticking, breaking the awkward quiet.

"Want me to drive you home?" he asked after a while.

"No, I'll walk. It'll give me time to think." I offered him a weak smile, but he just shrugged and crossed his arms again. I collected my things and quietly shut the door behind me. We didn't kiss or hug good-bye. I just left, and it was over.

I didn't cry on the walk back or even later when I curled up into my little bed. I wasn't sure how to feel about what had just happened. Tyler was right though, I'd never trust him enough to let him in. I knew he was a good guy, but I was just so damaged and empty. This probably would have happened to Tanner and me too if I'd stayed behind with him.

When thoughts of Tanner popped into my head, it was then that I did begin to cry. I didn't realize how much I missed him. I wondered where he was, what college he'd decided to go to without me. I hoped he'd gone off to Iowa State once I was out of the picture. I knew that was where he always wanted to go.

As time went on, I began to feel emptier and emptier. Without Tyler to make me laugh, to make me feel human, I began to feel lost. I once again had to drag myself out of bed in the mornings, fighting for a reason to live.

I felt so distant from everyone now. Melissa and Casey talked to me at work, and Britt tried to talk when I joined her in the living room to watch TV, but I couldn't really connect with them anymore. I tired of Melissa banging on the bathroom door, demanding I save hot water for everyone else when I barely stood in the shower long enough to rinse the shampoo from my hair. I tired of Casey coming in late at night, drunk and stumbling over furniture. And recently, the girls started bringing alcohol into the apartment, inviting too many people over and playing the music too loud. Every weekend, there'd be new people, more hangovers the next day. I'd just about had enough.

It was after a nasty fight with Melissa that I finally packed and left. Casey had come in late one night, drunker than normal and swearing like a sailor. In the morning, she was so sick, and she hadn't made it to the bathroom before she threw up all over my side of the bedroom. I lost my temper and laid into her pretty good, releasing all my pent-up anger onto her, and that hadn't gone over well with Melissa. After a screaming match, I quickly packed all my belongings and shoved them all in my car. I told them I wouldn't be coming back, that I just couldn't handle living here anymore. And I ran. Again. No plan, no clue where I was headed. Anywhere other than here was preferable.

I stopped by the bank for the money I'd managed to save over the past year. It hadn't added up much because I had to pay rent, and waitressing didn't pay very well. I decided it was fine to keep my little TracFone; I'd just delete all the contacts I'd added while living in Minneapolis. No one from Oak Ridge had this number, and no one from Minneapolis would ever try to contact me again, I was sure of it.

So with all my possessions piled in the back of my little car and a purse full of cash, I hit the road again. When fleeing from Oak Ridge, I'd gone north and landed in Minnesota, hoping to blend in and disappear in the cities. It had worked too. Besides Tyler and the girls, I'd made no connections there. I'd vanished. But maybe that hadn't been such a good idea. I'd been so concerned about becoming invisible, about not letting anyone in that I'd been suffering alone for a year and a half. I hadn't let anyone in to help me bear the burden of what lay behind in Oak Ridge. Of what I'd done in that abortion clinic. That was too much of a load to carry alone; the weight was crushing me. But I'd refused to let anyone lift the load off my shoulders and transfer it onto their own. I'd locked everyone out and insisted on lugging it around myself through the dry desert that was my life in Minneapolis.

So maybe this time, I needed to go small. Maybe it was time for me to let someone in.

Maybe it was time for me to be found.

Part Three

Found

My heart has heard you say,
"Come and talk with me."
And my heart responds,
"Lord, I am coming."

—Psalm 27: 8

Twenty-Two

October 2009

I'd been living in Green Lake, Kansas, for a little over a month, and simply being around Mary Beth was healing my cracked and wounded heart, slowly but surely breaking down the thick walls around my heart. She'd taken me in like a lost, lonely puppy that September day I'd rolled into town looking for a job. From the moment I sat down in her little family restaurant, she knew I needed to be here. The first day I worked for her she told me, "I could see it in your eyes, little girl. You looked lost. I knew you had nowhere else to go. And besides, I'm getting up there in years. It's about time I brought in more help." Then, she'd smiled warmly, patting my shoulders, as I filled a pie with cherry filling.

Mary Beth made everything from scratch, even all her pie-crusts and fillings. She kept the place spotless. The floors constantly shone, my shoes never stuck to leftover grease. And she treated me and Albert like family. Albert was an older gentleman, and he worked as a busboy. He was slow and clumsy, but Mary Beth loved him and never got on his case. My mind wandered back to Gavin, the poor little busboy at Frankie's. Melissa and Casey and the rest of the girls constantly picked on him. He was a sweet boy though, and I'd grown fairly close to him while working there.

I'd stepped out back for a moment on a particularly busy night and found him sitting on the dirty pavement smoking a cigarette. He looked up in fright, sure that one of the girls had noticed he was gone and come to chew him out. When he saw it was me, however, he sighed and relaxed. I never picked on Gavin because, in real life, we were almost the same age. I was technically still a high school student like him. I gave him a smile and plopped down right next to him. We were exhausted; both of us had been there most of the day and couldn't wait to go home.

Gavin really opened up to me that night. I asked him why he worked so much, and his eyes filled with tears. I choked up immediately; there's something about boys crying that really gets to me. He explained that his mom and dad had a surprise pregnancy a few years back and had a baby girl, Natalie. Gavin adored her, but at age three, she'd been diagnosed with leukemia. He was working all the hours he could so the family could continue fighting the disease. But the more he worked, the less time he was able to spend with her, and it was difficult for him. He was also trying to put a little money away for college, but he admitted that if she didn't get better before he was supposed to leave, he wouldn't go.

"I couldn't live with myself if she died while I was away, ya know?"

I nodded, tears spilling onto my cheeks. He was fighting so hard for his baby sister, and only months before, I'd aborted a perfectly healthy baby. Some family out there would have loved and fought for my baby, but I'd gotten rid of her. It was a hard conversation, to say the least.

We sat there in silence for a bit until Gavin finished his cigarette then headed back into the chaotic mess we called work. I kept up with what was happening with Natalie, but I knew a few weeks before I left, she hadn't been doing well. I wondered what had happened, if she'd somehow gone into remission or if in the end the cancer had gotten the best of her. Maybe someday, I'd try and find Gavin again, see how everything had worked out for his baby sister.

Working with Albert was pretty much the polar opposite of working with Gavin. I wasn't sure how old Albert was, but he had to be nearing eighty. He was the sweetest thing though. He was constantly teasing me, all in good fun of course, and he always had a hard caramel candy to slip into my front apron pocket. And when he asked me how I was doing, he looked me straight in the eye and grabbed my hands in his withered ones. I knew he genuinely wanted to know how I was doing, and I felt a little bad lying to him saying I was fine when, in reality, I was far from fine.

I was staying in the same dirty little motel I'd stayed in the first night I rolled into Green Lake. Until Mary Beth found out. Staying in a motel is expensive, and I was getting worried about my money running thin. Mary Beth sensed my unease and drew it out of me one afternoon, and when I told her I was staying in that motel, she scolded me for not saying something sooner.

"For goodness's sake, Molly, that place is a dump! The church I go to rents out a little house for people who have nowhere else to go, and the lady who was living there with her kids just got a Habitat for Humanity house, so it's empty. It's very affordable. Just let me take care of it, dearie."

I tried to protest, insisting I could figure it on my own, put Mary Beth just swatted me with a dishtowel and clucked her tongue. You just couldn't say no to this woman, and the next thing I knew, I was settling into the church's charity house. It came furnished though; I didn't have to worry about finding a kitchen table, couches, and a bed, which was nice. I could take charity from the church if they gave me a low-rental, fully furnished house. No problem.

It was weird being in a house all by myself. I'd never had a place all my own before. I'd gone from living in my parents' house to living in an apartment full of rowdy college-aged girls. And now, here I was, twenty years old, living in an empty house. In a way though, it was helping me heal. I didn't have to hide here. If I was feeling down, I just cried as loudly as I wanted and didn't worry about anybody coming in and asking what was wrong. I didn't worry about someone pounding on the bathroom door, yelling that I was hogging the hot water. I stood under the hot stream of water as long as my heart desired.

There was no TV though, and at night, it was strangely quiet. There was a bookshelf full of books, but when I scanned the titles, nothing really caught my eye. The church must have stocked it, because it was full of Christian books, from authors like A.W. Tozer or C.S. Lewis, and there was no way I was picking up anything like that. There was also a few different translations of the Bible, which I didn't even bother taking from the shelf either. I still wasn't ready for God quite yet. So reading was out of the question.

I wandered around the little house one lonely night, and I stumbled upon the little beat up box that I kept my childhood knick-knacks and some other personal items in. I pulled out a few spelling bee ribbons and other school awards, smiling at the fond, simple memories they brought up. Memories of me and Tanner at a time where we were simply friends growing up together. There were also a few ratty stuffed animals nestled inside, and I considered just throwing them out. They held no special memories for me, yet I couldn't bring myself to do it. A little ceramic pot I'd made and painted in elementary school held all my baby teeth, and I laughed at how disgusting that was. But

I didn't throw them away either. I just couldn't get rid of anything that lay in this little box.

Next, I pulled out two picture frames. One was a brown store-bought frame with the words *best friends* etched into the wood. It was that stupid picture of me and Tanner my mom had snapped. The other picture frame was heavy, black, sleek, and more artistic than the brown one. It held the photo of me that Tyler had taken and hung on his amazing wall of pictures. He'd stopped by the diner one night to give it to me, a bittersweet moment. It was nice to have some closure with Tyler, and the photo was beautiful. But Tyler had left a void in my heart, just as Tanner and Jason had too. I was getting emptier and emptier each time I put myself out there with a boy.

Each time I ran, I thought I would be escaping and starting over. I thought I could forget about what I was running from. But that was the furthest thing from the truth. I dragged everything with me when I left; there was no escaping the past. It just kept piling up, heavier and heavier, and I was forced to drag it behind me everywhere I left. Jason, the rape, the pregnancy, my split with Tanner, the abortion, my empty relationship with Tyler—it was too much for one person to handle on their own. Yet, here I was in some tiny town in Kansas, left to somehow deal with my load all by myself. Again.

Mary Beth watched me with concerned eyes. She could sense my brokenness, could see the hollow look inside my eyes. She knew that I had nothing left to live for, so naturally, she stepped in to help.

"Molly, honey, why don't you come with me to church on Sunday?" she suggested. "You're all alone in that house. It's not good for you. You need to go out and meet some people, get connected with the folks here."

I looked up to Mary Beth's expectant eyes from the stalk of celery I was chopping up. I hated to tell her no, but I wasn't ready for that yet. "I don't think so. The church isn't exactly the place where I want to be meeting people."

"Why not?" she protested loudly. "The church is a *wonderful* place to meet people!"

I decided to be somewhat honest with her. "I've had a really bad experience with some people in the church, Mary Beth. I made a mistake, and they treated me like I was some kind of horrific sinner, like I wasn't worthy of being in the church anymore." That was at least true of Kristina, not necessarily Tanner, but still.

I continued, "And I was always taught that God loves me, and that he has my best interest in mind. But something really terrible happened to me, and I just don't see how a loving God lets something like that happen to anyone."

She was silent for a moment. "Do you want to talk to me about what happened to you?" she asked softly.

I was right. What was so easy to do in a large city was impossible to do here in this tiny little town. I couldn't disappear around these people; they wouldn't let me. I felt a little tug, a small desire to spill my entire story to this woman, to finally let myself be found. But I was still terrified. I had been trying so hard to bury what lay behind me, and digging it back up would be hard. Maybe I wanted to be found sometime, but it was still too soon.

"Maybe sometime." I offered. "I'm still trying to work through it, though."

She nodded and smiled warmly. "Okay, sweet girl. But I'm not giving up on you," she said, wagging her finger at me.

And Mary Beth was certainly a woman of her word. Each week, she asked me to go to church with her; and each week, I told her I wasn't ready. During the last week of October, she asked me to go to the church's Halloween party. I guess she figured I'd be more inclined to go since it wasn't actually a church service.

"There's someone I really want you to meet," Mary Beth pleaded. "Her name is Delilah. I think you'll really like her."

Mary Beth's eyes were so full of hope and excitement that I just couldn't say no. And she was constantly badgering me to meet this Delilah person. If I just met her, maybe Mary Beth would let it go.

When I agreed, she jumped and clapped her flour-dusted hands in delight. "I'm so happy! I'll pick you up at seven, okay? You don't have to dress up, unless you want to. Albert is going as a wolf, and I'm going to be Little Red Riding Hood. It'll be such fun!"

I wasn't really sure what was so fun about a Halloween party at a church, but I had no other plans, no excuse not to go. So on Halloween night, Mary Beth and Albert rolled up in front of my tiny house, all decked out in costumes, to usher me away to the church party.

Mary Beth chattered the entire way there. "Now, you can either just mingle and try and meet some nice people, or you can volunteer to run a game station. Oh, and I'll introduce you to Delilah too. You'll just love her, won't she, Albert? Everyone loves Delilah!" She was absolutely gushing about this lady. I rolled my eyes. Probably just another stuffy church lady, just like the ones I'd grown up around in my own church, but I smiled and nodded enthusiastically for her.

"Oh, yes," Albert agreed. "She's a sweetie, that one."

The little church looked like something right out of a story-book. It was white, complete with a steeple, and tonight, it was absolutely crawling with people. Hay bales were spread around and little kids jumped and crawled all over them under the watch-ful gaze of their parents. A smoke machine was up and running and a little boom box spilled eerie Halloween noises and music all over the churchyard. This was not what I had expected; it looked so cute, and everyone looked like they were having a blast.

Mary Beth and Albert clambered out of the car like they were the little kids about to enjoy all this Halloween fun. I smiled and rolled my eyes again as I hesitantly made my way out of the car. Mary Beth looped our arms together and hauled me inside.

The church was small, the sanctuary immediately to my right when we entered the front door. The rest of the first floor had been cleared of all tables and chairs, and various booths and game stations occupied the room instead. It was hot and stuffy in here, even with all the windows thrown open. It smelled like childhood, like sticky little bodies mixed with the baked goods that overflowed from so many of the booths. Kids were dragging around huge bags of candy; they probably brought in a better haul here than going door to door in this little town.

Mary Beth could hardly contain herself. We went from booth to booth greeting people, but seeing toddlers waddle around in their bulky costumes was hitting me hard. My baby would have been fourteen months old this Halloween, and I could have dressed her up in a cute little costume like the babies I saw here tonight. People would have "oohed" and "ahhed" over her chubby little cheeks. Her eyes would have been wide and shining, taking in all this excitement.

I swallowed the huge marble that always caught in my throat when I thought about the child I had aborted. Thoughts of her always made me want to cry, to go back to that day and shake some sense into my terrified self. How had I let fear and desperation cloud my vision, my judgment? I could have figured something out, fought harder to keep my baby with me. I had rationalized that I needed to simply focus on myself, that this was the best thing for me. Well, here I was a year and a half later, so broken from that decision. It hadn't been the best thing for me. Not in the least.

Mary Beth pulled me out of my thoughts. "Oh, look! There's Delilah! Hello dear!" she called out. A young woman with jet-black curly hair turned around and gave Mary Beth a huge smile. "There's someone I'd like you to meet!"

Delilah bent down and hoisted a little boy dressed up as a pirate onto her hip. He looked to be about five years old. He was gorgeous with big brown chocolate eyes and brown ringlets springing from his head. Together, they stumbled through the crowd over to us. The little boy stretched out his arms to Mary Beth, and she gladly accepted the little pirate, nuzzling his face. He smiled and kissed her on the cheek.

"Whew!" Delilah huffed. "He's so huge I can barely hold him for five minutes anymore." She turned to me, smiled, and stuck out her hand. "Mom's been telling me all about you, Molly. I feel like I already know you!"

I turned and gave Mary Beth a sly look. She never told me Delilah was her daughter, and to be honest, she looked much too old to be her mom anyway. She ducked her head and giggled. "Uh-oh, Luke. We've been found out!" She tweaked his little button nose, and he chortled.

"Yes," I replied with a laugh. "She's been telling me all about you too. She just neglected to tell me you were her daughter!"

"Yeah, Mom's always been full of tricks." Delilah turned to her mother and asked, "Where's Albert?"

"Oh goodness!" she exclaimed. "I leave him unsupervised for five minutes, and he runs off on me. You two hang out, get to know each other. I'll go find him." And with that, she set Luke down and went huffing off in search of the mischievous old man.

Delilah shook her head. "Sorry about Mom. She's a little… crazy."

"Oh no," I said. "She's great. She took me in, gave me a job and a place to stay. I'm actually staying in the church's house right now."

Luke was getting impatient with standing around and talking; he wanted to run around and burn off the energy from all the candy he'd eaten.

"Mama, come on!" he whined, pulling on her slacks.

I don't know why I hadn't realized this little boy was Delilah's son. He looked just like her. But she looked to be only nineteen or twenty, and Luke looked almost five or six. I had first thought that maybe Delilah had been babysitting, so I tried to hide my shock when I found out the boy was her son. Not well enough, apparently, because Delilah smiled knowingly as she ushered Luke to a game station.

When she had Luke engaged in the game, she turned to me. "Don't worry, Molly. I get this a lot. Clearly, my mother didn't tell you the basic details about my life."

I shook my head. "No, she didn't. She didn't tell me you were her daughter. And…she didn't tell me you had a son. Not that it's a bad thing…" I sounded like an idiot, rambling on. But Delilah was so sweet; she took it in stride and shrugged it off.

"It's okay. Really. It surprises people that I have a son that old. I just turned twenty-one a few months ago. I had Luke when I was fifteen."

I was quiet as that information sunk in. I'd just turned twenty in August. I'd been eighteen when I got my abortion…and Delilah had given birth at age fifteen. She'd made the right choice at a time when it was probably so much harder to do so. She'd been a sophomore in high school. She'd probably struggled to just finish school. I had been three months from graduating, and I'd run away from all the possible scrutiny and made entirely the wrong decision. She was so much braver than I was. And a lot happier. Even though her life was probably nothing like she'd imagined it to be, love and adoration for her son shown through her eyes. She was head over heels in love with her little man; it was so obvious. And here I was, so empty and alone. I should have been able to make the same choice she did—to keep my baby. She'd had to struggle though two years of high school with her baby; I'd only had to endure three more months! I could have overcome that; I could have given birth! I could have made the right decision.

I pushed those thoughts out of my head and tried to continue chatting with Delilah. But she was a sharp girl. At the end of the night, with her son sleeping on her shoulder, she turned to me and said, "Something tells me you need to hear the rest of my story. I have a feeling my mom thinks the same. She may be nuts, but she catches things."

I blinked back tears. "Is it that obvious that I'm so...broken?" I asked, my voice cracking.

"Well...I can see it in your eyes," she admitted.

I laughed. "That's what your mom said too. She could see in my eyes that I needed to be here. That I needed to work at the restaurant."

"Like mother, like daughter I guess," she said with a shrug.

We agreed to meet up on Saturday to chat at the cute little corner coffee shop. So bright and early on Saturday, I sat in a booth waiting for her, and my mind started wandering back to my first date with Tyler when he'd taken me to the little jazz lounge coffee shop. Even though I'd let that relationship go on much longer than I should have, though it had eventually drained me more than I already was and left me feeling empty, those first few months had been magical. Tyler was a charmer, but in a sweet way. His goal wasn't to take advantage of me like Jason had; it was just his personality.

I checked the time on my phone and looked around. She was late. But Delilah finally breezed in, looking somewhat disheveled. She spotted me and waved happily then slid in across from me and huffed.

"Luke was being so fussy this morning," she explained. "Albert's watching him, and he loves that old man, but I don't know what his problem was! So whiny and clingy today."

"You leave him with Albert?" I asked, surprised.

She laughed. "Yes. He's old, but I trust him more with Luke than almost anyone. Mom and Albert always argue over who gets to watch him. It was his turn."

"He just seems…so *old!*"

"Yeah," she said with a laugh. "He turned seventy-eight right before you came. But he's young at heart. He brings out his old wooden cars and trains for Luke to play with, and he's down on the floor with him like a little kid, playing away. It's very cute."

If my baby had been a boy, my dad would have done the same. He would have been a great grandpa. But I didn't want to think about that now, so I jumped right in asking her questions.

"So not to sound rude or anything, but Mary Beth…she just looks…too old to be your mom." My cheeks burned, I felt disrespectful saying that about my employer.

Delilah gave me her wide, warm smile. "No, you're right. She's pretty old. My mom's story is pretty complicated itself, but she told me it was okay for me to share it with you. She had two daughters before me with a man she wasn't married to. They were engaged at one point, but when my sisters were in high school, he ran off and disappeared. Met up with some young chick and just left my mom and sisters. They weren't believers then, and my mom didn't take it very well. Started drinking pretty heavily to deal with it, and my sisters grew up really fast to take care of her."

From how Mary Beth acted today, I never would have guessed her past was so shaky. She didn't serve any alcoholic beverages in the restaurant. Perhaps that was why.

"Then she met *my* dad," Delilah said, rolling her eyes. "He was an even bigger loser from the sound of it. Anyway, she ended up pregnant with me at age thirty-seven."

My eyes widened and Delilah giggled. "Yup, so Rachel and Hannah became big sisters when they were sixteen and fourteen. But it shocked my mom back into life, and she started meeting with Pastor Dennis at the church. That's where she met Albert, and he adopted all of us. He was the only grandpa I ever knew because my dad didn't stick around either, and Mom's parents were both gone. We went to his house for every holiday, he was there for every one of my birthdays."

She smiled fondly at those happy memories, but then, her eyes darkened. The story must take a dark twist. She took a large breath and huffed again.

"So thanks to Albert, I grew up in the church, my mom and both my sisters and I became Christians. But you know how the teenage years are," she said sadly, and I nodded my head. "I met a boy. David. He was two years older than me and so cute and nice. I met him at church. I never worried that things would get out of hand, but of course, I *should* have worried."

She swallowed and took a moment. This part of the story was clearly hard for her to tell. "He took me to my freshman-year homecoming dance," she continued. "But we left early because David didn't really enjoy dances. He suggested we just go back to his house to hang out with his parents for a bit, so we did. But after a while, they went to bed, and it was just the two of us." She shrugged her shoulders. "One thing led to the other, and we ended up in his bed. He had a basement room all to himself, and his parents trusted us, they never checked on us. Ever."

She had tears in her eyes now. "When I found out a few months later that I was pregnant with Luke, he flipped out. He couldn't even look me in the eye, and he blamed it all on me. He made me feel so guilty, so I told him to just leave. That I would take care of it.

"I was so scared," she said, her voice quavering. "I didn't want to tell my mom because she was so happy in the church…she had made so many good friends, and I knew that once everyone found out, they'd think of her differently. They'd wonder why she hadn't raised me better. They'd judge her for my mistake. I felt trapped."

I related with Delilah on that point of her story. I had felt the very same way when I found out I was pregnant, I had experienced those same fears. While our pregnancies hadn't started the same way, she'd made a mistake with her boyfriend, and I'd been attacked, our stories were still similar. We both had been terrified. We both had felt so trapped. It had been a while since I'd given God a second thought, but maybe he'd sent me to Delilah for a reason. Maybe she was supposed to help me heal.

Tears started gathering in my eyes too as I remembered my own pain and confusion. But I kept quiet. Delilah wasn't finished yet.

She sniffed and continued. "I decided not to tell anyone else. David and I broke up, and I watched him go out and get another girlfriend a month after I told him I was pregnant. *A month later*," she said sadly. "I was devastated. When I saw him at school, he would look away. He never came back to offer any support, to ask if I was okay. He just left me to fend for myself.

"That was enough for me. I felt like I had no one, and every day became harder than the last. When I couldn't handle it anymore, I grabbed a bottle of aspirin and planned to kill myself. But as I sat there with the pills in my hand, my mom walked in with a laundry basket.

"She flipped, of course, and took me to the hospital even though I told her I hadn't taken any. Of course they made me pee in a cup, and that's how my mom found out about the baby. She was shocked of course but angrier at me for keeping it from her. She started making me do counseling with Pastor Dennis, which I of course resented. In the end, it was a good thing. I was able to work through it all, come to forgive myself and accept the forgiveness I knew Christ offers. And Pastor Dennis adores Lukey now."

I sat there in shock for a moment. She'd taken drastic measures too. I'd never gotten so desperate as to kill myself, but what I did was probably worse. I'd killed my baby.

"Wow." That was all I could say.

"Quite a story, huh?" she asked with a smirk.

"Yeah…" I felt like I should tell her my story, but something inside me made me hold back. I wasn't quite ready yet. Delilah saw it in my eyes. She reached over and took my trembling hand in hers.

"You tell me your story when you're ready. My mom and I haven't stopped praying for you. We want to help you overcome whatever it is you're running from. Running is a hard lifestyle, Molly. It's tiring. I think you'll find that stopping, turning around, and facing whatever giant is chasing you is much easier than running. You'll get there," she reassured gently.

I nodded and sniffed. In the year and a half that I'd left home, no one had ever expressed any desire to help me. Besides Tyler, I supposed, but that was more out of desperation of trying to fix our broken relationship. Mary Beth and Delilah, they just wanted to help me because they'd been through just as much trauma as me. They'd been in my place, running away from the bad choices. They'd felt the loneliness and desperation. They'd endured the sleepless nights.

They *saw* me. They saw the raw, hurting young girl that I really was. I couldn't hide around them anymore. I was found. I was finally found.

Twenty-Three

November

On the first anniversary of the rape, I had gone to work and tried to ignore it. But as this Thanksgiving drew closer and closer, the images started flooding back to me, and I couldn't seem to ignore it any longer. It had unknowingly been my last Thanksgiving with my family, and I had wasted it with Jason. And then that Saturday, he'd tricked me into going to his house. That's where this all had begun—this horrible journey I found myself on. All because I'd let Jason come in.

I'd be spending this Thanksgiving with Mary Beth and Delilah. I'd get to meet Rachel and Hannah and their families too. They both were married, with six kids between them—Rachel had four and Hannah had two. Add in Luke and there would be a houseful of noisy kids. Right around the anniversary I'd conceived my baby. Being around kids now was so hard; it would be a tough day for sure.

Working with Mary Beth was turning me into quite a cook, and even though I knew she'd be preparing an amazing meal, I still wanted to bring something. So I whipped up a cookies and cream salad to contribute to the feast; Mary Beth always complimented me on how well I made it.

When I drove up to Mary Beth's house that brisk Thanksgiving Day, my head was going in all different directions. I didn't really have a Thanksgiving last year, and the one before had been with my family. I sat in the car for a bit and braced myself for the chaos I knew lay inside. That's how it always was with kids around. Talking, laughing, screaming—pure chaos. I hoped I could handle it.

Delilah saw me walking up the sidewalk and welcomed me in with a hug. We'd fast become friends after that Saturday morning chat over coffee. She never pressured me about telling my story; she knew I'd tell her when I was ready. But she could see it written on my face that this day would be tough for me. She could already read me like a book.

Rachel and Hannah's families were beautiful. Rachel and her husband had three girls and one boy, spanning from the ages fourteen to seven. Hannah and her husband had twin boys, age five. Perfect playmates for little Luke, and you could tell that the young cousins adored each other. These people were raising their families right; you could feel the love that filled the room.

We used to have big Thanksgivings like this too, but over the years, the tradition began to die. My grandparents lived a few hours away, and when they couldn't handle so many people taking over their house for a weekend, all the aunts and uncles tried to take turns hosting it. But it slowly tapered off as each of our families grew older and kids busier. For the last few years, it had just been my family at our house, which was fine, just quieter and a lot less chaotic. So being here was a little overwhelming. I was out of practice.

I tried to fit in and join in conversation as we stood around munching on veggies, but everyone seemed to be talking all at once, and the girls were mostly sharing childhood memories and inside jokes. Rachel's and Hannah's husbands were great guys, but they'd been a part of this family for so long and didn't have a problem jumping into the conversation. I mostly stood there awkwardly, but it helped that Albert was there though. He smiled at me and gave me a caramel candy. I was relieved when Mary Beth finally brought out the turkey and shushed us.

We settled into Mary Beth's dining room, which was about to burst at the seams from all the bodies crammed into it. She sat at the head of the table; I sat by Delilah. The room fell silent, and I looked around nervously. Everyone else knew what to do, this was tradition. But I was the odd one out, and I panicked. Delilah smiled and took my hand; we were only going to say grace.

Mary Beth cleared her throat and began. "Dear Heavenly Father, we thank you for this beautiful Thanksgiving Day. We thank you for the abundance of food when we know many people in our country and around the world are in need. We ask that you would help us to be your servants in this world, to help those that are less fortunate. We thank you, Father, for the many blessings you've poured out on us. For my five wonderful daughters and sons-in-law, for seven wonderful grandchildren. For the gift of friendship we've found in Albert and Molly." My cheeks burned when she mentioned my name, but when I peeked to see if everyone was watching me, I could see everyone had their eyes shut tight. I closed mine again.

"We ask, Father, that you would help us to be thankful every day of our lives, not just on this day. Finally, we pray that you would bless this food we are about to enjoy and to make our conversation pleasing to you. In your precious name we pray, amen."

That was the first prayer I'd partaken in since the night I left home. My father had said grace before supper, and then later that night, I took off. Since then, I hadn't prayed or taken part in any kind of prayer so that had felt a little stiff and awkward, to say the least.

I also hadn't eaten this well since I left home. Delilah told me not to be shy about taking seconds, or even thirds, so I ate until I felt ready to burst. We stayed at the table chatting while the kids took off to find some other adventure. I wasn't allowed to help clear off the table or do any dishes.

"You do so much for me at the restaurant, sweet girl. Today, you're my guest, and I'll be serving you. Just sit!" Mary Beth commanded and shooed me away from the kitchen. The men headed for the couches to doze and watch football, and I was feeling awkward again. This down time was causing my mind to wander back home, and I didn't welcome those memories at all. I stepped outside for some air when I couldn't handle it anymore.

I didn't even hear Delilah come out and join me. She handed me a steaming cup of coffee and sat down on the patio steps beside me. She didn't talk, didn't pressure me to share what was eating me up inside. I so appreciated this about her.

I turned to her and gave a weak smile. "It's really hard for me to be around kids," I offered. "I made a really big mistake when I was living in Minneapolis…it's such a long story," I said glumly.

"Well, we have all afternoon. I'm a good listener." And with that she gave me her full attention because she realized I was finally opening up to her.

"Okay, well…" I hesitated, unsure if this was safe. If I could trust Delilah not to run out on me after I told her my awful story. But I went on…I took that risk.

"All these memories come back at Thanksgiving because that's where my whole story starts. The last Thanksgiving I spent at home was my senior year of high school. I was dating a guy named Jason then. My best friend, Tanner, hated Jason—he kept trying to tell me what a jerk he was. But of course, I didn't listen. I was so caught up in his charm and good looks, and it was fun to rebel a bit, to date someone my friends didn't approve of. And I knew he probably wasn't the best person to be dating, but I ignored it.

"Anyway, the Saturday after that Thanksgiving we were out on a date, and he kept pressuring me to go home with him to meet his dad. Except I knew his dad was out of town, but Jason told me sometimes his dad came home early. He was getting really upset about it, so I finally agreed."

Delilah winced. "Mistake?"

"Big time," I said sadly. "His dad wasn't there, but he convinced me to come in and wait for a bit. That's where the similarities between our stories stop. Because Jason and I didn't sleep together. He…he raped me." I croaked. This was the first time I'd ever said out loud what Jason had done. It was the first time I'd ever told another person.

Delilah took a sharp breath in, and her eyes filled with tears. "Seriously, Molly? Did you report him?"

I shook my head no. "Just the opposite really. I pretty much did everything you're not supposed to do. I showered, tossed my clothes. That night was awful…I felt so alone, and I had this overwhelming need to be with my mom. You know, like in elementary school when a mean boy picks on you and makes you cry, and all you want is for your mom to hold you and tell you everything will be okay?"

She nodded. "I know the feeling. When I found out I was pregnant, I felt the same way. I just wished I could be a little kid again."

I took a deep breath and forged on. "I didn't go and get my mom though. I didn't think I could tell anyone…Jason convinced me no one would believe me. And I thought he was right. I'd ignored the warnings of my friends, I felt like the whole thing was my fault. But I didn't want to be alone, so I went to Tanner.

Our houses are right next to each other, and our bedrooms are both on the first floor facing each other," I explained. "I crawled into bed with him that night and he held me until the morning. I just told him Jason broke up with me. That's what I told everyone, and they bought it, but I felt so dead after the rape, I never returned to normal. After a while, Tanner started to get suspicious, but I just worked harder to try and appear normal, even though I was dying inside."

Delilah looked overwhelmed. This was a tough story to tell and to listen to. "Did you and Jason go to the same school? I can't imagine seeing him ever again!"

I nodded. "Yup. I switched my whole schedule around to avoid him, but occasionally, I still ran into him. After Christmas, I started to feel better, but...then, I found out I was pregnant."

"Oh, Molly, no!" Delilah cried. "That's too much."

"I know. I felt like I was drowning. I kept it a secret for as long as possible, but one morning, I threw up on the way to school with Tanner, and I felt like I had to tell him at least. He was heartbroken. Tanner's always loved me," I explained sadly.

Delilah nodded sadly. "What did he do?"

"Exactly the opposite of what I thought he'd do. He stayed. Told me he loved me...offered to stay with me and raise the baby with me."

She melted. "Really? Wow. David wouldn't even look at me after I told him about the baby. And it wasn't even Tanner's baby, and he wanted to stay?" she asked, clearly amazed.

"Yup. He was even getting excited. Wanted to name it Eden if it was a girl. So we told our parents we were dating and that Tanner wanted to raise the baby. His parents were okay with it, but mine struggled. We got an ultrasound and started planning. But then..." My voice took a hard edge. "Tanner went and told Jason about the baby. I never wanted to tell him because I knew he'd be furious. And I was right. He cornered me one day after school and demanded I get rid of the baby. Gave me a few hundred dollars for an abortion. I was terrified. He threatened Tanner…my family…I didn't know what he was capable of. He'd attacked me, what was stopping him from attacking them?"

She nodded, silent, so engrossed in my story. "That night, Tanner and I got into a big fight. He wouldn't own up to the fact that he'd made a mistake. He kept saying he never said anything to Jason, but Jason *told* me that Tanner had let him in on the news. The fact that he went behind my back and then lied about it was too much. We were both furious…after all these years we finally owned up to our feelings for each other, and it was all being ruined. He left all angry…and I packed and ran. Three months before graduation.

"I ended up in Minneapolis, and through a series of really crazy events, I ended up living with some girls and working in a junky little diner. I felt like I didn't have any other option after I left home, so I took the money Jason gave me, and I got an abortion," I whispered, ashamed. I fell silent for a moment, then, continued. "And that's why…why it's so hard to be here. Around so many kids. I should have a baby with me here today….but I don't. I aborted my baby."

I couldn't go on anymore. A river of tears streamed down my face, and Delilah put her arm around me and squeezed. Neither of us said anything. There were no words.

When I composed myself, I continued, hiccuping in between sentences. "It was awful. I had nightmares…I heard babies crying at night. I felt even emptier than before. Then, I met another boy and messed around for a year, letting things get way too out of hand. I spent every weekend with him, and every time we slept together, I felt dirtier and dirtier. After a year and a half in Minneapolis, I couldn't handle it. Tyler broke up with me because I wouldn't let him in. He knew I'd never trust him enough to really open up, and that frustrated him beyond belief. I stuck it out there for a few more months, but after a fight with one of my roommates, I packed and left again. I just couldn't handle living there…everything was piling up on me, especially the abortion. I just couldn't stand it there anymore."

"And you ended up here?" she asked surprised.

I let a small laugh escape my lips. "Strange, I know. The first time I ran, I wanted to disappear. I knew that would happen easily in a big town. But it hadn't helped me heal at all. If anything, I was worse off in Minneapolis. I thought maybe a small town was the way to go the second time around. Something told me… that I just needed to be found. And then, I met your mom," I said with a smile. Meeting Mary Beth had been the best thing that had happened since I left home. It had led me to Delilah, the closest friend I'd ever had, besides Tanner.

Delilah smiled back and gave me another hug. The weight of my heavy story hung thick in the air. I could tell she was searching for the appropriate thing to say.

"You're the first person I've told my story to," I admitted. "I never told anyone about the rape. Not my parents, not Tanner, not the girls I lived with, not Tyler. You're the only one who knows."

"Wow. I…I don't even know what to say, Molly."

"I know, I know. I don't expect you to work some miracle or fix anything. But it just feels nice to finally share this burden with someone, you know?"

"Oh, believe me, I know. I felt the same way when my mom finally found out about Luke. It was like the door of some horrible prison I'd locked myself in was finally swinging open."

"That's a good way to put it," I agreed.

"I'm glad you told me your story, Molly. It was hard for me to share mine with you, but now that they're both out in the open, we can really start to help each other heal."

I looked at her quizzically. "It certainly looks and sounds like you've already healed to me."

"Far from it," she said with a laugh. "Healing is a process, Molly. I've been healing for years now. My mom was a big part of my healing process. And Pastor Dennis. They talked me through everything, helped me make the decision to keep Luke, even though I was only a sophomore in high school. I missed the last semester of school when Luke was born, but my mom helped me go back and get my diploma. Which was far from easy because, boy, did the rumors start flying about who the father was. David never did step up and take credit for it, and I begged and pleaded with my mom not to push it on him."

Another area I could relate to. "I felt the same way about Jason. I was terrified to even tell my parents about the baby because I figure they'd want to make Jason help me out, and after the rape, I couldn't even handle seeing his face, but I couldn't tell my parents why."

"Why did you feel that you couldn't tell anyone about the rape?" she asked softly.

"Because it was my fault in the first place. I should have listened to everyone who was telling me to get out. I should have seen that Jason was trouble."

She was silent for a moment. "There's no way you could've known, Molly. You can't keep thinking that. You'll never move past this if you do."

I shook my head. "It's hard. I've always been taught to own up to mistakes, and I know Jason was a mistake. When I told Tanner about the baby, I *wanted* him to walk out of me. I *wanted* him to give me what I deserved. When he didn't, I felt so guilty and unworthy. I wanted to suffer for what I'd done."

"Don't you think keeping the rape a secret caused enough suffering?"

I hadn't thought about it that way. Delilah could be right. But that didn't make the shame go away. Every time thoughts of the rape popped into my head, I wanted to crawl out of my skin because I felt so dirty and ashamed.

"Plus," Delilah continued, "reporting him could have saved other girls, Molly. Maybe he did the same thing to another girl once he saw how he could control you. He knew you were scared enough to do anything he said, including keeping quiet about the rape and the pregnancy."

My heart sank at this information. She was right. Jason was a monster; he very well could have gone out and done the same thing to another innocent girl at my high school. If I'd stepped up and reported him, if I'd overcome my fear of him and what he was capable of, I could have stopped him from inflicting the same nightmare on another girl. What had I been thinking back then? I'd let emotions get in the way of standing up for what was right. What a coward.

I nodded. "You're right," I said slowly. "I should have stepped up. But I was just so blinded with fear and shame...I was afraid no one would believe me. I was afraid people would think I was just trying to get him into trouble. And I was embarrassed."

"Molly, it's okay," Delilah said reassuringly. "I shouldn't have said that. You were young. You were terrified. I look back on my actions and wonder why I did things the way I did too. Like, why did I think suicide was even an option? But if we get stuck up on the past, we can never move forward."

"I might be able to move past the rape...to heal from that... but I don't think I'll ever move past the abortion," I mourned. "Did you ever think about abortion?"

"Briefly," she admitted. "But I didn't have the money for it, and there aren't any clinics close to here. Couldn't ask my mom, and I knew that even though David didn't want anything to do with the baby, he wouldn't help me get an abortion. That's when I resorted to suicide."

We sat there in the chilly autumn air. Delilah had finished her coffee while she listened to my story, but mine was forgotten and cold. "We both fell pretty hard, huh? Hit the lowest of the lows."

"Yup. We sure did," she agreed sadly. "But I climbed out of that pit, Molly. And I know you can too."

"I'm really not sure I can," I said with a sniff.

"Sure you can," she urged. "The problem is…you've been try-ing to climb out on your own for all this time. But I'm here now. Mom's here. And Albert. And who knows…maybe, you'll change your mind about God. Pastor Dennis turned me around and pointed me back toward God…maybe you'll turn back to him too. God's the ultimate healer, Molly, if you let him do his work."

I nodded. At one point, I had believed that. I'd grown up in the church. Once, I had trusted God to take care of me and heal me from whatever life handed to me. But I'd been handed blow after blow, and I was beaten. My trust in him was so severed; it would take a great deal of time before I was ready to let him in again.

"Maybe. We'll see." I heard the sliding door open up behind me, and we both turned around to see a sleepy Luke walk out, dragging his blanket behind him. He rubbed his eyes.

"Hey, buddy. What's up?" Delilah called out.

"I couldn't find you," he mumbled.

"Aw, Lukey, I didn't go anywhere. Just talking with Molly, that's all. Come here." She opened her arms, and Luke fell into them. Delilah stroked his curly hair and whispered little com-forting murmurings. Something only mothers know how to do.

"Just keep an open heart," she whispered to me over Luke's little head. "That's all it takes. Now, let's go in for dessert, and then, I'm sending you home from all this chaos. You've endured enough for one day."

I offered a small laugh, and we stood up together. Delilah rearranged Luke and gave me the best hug she could with her full arms and whispered, "Thanks for letting me into your world. I'm here for you. We'll get through this, Molly. We will."

After all the false hopes I'd endured in the past two years, this time, it felt different. Maybe this time everything would change for the better. Maybe this time, I wouldn't run into another dead end, but I'd be able to go down a path that led to freedom from the demons that tormented me day in and day out. Could I finally be on the edge of the desert, finally taking my first faltering steps out of the wilderness?

Real hope. I savored the feeling in bed that night. For the first time on this horrifying journey, I could taste real hope. It was like a refreshing gulp of water quenching the thirst of my dry and cracked heart.

I was beyond ready to say good-bye to the desert and say hello to a new life.

Twenty-Four

Tanner

March 2010

It was unusually warm for March. I sat on a park bench in Oak Ridge, fingering the little felt box that held Leah's engagement ring. Today was our one-year anniversary, and I was planning on popping the question tonight. We were going fishing, our favorite thing to do together. Our first summer together; we'd spent every night we could out on the edge of the little lake in Oak Ridge with our poles in the water, sharing pop and candy. We never caught much, but it was that much more exciting when one of us did reel in a big catch. Leah's face would light up whenever she felt the slightest tug on her line, and when she reeled a big one in by herself, she'd jump around all excited and then gloat about it for the rest of the night. She was adorable.

Leah and I had gone to the same small Christian college the fall of 2008. All throughout high school, I always planned on going to Iowa State…but then things with Molly got all complicated, and I'd declined the scholarship package they'd offered me. The scholarship would have allowed me to easily pay for my entire year of college…my grades and ACT score were that good. But I'd dropped everything for Molly, decided to stay close to home to be there for her and the baby. I'd given up my dream of becoming a Cyclone just for her.

But then something weird had happened. Her pregnancy caused her to be a little overdramatic, and she was super stressed out about finishing school, giving birth, and then figuring out what to do with her life after that. And although I was an expert at maneuvering her mood swings, one night in March, she'd absolutely snapped, claiming I went behind her back to tell Jason about the pregnancy. But after twelve years of being best friends, I knew when it was appropriate to overstep the boundaries. Telling Jason was clearly an inappropriate overstepping of the boundaries, and even though I disagreed with her about keeping the pregnancy from him, I hadn't told him. I *considered* it, but I hadn't told him.

Molly hadn't even let me explain myself; she just kept accusing me of lying and betraying her. We'd both said hurtful things, but the last thing Molly said to me that night haunted me for months. She'd said she never needed me.

There's nothing worse than loving someone so much for so many years and then having them throw that in your face. When Molly had finally told me she loved me back, I'd felt the rush of excitement knowing that she wanted me. That she *did* need me. And when she'd casually thrown that out in the air—that she didn't need me—it had been heartbreaking. So I left.

That was our first major fight. And our last major fight because Molly took off that night. It hadn't concerned me when she didn't text or call that night because we were both very hurt and angry. I thought she was just being stubborn in the morning and not texting, so I'd texted her. No reply. I wasn't going to chase after her this time though. If she decided she did need me, I'd let her come crawling back to me this time.

Around eight that night, Molly's parents came knocking at my door, wondering where Molly was. I explained we'd gotten into a fight and hadn't spoken since last night. It was then that we realized Molly's car was gone, but I reassured them that Molly was probably just out at the lake trying to clear her head. That's where she always went to think through things.

But her car never returned that night, so we decided to investigate her room. Sure enough, her bed was stripped, clothes were missing from her drawers and closet. She had run away.

I collapsed on her bedroom floor. I hadn't realized how serious it was to Molly that Jason knew about the baby. Why did he have such a strong hold over her? Whenever he was near, she cringed and tightened up in fear. I wondered if he'd ever done anything to harm her when they were dating. An ex-boyfriend should not have this much power over her.

Molly was smart about running away. Since she wasn't a minor, the police couldn't do much. Legally, she could leave without telling anyone if she wanted to. I figured she found a cheap phone and got a new number; she'd probably traded in her car so we couldn't trace her license plate. We all decided that trying to find her was useless; she'd come back if she wanted to. She'd just be mad if we tracked her down. But it was so puzzling to all of us why she had run away in the first place. Sure, she was under a lot of pressure, but we were helping her through it. And one fight with me wouldn't be enough for her to want to run away. We'd had spats before, and yes, this had been the worst, but certainly not enough to make her run.

So something had to have happened between her and Jason. He was the only one she really wanted to get away from, I guessed. I needed to figure out exactly what had gone down between them, why Molly was so terrified of him.

My confrontation needed to happen in public, and I caught a break at lunch that Wednesday after she ran. Jason was sitting at a lunch table all alone, and I plopped my tray down across from him and sat down. He looked up in surprise, but then smirked when he saw it was me. Gossip was flying about Molly's disappearance. I'd been getting strange looks all week from people. I could tell so many of them just wanted to come up and ask me what I'd done to cause her to run away. I kept silent about it though. It was none of their business.

"Well, well, well. Never thought I'd see you here. What can I do for you, sir?" he'd said sarcastically.

"Cut it, Jason. I'm not in the mood. I just need some information from you."

He smirked again and sat back in his chair, amused. "I'll do my best."

"What'd you do to Molly?" I asked, wasting no time.

"Nothing," he snapped, folding his arms tightly across his chest.

"Wrong answer, Jason," I spat. "Molly flipped out last Friday, accused me of telling you about the baby. She wouldn't even let me explain myself. She just took off and ran away. There's no way one fight with me caused her to leave...and we were all helping her deal with the pregnancy. You did something to her. Now tell me." I was seething, my eyes narrowed in anger.

He leaned forward. "Hey, you have no right coming over here and accusing me of that, Tanner. Molly was psycho. I was lucky to get rid of her when I did."

Suddenly, I wished I'd chosen to have this conversation in private because I wanted to reach across the table and strangle him. He was talking about the girl I desperately loved—calling her psycho caused my blood to boil. And he held the answer to why she'd run, I just knew it.

I tried a different approach and softened up. "Please, Jason. Molly is my world. You don't even know what a great person she is—you never knew the Molly I knew. The Molly I grew up with. The Molly I was planning on spending the rest of my life with. Now she's gone, and I just want to know why. I want to know if I caused this. Please."

He laughed cruelly. "Wow. Pathetic." He rubbed his neck and sat back again. "Fine. I found out about the baby from Kristina. I was getting a drink from the fountain at the end of the science hall, and she and a bunch of her friends were talking around the corner. She spilled the news then freaked out because she realized it was supposed to be a secret." He rolled his eyes. "Girls are so dumb. Anyway, so Kristina's freaking out, telling her friends not to tell anyone. But I heard it all. I figured Molly was never planning on telling me. I knew you guys were together, that you knew about the kid and were probably planning on sticking around. But I didn't want some brat trying to contact me later in life, on some deep journey to reconnect with their birth father. And I didn't want to risk you dumping her and then having her come after me for child support. I've got too much at stake.

"So I convinced her you told me because I knew she'd freak out. I wanted her to get rid of that baby, and getting her mad at you was the ticket. Apparently, it worked."

I just stared at him. He was a monster, plain and simple. What a devious plot using me to manipulate Molly. My eyes were darting everywhere as I pieced all the information together. She felt betrayed by me and threatened by Jason. She was scared about what he'd do if she didn't listen to him if she didn't get rid of the baby.

So maybe she'd run away because of a combination of two reasons. First, she was mad at me. I couldn't ignore that anymore; she was mad that I went behind her back, even though I really hadn't. Secondly, she wanted to save the baby. Abortion had never been an option for her, but she knew if she didn't do what Jason wanted, he'd come after her. I could see it in his eyes. He would do whatever it took to make sure he was safe from paying child support and from the baby growing up and coming to look for him. So out of fear, she had probably run to protect both her and the baby.

My heart was breaking because my sweet girl thought I had betrayed her. And she was probably terrified, all alone and facing this huge mountain by herself. I wanted to gather her up in my arms and whisper that everything would be all right. That I was there for her.

I was angry though, that she hadn't trusted me enough to share her fears with me. She should have just told me about Jason's threat. He couldn't force an abortion on her. I would have made sure he couldn't come anywhere near her or the baby. The baby was more mine than his anyway.

It dawned on me that I would probably miss the birth. If Molly was trying to protect the baby, she'd make sure she was far, far away from Jason. Without a high school diploma though, it would be hard for her to support the baby when it came. How would she pay the hospital bills? How would she afford diapers, clothes, all that baby stuff? We hadn't bought anything yet for the baby. She had nothing.

Perhaps she'd choose adoption. Though it would break her heart, if it meant the baby was safe, she'd do it. And this made me mad because once Molly and I were together, the baby became mine. At least in my heart, it was mine. I hadn't fathered it, but I was planning and dreaming about being the father. It wasn't fair that she'd just run off, without letting me have any say about it whatsoever. It made me mad that I didn't have the chance to protect her now.

I stood up quickly and left without saying anything. I was beyond angry at him, but I was also fighting tears because I knew my girl was out there alone somewhere. We were always supposed to be together, and once it finally happened, Jason had swooped in and ruined everything. Who knew if she ever planned on coming back?

Calling and texting was no use. She never returned any of them. The months crawled by, and suddenly, I was walking across a stage receiving my diploma. Molly and I had looked forward to that day forever, and I was experiencing it alone. Her parents still came and supported me, but tears were streaming down their faces the whole day. Molly should have been there.

Summer was no better. I worked all day just to keep my mind off of her, but each day I crossed off my calendar meant that August 18 was drawing nearer and nearer. Molly's due date. When the day finally came, I sat around the kitchen table with Molly's family. We all wondered if they baby had decided to come that day, or maybe if it had come early. Or maybe it was late, and it would happen in a few days. It was torture not knowing for sure. My heart was broken and bleeding, my arms ached with emptiness. I wanted to hold the baby in my arms, look into her beautiful eyes. She wouldn't biologically be mine, but in my heart, she belonged to me. She'd always belong to me.

Time didn't care that we were broken though, and suddenly, it was time to pack up and leave for college. I'd only be going forty minutes away, but I'd be living on campus now that Molly was gone. Originally, the plan had been to live at home and commute so I could care for Molly and the baby. But after she left, my parents convinced me to stay on campus, get the most out of my college experience.

This was hard though because I'd always pictured Molly beside me having all our college adventures together. I felt so empty now that she was gone. I'd never fully enjoy college without her and the baby in my life.

I tried my best to muster my way through the first semester, to connect with the guys in my dorm. It was a small Christian campus, much like my high school. One day, I bumped into Kristina's friend Leah; I'd gone to youth group with her for years. I had no clue she went to the same college as me. I was sitting alone at a table in the coffee shop area and she joined me and we chatted for a bit.

The next semester, we had a class together and were partners for a project. Then, we started commuting home together and hanging out a ton. We'd spend the weekends at my house doing homework and watching movies together, then, go to our hometown church on Sunday mornings. We ate every meal together, and suddenly, our roommates and friends started hinting that we should be dating—we were always together anyway—and we seemed compatible. We laughed it off for a while, much like Molly and I had always done, but then, I realized I didn't want to play this game anymore. I *did* have feelings for Leah. She was sweet, pretty, and tons of fun to be with. She made me laugh and smile. She made me forget about Molly.

I waited a bit to ask her out though. I didn't want to use her just so I could forget about Molly. I wanted to tell Leah I liked her when I was absolutely sure I was over Molly.

So I spent a weekend home alone, much of it in Molly's favorite bench at the lake. I let myself really mourn my loss of her. I cried out to God, asking him why he'd taken her from me when we'd finally found our way together after twelve years. I searched the scriptures for comfort and prayed until I grew tired of pleading the same thing over and over.

As I drove back to campus, I shut the drawer full of Molly's memory completely closed. If I wanted to move on, it needed to be done. I would never forget about her or the baby—that would be impossible—but I gave up hope that she was coming back. I couldn't wait around for the impossible forever. Once that drawer was shut, I opened up a new one, one that held the hope and excitement of a future with Leah.

On a rainy March day, I took Leah's hand and told her I wanted more than friendship with her. It was fun to tell a girl I liked her without being in the midst of a crisis. We were able to smile, laugh, and enjoy the excitement of the beginning of something wonderful. That's the way I'd always wanted it to happen with Molly, but since that hadn't worked out, I was now getting a second chance.

So we spent the next few months falling in love. We went fishing every chance we could, watched countless movies, and took midnight walks on the bike paths that crisscrossed Oak Ridge. Time flew by, and we were in school again. We spent our first Christmas together, and I gave her a promise ring. Her face lit up in joy as I slipped it around her finger and kissed her gently.

Now I was fulfilling that promise. I was asking her to be my wife. I couldn't imagine living life without her, and since we lived so close to home, we'd be able to get married this summer, live in Oak Ridge, and commute to school each day until we graduated. So on this first anniversary of dating, I was taking the biggest leap of my life and asking her to marry me.

To many, it would seem a whirlwind relationship, that we were too young to make such a big decision. But to those who knew us best, this was a great thing for Leah and me. We adored each other, and we were mature beyond our years. We'd had more than enough of dorm life too. And technically we'd grown up together—I'd known Leah for years.

This was the right thing, the right step for us to take. So I spent the rest of the afternoon praying and preparing my heart for what I would do tonight. I headed home around four, changed, and got all the fishing gear ready. I slipped the ring into my tackle box. Tonight, after fishing for a while, I'd decide to switch out my small bobber for a bigger one, and I'd ask Leah to open up the tackle box and hand me one. She'd see the velvet box nestled inside, and then, turn around to see me on one knee. It would be perfect.

When I picked her up, my heart was pounding. She had no idea what was coming, she was just excited because it was our first anniversary. I gave her a kiss when she slid in next to me and we took off.

It was a bit chilly that night, so I draped my jacket over her. When I couldn't wait any longer because my heart was about to beat out of my chest, I went for it.

"Hey, Leah, hun, could you look in my tackle box and hand me a bigger bobber? I keep losing sight of it out on the water."

She smiled. "Sure, babe. But you know a bigger bobber won't help you at all. I'll still catch more," she teased.

"I'll take my chances." I was going crazy as she turned around to open the tackle box. I moved quickly, getting on my knee behind her as she gasped. She slowly picked up the little box and turned around with big shining eyes.

"What...what's this, Tanner?" she asked softly.

"Open it," I said excitedly.

She gasped again, her eyes even bigger than before when she saw the solitaire diamond ring sparkling up at her.

"Leah, I love you. I can't imagine living life without you, so will you marry me so that I won't have to?" I kept it simple, I didn't want to have some big speech planned out, only to forget it and sound silly.

"Yes! Of course!" she squealed.

We both laughed, and I got up and slipped the ring on her slender finger. We shared a kiss, and then spent the next half hour admiring how beautiful the ring looked on her finger. We laughed about how big her eyes had been, wishing we'd had a camera to capture the look on her face when she saw the ring in the tackle box. We forgot about our poles in the water until my line got a giant tug.

"Tanner!" Leah screamed. "Fish!"

I jumped up and grabbed my pole, then, reeled in our only catch of the day. A tiny little bluegill, not even worth keeping.

Leah laughed and teased me as I removed the hook from the fish's mouth and threw him back in.

"Guess that bigger bobber didn't help you after all."

I chased her, and she ran and squealed. I grabbed her from behind and swung her around as she screamed and laughed, then whirled her around and locked her in a tight hug and kissed her smiling lips. This night had turned out exactly how I'd always dreamed it would.

We packed up and left, then, headed to her house to show off her ring to her parents and little sisters. The rest of the night was spent retelling the story and making plans to get together soon to start planning. We wanted an August wedding, six short months away. Leah and her sisters talked excitedly about going wedding dress shopping, and Leah's dad wished me luck with all the planning. We relished this excitement, all the love and joy that was circling the room.

Leah and I stayed up talking late into the night, holding hands and making plans. We wanted to enjoy every step of the planning, after all, we'd only be doing this once in our life. I looked at my future bride, and my heart flip flopped. God had truly blessed me.

Twenty-Five

Molly

September 2011

"Is that the last box?" Delilah asked.

"Yup, I think that's everything. Man, when I left home the first time, my stuff barely filled the backseat. And now look at it all! My whole car is stuffed!"

Delilah laughed. "Well, your house was pathetic when you first came here. But that's what happens when you *really* live somewhere. You start accumulating stuff."

She was right. When I'd lived with Melissa, I'd never decorated, never really unpacked and made myself at home. I knew that's not where I wanted to stay for a long time, and it had made it so much easier to run. I'd been doing the same thing before Delilah and I became so close—I didn't put up any pictures, didn't hang my clothes up in my bedroom closet. When she came over one night to watch a movie with me, she walked around my bare house and turned to me with her arms crossed.

"Really, Molly?"

"What?" I asked, pretending I had no idea what she was talking about.

"You know what I'm talking about. This place is a skeleton! Have you even unpacked?"

"Sort of." I shrugged. "It still feels weird being here alone. I don't know…I have no excuse I guess."

"That's right!" she teased. "Now, before we watch this movie, let's do some work here first. Come on!" And she dragged me into my bedroom where we unpacked everything I'd brought with me. That weekend, she took me out shopping for towels and bathroom stuff, dishes and kitchen supplies, and some small decorations. And from then on, whenever Delilah come over, she'd bring me some sort of decoration or trinket. Slowly but surely, my little house came alive. I had quilts hanging over my couches, bright and cheerful candy bowls scattered about the house, and vases that Luke always made sure were filled with flowers. Well, mostly weeds, but it was still sweet.

One day, when she was stuffing towels into my linen closet, she saw that stupid box. She hadn't meant to upset me, but seeing those things was always hard. Especially the pictures.

She pulled Tyler's photo out. "Whoa, is this you?" she asked, clearly impressed with Tyler's work.

"Yup. Tyler took that—he's the guy I was seeing back in Minneapolis."

"Oh…he gave it to you before you left?"

I let out a sad laugh. "Yeah. Talk about awkward. He made it very clear that night that we were over...that he had no room in his life for me, you know?"

She nodded and then pulled out the other cheap frame. "And is this..." Her question hung in the air because from how I'd described Tanner to her; it was clear in this picture that it was him. I simply nodded, not wanting to dig up those memories right then. She settled the pictures back into the box and slid it to the back again. Together, we were working through all our emotions and issues, but she understood that some things were just too much. I just couldn't hang those pictures up anywhere. I didn't belong in those people's worlds anymore.

Little Luke, surprisingly enough, was the one who helped heal me more than anyone else. It took him a while to warm up to me at first, but that was just because I didn't feel comfortable around him. Seeing Delilah pick up her little boy, swing him around, and nuzzle his chubby cheeks was too much for me to handle when I first started hanging out with them a lot. My arms would start to ache with emptiness because I should've had a little girl in them. Delilah saw the pain in my eyes, but I did my best to just work through those feelings.

But one night, I babysat Luke, and after that, I softened up to him quite a bit. I'd given him a bath and snapped him up in his pajamas, and then, he insisted I read him a story. So we snuggled up in his favorite chair, and he handed me a worn-out picture book. It was a children's version of the prodigal son. I made it through most of the book, but one passage was particularly hard to read. "We must celebrate...for this son of mine was dead and has now returned to life. He was lost, but now he is found."

I stopped with those words hanging in the air, and Luke squirmed in his chair and looked up at me. He clearly knew this story by heart; he knew it wasn't over yet.

"It's not done yet," he said bluntly.

"I know, buddy. Sorry, that was just a hard part for me to read."

"Why was it hard?" he asked curiously, batting his thick eyelashes up at me.

"Well," I said slowly, "I kind of feel like the boy in this story."

"But you're not a boy," he said innocently.

I smiled. "No, I'm not. But I ran away like the boy in this story. And I feel really bad about it. I miss my family very much sometimes. And see how the father here says that his son was lost but then he got found?"

He nodded solemnly.

"Well, that's how *I* am too. I feel a little lost. But after I came here and met your grandma and mommy, I started to feel a little less lost. I felt like someone found me."

"Like hide-and-seek?" he asked.

"Kind of. For a long time, I kept switching hiding places though. And that's cheating, right?"

He nodded again. "Cheating is mean."

"It sure is," I agreed. "But your grandma and mommy found me anyway, even though I was cheating. And they've been helping me play by the rules. I can't hide anymore. Once you're found, the game's over, right?"

"Yup." It made perfect sense to him.

Later on I tucked him into his bed, and when Delilah came home, I shared our sweet conversation with her. She smiled and said with pride leaking out of her every word, "Yup, that's my boy. Such a good listener. He'll make a fine husband one day."

She was right. Luke was so sensitive, so willing to listen even though he couldn't fully understand the depth of the issues. He'd snuggle up to me sometimes, or bring me some flowers and/or weeds to fill my vases with, and my heart melted each time. So when he asked me to go to the Easter service with him, I couldn't say no. How could anyone look at his adorable little face and say no? I didn't know how Delilah did it.

Mary Beth and Delilah were ecstatic about my decision to finally join them at church. I put on a springy dress, and my heart was pounding when Mary Beth and Delilah picked me up that beautiful morning. It had been so long since I had stepped foot into a church, since I had even given God a chance to change my mind about him.

I went in with a resistant heart, but it was like God himself had told Pastor Dennis my heart was hardened. The whole sermon seemed to be pointed right at me. If God had been slowly picking away at the brick walls around my heart over the past two years, he was trying a new tactic now. He was using a sledgehammer, absolutely hammering away at the thick walls. Demolishing them. They didn't stand a chance.

After a lengthy and very lively time of singing, Pastor Dennis stood behind his podium all dressed up in his Easter best, a light gray suit with a lavender shirt and purple tie. Very Easter-y. I'd never had the chance to talk to him one-on-one, but he looked like a nice guy; he was probably in his late fifties or early sixties. His salt-and-pepper hair was slowly but surely receding, but he obviously didn't care about hair loss. You could tell just by looking at him that all his thoughts, all his energy, were focused on Jesus.

He gripped his podium and smiled out at us. "Welcome!" he boomed. I sat back in surprise, and Delilah giggled. I hadn't expected such a big booming voice to come out of this meek-looking man. "I always expect a full house on Easter Sunday, and let me tell you"—he looked around slyly—"you didn't disappoint! Take a look around, folks! Better yet, let's stand up and greet those around us. I guarantee, you'll meet someone new today! He is risen!"

"He is risen indeed!" the congregation responded, and then we all greeted one another, which I've always felt awkward about. I didn't move very far as I awkwardly shook hands with strangers before I sat down again.

"Did you meet some new people today?" Pastor Dennis asked enthusiastically.

The congregation responded all at once in agreement.

"Wonderful! It's always good to gather together in worship, to be in communion with fellow believers, especially on this very special Sunday of celebrating Christ's resurrection and his victory over sin and death. But I'm not naive. I wasn't born yesterday! I know that many of you here today are not believers. While that would make my heart leap with joy, I won't kid myself. Some of you are only here because you feel obligated to. I'll only see some of you on Christmas and Easter—and that's good! I'm glad you join us on those two important days. But I'd love to have those of you who only come on those days to consider joining us on a regular basis though. There's something special about getting connected with God's family. We've got something good going on here. If you don't believe me, you're left with no other choice but to come and find out!"

The congregation laughed softly, but I squirmed uncomfortably. While in high school, I'd always inwardly judged those people who only showed up for church services twice a year. You could easily spot them in the sanctuary, sitting stiffly in nice clothes next to their families who were often regular attendees themselves. I looked around sneakily to see if anyone in the sanctuary could spot me, someone who was only here out of obligation. No one seemed to notice how out of place I was though, so I relaxed.

When the congregation quieted, Pastor Dennis opened up his Bible. "Some of you may be here out of curiosity though. Perhaps a friend or relative has been sharing Jesus with you, or you've suddenly gotten curious about Christianity. You're here because you're wondering. Or maybe you're here because you've fallen away, but you're thinking about coming back." Pastor Dennis's eyes scanned the room and seemed to stop on mine. *Is he looking right at me?* I wondered; my heart was basically pounding out of my chest.

"Faith is a hard concept to grasp. Today, we remember Christ's resurrection, his victory over sin and death. It takes a great deal of faith to believe this happened, and it's not easy! Let's take a

look at John 20:24–9, at an example of one of Jesus's own fol-
lowers who struggled to believe in what Christ had done, that
he had overcome death." Everyone pulled their Bibles out and
flipped to the passage. Delilah shared her Bible with me. Pastor
Dennis read out loud, "One of the twelve disciples, Thomas, was
not with the others when Jesus came. They told him, 'We have
seen the Lord!' But he replied, 'I won't believe it unless I see
the nail wounds in his hands, put my fingers in them, and place
my hand into the wound in his side.' Eight days later the disciples were together again, and this time Thomas was with them.
The doors were locked, but suddenly, as before, Jesus was standing among them. 'Peace be with you,' he said. Then he said to
Thomas, 'Put your finger here, and see my hands. Put your hand
into the wound in my side. Don't be faithless any longer. Believe!'
'My Lord and my God!' Thomas exclaimed. Then Jesus said to
him, 'You believe because you have seen me. Blessed are those
who believe without seeing me.'"

Silence settled over the room as those words echoed in the
sanctuary. "I know many of us in this room are like Thomas.
We doubt because we cannot see. But look what Jesus says here!
'Blessed are those who *have not seen* and yet have come to believe!'
Thomas needed to see Jesus before he believed. He needed to
touch the wounds. That's how all humans are—we all crave the
proof. We all want to know for sure that what we believe is real.

"And this is where faith really comes into play. Because faith is
the assurance of things we can't see. Let's turn to Hebrews 11:1."
More page flipping. "It says, 'Faith is the confidence that what we
hope for will actually happen; it gives us assurance of things we
cannot see.' That's a hard thing to swallow, right?"

Someone yelled out, "Amen!"

"Right!" Pastor Dennis agreed with a small jump, and everyone laughed again. "Why should we just blindly accept something we can't see? That's where a lot of Christians get into trouble. Have any of you ever had a friend go through something

really hard, and they come to you with all sorts of questions about why this is happening to them?"

Heads began nodding. "And how many of you have told that hurting friend, 'You just need to have faith?'"

More heads nodded, and murmurs of agreement ran out.

"Well, I'm here to tell you today that it *is* okay to question! Questioning doesn't mean you doubt, it means you're seeking out the truth! Think about Job! His whole life was taken away from him. Does he just sit around and say to himself, 'I just need to have faith?' No! He certainly does not! Go home and read the book for yourself, and you'll see that Job asks God all kinds of hard questions. And that's okay! It doesn't mean that Job doesn't have faith. Faith doesn't mean we just blindly accept things. It's okay to question!"

My heart was pounding. I'd been doing a *lot* of questioning lately. But the way I'd grown up, I felt like a bad person to question God. I'd grown up believing in blind faith, that I just had to accept what happened to me and have faith that God would work it out. But now I was realizing that it was okay to question, to cry out to God. Job did it. And the Psalms were full of questions to God. Maybe I wasn't too far gone. Maybe I *could* come back.

"I know faith is hard, people. I know it's sometimes hard to accept what God gives us. Sometimes, we go through dry spells—periods in our lives where it feels like God is absent—and we are thirsty for his love and mercy. We've all been there, right?"

More murmurs of agreement.

"But we can live between the rains, my friends! We can. Let's take a look at James 5:7–8." He waited a bit for people to find the passage, then, read aloud, "Dear brothers and sisters, be patient as you wait for the Lord's return. Consider the farmers who patiently wait for the rains in the fall and in the spring. They eagerly look for the valuable harvest to ripen. You, too, must be patient. Take courage, for the coming of the Lord is near."

He looked up solemnly. "We all go through dry spells, folks. Jesus doesn't promise us a life of luxury or easy living. No, we are called to daily pick up our cross. We are called to live through dry spells. At times it feels that God is drowning us in mercy and kindness, and other times, it feels like we're just wandering in the wilderness. Wandering around in the desert."

My head snapped up when he said this. That's exactly what I felt like right now. For the past two years, really, I felt like I had been in the desert. I was definitely living between the rains.

"But, folks, if we're all going to experience the dry seasons in our life, should we not accept the beauty of it? Think to the last time you were in a desert. When the rains returned, did you not dance for joy? Did you not fall on your knees in gratefulness when you finally understood why it was necessary to go through that? It *always* strengthens our faith, always makes us grow in him. It is a beautiful process! So accept the beauty!"

Wandering in the desert didn't seem beautiful, not in the least bit. But would it be worth it in the end? Would I be grateful I'd endured this dry spell later? Would I be a stronger person having gone through this trauma?

"While in the desert though, we must acknowledge God's faithfulness. We know the rains will always come! Trust that God will see you to the end. Question him, cry out to him, but in the end, know that he is in control and he will send the rains again. Listen to the beautiful words of Hosea 6:3: 'Oh, that we might know the Lord! Let us press on to know him. He will respond to us as surely as the arrival of the dawn, or the coming of the rains in early spring.'

"Long for him in the dry spells, my friends! Let him know of your desire to be drenched in him. God loves it when his people desire him. And he promises he will come through like what? 'The arrival of the dawn, or the coming of the rains in early spring.' How many of you remember a day when the dawn didn't come? Or how about a spring without rains?"

The congregation laughed softly again.

"That's right! No one can remember because it hasn't happened. God always follows through on his promises, my friends. He will see you through the dry spells. He will."

Tears were forming in my eyes now. I'd been in a dry spell for so long; I didn't know if I dared trust that God would again send the rains of his love and mercy. My heart thirsted for those rains; it so badly needed to be quenched. Would God really follow through with me?

Pastor Dennis moved to the front of his podium and looked at us with such love in his eyes. He desperately wanted us to understand this.

"We all go through hardships. Like Job, we wonder why terrible things happen to us. We cry out to God and ask him why. But remember that faith involves questioning. Faith *directs* our questions—it helps us draw closer to God in the dry spells. We can take heart knowing that our fellow brothers and sisters here today have gone through dry spells too. Maybe some of you here today *are* in the midst of a dry spell. And if you haven't been there, you will. But we can trust our great God."

Pastor Dennis began pacing. "I want you all to know, people, that faith is necessary for salvation. We have two great needs in this life: to have our sins taken away so that we can have a right relationship with God established and the need to overcome death. We *all* need that, and we all have the hope that those needs will be met through Christ's death because he overcame our enemies of sin and death. The gift of salvation is offered to us all, but we have to reach out and take it. We have to have the faith that he will see through to those promises.

"But we all know that we don't have Jesus with us here physically today—we can't put our hands in his wounds like Thomas. Sometimes, we must trust and believe what we can't see. Yes, we can ask questions, we can doubt. But what it boils down to, folks, is what we choose to believe. We can believe that Jesus died for us, that he rose to conquer death and save us from our sins on this glorious Easter day. Or we can sit around and demand proof. But God proves his love each day by sending the sun, by sending the rains in the spring. So really, we have no excuse not to believe. Because we see the proof of his love every day of our lives, people. Every single day."

I squeezed my eyes shut to stop the tears from flowing. I thought back to the many things I'd endured in the past two years, trying to pick out the places God had been there for me.

Meeting Melissa—God must have been the mastermind behind that whole crazy deal. She'd given me a job and a place to stay.

Tyler. He'd given me love, someone to help me smile and make me feel human again. While it wasn't exactly a godly relationship, God may have used Tyler to drive me closer to him. Mary Beth. Albert. Delilah. Luke. All these people God had given me to draw me out of the desert and into the rain. He was there. He'd always been there. Even through the times I'd rejected and disobeyed him—running away, getting an abortion, and abusing sex—he had been there through it all. He'd been there all the nights I cursed him. He'd been leading me through this dry spell so at the end maybe something beautiful would come out of it.

Pastor Dennis returned to his podium and softened his voice; I leaned forward to drink in what he was saying. "God keeps his promises, my friends. Just like he promised Israel in Isaiah 61:3, 'To all those who mourn in Israel, he will give a crown of beauty for ashes, a joyous blessing instead of mourning.' He will turn your mess—your ashes—into a crown of beauty. Instead of mourning, we will have a joyous blessing.

"That's what Christ did on the cross for us, my friends. He took us—ugly and broken sinners—and ransomed us. He turned our mourning and suffering into beauty. And if we put our trust in him, if we have faith even when we can't see or understand, one day we will enjoy him forever. If we allow him to lead us through the dry spells and if we believe in him even when we can't put our fingers in his wounds, we will grow and develop great strength.

"So take heart, my dear brothers and sisters. If you are in a dry spell, trust that the rain will come. If you're dancing in the rains right now, keep rejoicing. Soak it in because another dry spell may be coming, and you'll want to remember the joy of being drenched. It will keep you going when your heart is thirsty and when you start asking the hard questions."

He smiled at us. "Enjoy this Easter day, my friends. He is risen!"

"He is risen indeed!" we all responded. Even me.

When the sermon ended and the last worship song was sung, I just sat there with tears running down my face. Little Luke looked up and asked, "Are you okay, Molly? Here's a tissue."

I sniffed and gave him a smile. "I'm okay, buddy. I just really liked what Pastor Dennis told us today."

Delilah put a hand on her son's shoulder and said, "Jesus was talking to Molly today, Lukey. He was telling her how much he loves her, how much he wants her to come home to him. What do you think she should do, sweetheart?"

"I think she should come back to Jesus. I have Jesus in my heart, and he always takes care of me, even when I think monsters that want to eat me are under my bed at night. But they never do. That's because of Jesus, right, Mommy?"

She laughed. "Right, kiddo. Jesus always takes care of us."

I took little Luke's advice, but not right away. I always wanted to do things the hard way lately, it seemed. But being on the run for so long had given me a heart of fear, and I was terrified of returning to God. I felt that he hadn't protected me when I needed it the most that night at Jason's. Even though I had walked right into that trap, I still felt God could have stopped Jason from raping me. So it was hard for me to open my heart up to him again.

On a rainy night a few days after Easter, however, everything changed. It had been a pretty busy day at Mary Beth's little restaurant, and I was exhausted. I sat on my living room floor in my coziest pajamas with the lights dimmed and candles burning throughout the room, trying to clear my swirling thoughts. The dimmed lights and flickering candles made the room feel so...safe. And for a while, I just sat there listening to the rain pound the roof, not really thinking about anything, until I had this strong desire to pull out my Bible...and this quiet voice kept urging me, "Come and talk with me." I looked around the room, trying to figure out if I'd really heard a voice or if I was simply going crazy. But I slowly crawled to the closet, pulled from the back the box that had been haunting me for the past three years, and rummaged through all the stuff until my fingers found the worn leather Bible I'd used in high school.

I held that book in my hands for the longest time before finally taking it back to the living room. I began flipping through the pages, and I saw all the underlining and circling I'd done when I had read my Bible as a teenager. There had been a time in my life where I was so hungry for the word of God; I simply couldn't get enough. I hadn't had that desire in so long, and I missed desiring God! I missed the thrill I used to get when I'd read something over and finally understand what it meant. I missed feeling close and connected to God.

My fingers were suddenly turning to the Old Testament, which I hadn't read much of in high school. But one lone underlined verse caught my eye, so I flipped back until I found it again; it was Ezekiel 36:26. "And I will give you a new heart, and I will put a new spirit in you. I will take out your stony, stubborn heart and give you a tender, responsive heart."

I have no idea why that verse was underlined. I hadn't written anything next to it, which I'd often done if a verse spoke to me in any way. I don't remember ever reading through Ezekiel. Maybe a camp speaker or a Sunday school teacher had taught about this verse once, and I'd underlined it. It didn't really matter, but I sat there rereading it over and over again until something dawned on me.

I'd known about God my whole life. My parents were Christians and had taken me to church my whole life. I'd grown up going to church every Sunday and Wednesday, and my summers were spent running around at church camps. I'd gone to youth group and had done a few missions trips. But even though I'd been surrounded by God my whole life, I'd turned away immediately when something bad happened to me. I lost all faith and trust after one night, one event. Granted, it had been a very traumatic event, but think of how much easier this all could have been if I had just let God handle the situation.

But maybe, I needed to go through all this to finally realize that even though I'd been surrounded by God my whole life, I'd never really responded to him. Sure, I'd probably uttered some prayer as a little kid out of fear of spending eternity in hell, but the more I thought about it, I knew that I had never really given God my whole life. I'd played the part very well, up until the rape of course, but I'd never surrendered myself to him. With this realization swirling around in my head, sitting on my living room floor with all those candles flickering around me, I began to weep. This was not just crying, like I'd been doing for years now out of desperation. This was weeping, crying out to my savior to take my stony heart and replace it with a tender one. I was tired of running, of hardening my heart and, then, building walls to protect it. I wanted a new heart; I wanted to go home to Jesus, just like little Luke had advised me to do.

So I did. On that night, with the rain pouring down outside, I let God break down the rest of my walls to transplant my heart of stone with a tender, responsive heart. I came home to Jesus.

Returning to Jesus was a slow process though, a jumbled mix of emotions. I felt tremendous joy at first because I knew I was once again on the right path running straight to God.

But it was also hard. I let myself question God, just like Job. I cried out in pain and confusion. In the end though, I decided to believe. I'd grown up in church; I knew the power of the cross. I knew that through Christ's resurrection, I was free from sin and death. Once I forgave myself for what'd I'd done, I allowed myself the peace of knowing Christ had forgiven me too. And I decided to trust that one day soon I'd be dancing in the rain, that I'd be out of this desert for good, that I would be stronger for having gone through this. And maybe, if I hadn't gone through this whole ordeal, I never would have truly responded to God, and I'd still have a heart of stone—maybe a traumatic experience was what I needed to really and truly accept him.

Over the next few months, I let my heart finally heal. I slowly but surely began to reopen my heart to Jesus, once again seeking and desiring his word. And nothing had ever felt so refreshing in my life. At night, sometimes, I would weep at all the time I'd wasted pushing him away, but it was always followed by rejoicing because I was once again on the right path.

I knew the next step, but I was reluctant. If I wanted to heal completely, I needed to turn around and go home. I needed to face all that I was running away from back in Oak Ridge. I needed to forgive Tanner, to look him in the eye and tell him I forgave him. I needed to explain to everyone what had happened to me. Every part of the story, even the darkest parts. I needed to get it all in the open, to release the pressure I'd allowed to build all this time. I knew it was the final step in the healing process.

But I was scared out of my mind. So much time had passed. Tanner would have moved on or maybe he was still mad at me. When I'd left, my parents' marriage was strained; I wondered if after I'd left it had been the final straw and they'd separated. Josh and Savannah would be all grown up and probably furious at me for leaving them to deal with mom and dad.

Mary Beth was the one who pushed me to step out of my comfort zone and return home. We were working in the kitchen on a slow afternoon in late August, and I'd sighed in frustration.

She smiled up and me and said, "You'll never fully heal until you turn around and face it, baby girl. It's always gonna be following you around if you don't go back."

"I'm scared." I croaked.

She put down the wad of dough she was kneading and focused on me. "I would be too. But you won't be doing it alone. You've opened up your heart again, you have Christ in you once again. And with him, all things are possible, right?"

I knew she was right. I'd never have the courage to come home without Jesus. I wouldn't want to go home at all if I hadn't returned to him. But after I rededicated my life to him and vowed to stop running away, he'd placed this overwhelming need in my heart to return home and make amends. That need consumed my thoughts day and night, and just like Mary Beth said: if I didn't face it now, I'd always have it looming behind me. Sooner or later, I'd need to go back and tie up all the loose ends, to look everyone I'd run from in the eye and forgive them, and to ask for their forgiveness in return. If I wanted to truly heal, to truly step out of the desert for good, I needed to go back.

So on a warm and sticky September day, Delilah and Luke came over and helped me load my little car up. It was fuller than when I had come because I'd opened myself up to these people. I'd allowed myself to really live here. I'd found real love here in Mary Beth, Albert, Delilah, and Luke. The car was full of memories, of love. I was sad to leave this place, but it felt good to be leaving for the right reason this time. I wasn't running away anymore. I was done with that for good.

No more running. I was finally going home.

Twenty-Six

The drive home was extremely nerve-wracking. I had no idea what lay in front of me. I'd left at such an emotional time, and now, it was three years later and the world I'd left behind would be gone. Everyone I knew from high school had graduated and probably left our little town of 1,300 for a larger city with more opportunity. Josh would be graduating this year, and Savannah would be in high school now too. Who knows what had happened to my parents, how awkward to come back and find them divorced. And Tanner. Hopefully, Tanner had gone away to Iowa State; I wasn't sure if I was ready to face him yet.

Facing Tanner would be the hardest because he had been the hardest to forgive. After all, if he'd never told Jason about the baby, I wouldn't have run. I wouldn't have gotten the abortion. I'd have stayed, given birth, and probably married Tanner. My life would be so different now if he hadn't told Jason.

But I'd worked through it, with the help of Pastor Dennis. I knew I couldn't blame what I'd done on Tanner. Yes, he'd played a role in my decisions; but ultimately, they'd all been *my* decisions.

And I'd laid down all my mistakes at the feet of Jesus and left them behind. I'd never forget what I'd done, but I could move on from them knowing that Christ had died to free me from those mistakes. They were too heavy to lug around anymore; casting them on Jesus had been one of the most freeing experiences of my life.

I reached over to the passenger seat and pulled out a CD from my purse. On my last night in Green Lake Delilah slept over, and we'd sat on the living room floor with all my boxes stacked up around us. With tears in her eyes, she gave me this CD.

"It has songs on it that really helped me when I was going through the darkest days of my life. I'd lie in my bed at night with my hands on my huge pregnant belly and listen to them over and over again. I felt so low and alone. So worthless. But my mom made me a CD with these same songs on it, and it helped so much."

I swallowed and nodded; tears were making it hard to talk right now.

"Healing is a long and slow process, Molly. So on the days it feels impossible to go on, just pop this in and focus on the words. And don't ever forget—with God, all things are possible, right?"

"Right," I agreed. This road ahead of me would be hard, but I had the love and support of Mary Beth and Delilah to keep me going. Delilah and I promised to keep in touch, to help each other on the never ending journey of spiritual healing. We already made plans for me to come back and visit next summer.

The CD held a mix of different Christian artists, artists Tanner and I had enjoyed in high school. But back then, my life had been simple and easy; I hadn't gone through these dark days, and the words hadn't meant much then. Now though, these lyrics about Christ's wonderful, redeeming love were everything. Six months ago, I would have been unable to sing along with theses praises, but now, after I'd reopened myself to Christ, I threw my head back and sang out to my redeemer like I'd never done before. It was so much more powerful, so much more meaningful, than the worship I'd experienced in my younger years.

When I pulled into Oak Ridge hours later, the fear returned, gripping my heart and making me want to turn right back around and drive straight back to the safety I'd found with Mary Beth and Delilah. And because I was so scared, I didn't go home right away. Instead, I drove out to the lake and found my little bench. I just needed a bit of time to clear my head, to prepare myself for the emotional mountain I knew I'd be facing in the next few hours and days.

I took the time to open myself to whatever God wanted to lead me through. Trusting him was still a bit hard for me to handle, but if I'd learned anything in the past three years, I knew trying to handle it on my own would end up disastrous. He knew the ending of my story, so why not let him lead me through this now? His plan, his ending, was better than what I could ever imagine, so I decided to take the leap and go his way this time.

So after a long hour of prayer and searching his word for courage, I took a deep breath, got back in my car, and drove the familiar roads back home. The closer I got, the harder my heart pounded. It all looked the same; it was like I'd never been gone. It was still the same sleepy little town I'd known my entire life.

I didn't pull into the driveway because I'd been away for so long and this place didn't feel like home anymore. I walked up the narrow sidewalk leading up to the front porch, and paused a minute before I knocked on the door. Someone would be home on this Saturday afternoon, but I couldn't just walk in. It wasn't my house.

It took so long for someone to reach the door that I almost turned around and gave up. But right as I was turning to leave, the door flung open and my flustered mother opened the door. And she didn't recognize me.

"Hello? Can help you?" she asked, squinting at me. She looked at me like she sort of knew me but couldn't quite place where she knew me from. Like when you run into someone at the grocery store and they wave and say hi, but you walk away feeling bad because you don't quite remember where you know them from.

That hurt a little bit, but it was understandable. I'd been gone for so long; they all probably had given up hope of ever seeing me again. And I knew I didn't look the same as when I'd left. I wasn't the innocent young girl they'd known. I was broken, harsher than they remembered. It was only in the past few months that the light had slowly been returning to me eyes. I knew I looked much different than what they remembered.

I smiled weakly and said quietly, "Mom. It's me."

Her eyes widened as big as saucers, and she took a few faltering steps backward and clutched her neck. After she got over the shock, she lurched forward and threw her arms around me and sobbed. I hugged her back, and we stood in the doorway for the longest time locked together like that, swaying and crying together. That longing for my mother on the night of the rape never quite left me. For some reason after that happened, I needed her so badly, craved her loving arms to soothe my hurting heart, but I'd never reached out for her help. But now I was finally in her arms, and it felt so right. As we swayed back and forth, it felt like she was rocking me, like she used to do when I'd get hurt to stop my crying. She stroked my hair and breathed in the scent of me, her arms locked around me like she never wanted to let go.

She finally drew back and held me at arm's length, and the tears were still coursing down her cheeks. "You're back," she said simply, like she couldn't quite believe it, and she had to make sure I was really in her arms, that she was awake and this wasn't some sort of crazy dream.

"I'm back," I replied.

She laughed and pulled me into the house, and I was shocked at how different it was. New furniture. New paint on the walls. A brand-new kitchen complete with the shiny black appliances she'd always wanted. It was completely different.

"I went through a bit of a midlife crisis after you left," she explained as she put the kettle on to boil for tea. I nodded as I sat down at the new kitchen table. "I needed to change everything up, and I needed a project to keep me busy," she said with a sad smile.

"Mom," I croaked. "I'm...I'm so sorry. I must have put you through so much..."

Tears filled her eyes again, and she nodded. She couldn't lie about this to make me feel better. When I'd left, I'd selfishly only thought of myself. I hadn't once considered what it would do to my parents and my siblings. I hadn't even had the decency to leave a note! I'd just disappeared from their lives without a single explanation. They knew nothing of the fight Tanner and I'd had or about the deeper reason that drove me away. The rape. I'd thought leaving would protect them from Jason, but after the abortion, I realized that he really couldn't have done anything. If I'd just *told* Tanner and my parents about the rape, if I'd let them help me deal with it, we could have dealt with Jason. He only held power over me because I hadn't told anyone, hadn't reported him. He knew that as long as I was alone in it, he was in control. If only I had told someone! How different my life would be right now...

"Why, Molly?" she asked, the hurt in her voice spilling out. "Tanner told us you had a fight that night, but I know you. One little fight wouldn't make you run. What was it?"

The story wouldn't come any easier telling it to my mother. But she needed to hear it all. So once again, I went back to that rainy November night and let her in to the dark world I'd been slugging through for the past three years. I told her about my terror, about how just when I started to feel somewhat normal again I found myself pregnant. I spilled all of Jason's cruel threats, and how the fight with Tanner had been the last straw.

She closed her eyes in pain. "Tanner never told us that he'd told Jason…I can't believe he did something like that. That was wrong, baby girl. I'm sorry."

"Me too." I mourned. I continued on, telling her about how terrified and alone I'd felt running away that night, but that I'd met Melissa, gotten a job, and settled in Minneapolis. It had all sort of fallen into place.

But then I stopped because the next part of the story was the darkest, most painful part, and I was ashamed to have to tell her what I'd done.

She waited with questioning eyes for me to continue. I'd obviously been pregnant when I ran, but I didn't have a toddler here with me today. She wanted to know where my baby was. When I didn't give any information, she went ahead and asked.

"What about the baby, Molly?" she whispered, anxiously sitting forward in her seat.

I hung my head in shame and swallowed. I didn't want to say it, so I just looked up and hoped the raw pain in my eyes would say it all. And it did because the tears spilled onto her cheeks. It was then that I saw the ultrasound pictures still hanging on the shiny new fridge.

I watched my mother's world come crashing in around her. She got up slowly and brought the ultrasound pictures to the table, and her hands shook as she traced the outline of my baby's tiny face with her fingers.

With a shaky voice, she whispered, "I fell in love that day, Molly. Your pregnancy was so hard for me to swallow at first… but then I saw the little face…heard the heartbeat. How could I not absolutely fall in love? We all did. We started to anticipate a new life…a new family member to love."

She smiled sadly and continued tracing my baby's little profile. "We prayed for you and the baby so hard the week of your due date. We hoped that maybe you might send us some pictures…or that one day, you'd bring him or her back to meet us."

Her words cut like knives. Again, when I decided on abortion I'd only thought about myself. I didn't think about how my decision would affect my family. I hadn't stopped to think about how my parents would feel about losing their first grandchild. The thought hadn't even crossed my mind. I had been completely focused on making my life easier, on trying to cut all ties to Jason forever. But my decision was breaking my mother's heart. She'd never rock that little baby in her arms like she'd just rocked me... never hold her little hands or tell her "I love you" as she tucked her into bed. The little life she'd prayed for and hoped to one day meet was gone, and she'd never get the chance to pour out all her love onto my baby girl.

"I wish I could take it back, Mom, I really do," I choked. "I made the wrong decision at a time when my mind was so messed up. But there's no excuse good enough for what I did, I know that. And it's taken me *so* long to put it behind me...to forgive myself. I honestly don't know if I'll ever fully forgive myself for what I did...but..."

She reached across the table and took my hands in hers. "What's done is done. We can't go back. We have to figure out how to move on from this together. And we will. Sounds like you've already started, and that's good."

I nodded, grateful for her gentleness and understanding. Her heart was broken, but she realized there was no sense dwelling on the enormity of my mistake. We could only leave it at the foot of the cross and let Christ heal us. The burden was too big to carry alone; I knew that all too well. He was the only one strong enough to do so.

The rest of the story came easier. I told her about my remaining time in Minneapolis, about Tyler and our broken relationship. I told her about my second running away and smiled as I told her about meeting Mary Beth. She smiled too as I told her all about the wonderful people I'd met in Green Lake, especially Delilah and little Luke. I cried as I told her about that glorious

Easter day, about the rainy night I'd returned home to my heavenly father and decided to stop running. And the story ended right there at the table, sitting with my mother. I didn't know what lay ahead for me now, what the ending of my story would look like. But the final leg started right here, with me facing what I'd run away from three years ago.

We sat in silence for a while as my mom processed all I'd told her. I could see it in her eyes how much she hurt for me.

"I'm sorry you had to struggle through all of this alone. It just breaks my heart, all that you went through. Especially the rape, honey. We would have helped you!" she cried desperately, wiping the tears away that never seemed to stop spilling out of her tired eyes.

I wiped the tears from my own eyes and nodded. "I know. But back then, Jason had me convinced no one would believe it. And I'd destroyed all the evidence. And I thought people would treat me differently if they knew, that they might think I was just making it up to get Jason in trouble. I honestly thought telling you wasn't even an option."

She nodded slowly. Getting people to understand about the rape was hard; they automatically thought I should have reported him, that I should have known better. I realized that now, but back then, I'd been too scared, plain and simple. I was embarrassed and ashamed. I truly felt like I had no options.

"So fill me in on what's been happening here," I suggested, trying to steer the conversation away from me; I didn't want her telling me more of what I *should* have done. "I feel like a stranger here, not knowing anything about anyone anymore."

She took a deep breath and said, "Well, it's definitely been a rough few years, but…they've kind of been good for us." She smiled a little, a twinkle in her eye.

"Oh?" I asked.

"Yeah. It was pretty hard for me and dad at first. We were all just really angry and confused. But we got to a place where we realized that if we wanted to get through your leaving, we needed to go through it together. We wanted to be there for Josh and Savannah, and we couldn't do that divided. So as bad as this sounds, your leaving kind of saved our marriage, Molly," she said sheepishly.

I laughed. At least *something* good happened. "I'm really glad to hear that, Mom. I'm kind of surprised. To be honest, when I was driving back, I sort of figured it might be over between you two. It was pretty rough back then."

She nodded. "It sure was. But it's nothing like that anymore. We started doing counseling at the church, and our relationship has never been stronger. God is good."

In all my life, I'd never heard my mother say that before. I knew she was a woman of God, but she was quiet about it. I couldn't contain my joy as I listened to my mom talk about her renewed relationship with dad and with God.

She continued filling me in on all that had happened in the three years since I'd left. Josh had taken my leaving the hardest, which didn't surprise me the least bit. Josh and I had been so close as kids; he always tagged along when Tanner and I played together. And we just had this strange connection, though we were three years apart. When he got scared at night from thunderstorms, he wouldn't go running to Mom and Dad's room, he climbed into my bed and I'd whisper made-up stories in his ear until he calmed down. He talked to me about everything and always sought my approval. When I had gotten pregnant, he'd taken it the hardest then too. I knew he had been disappointed. My heart ached when I thought about how he would respond to my coming back and the news of the abortion. If he was still mad at me for running, who knows how he would respond to my return and to that sad news. I shuddered.

He'd moved on eventually, and from the sounds of it, he was doing great. He was graduating at the top of his class, and he was dating a nice girl from the church. From the sounds of it, things were pretty serious between Josh and Caitlin. My mom speculated that they'd go off to school together and be married within two years.

I stared at her in surprise. "Wow! That serious, huh?"

She smiled and said, "Yup. She's a sweet girl. I approve."

Savannah was a freshman this year; she had bounced back from the shock of my leaving faster than anyone else, my mom told me. She had been sad, yes, but mostly because she had wanted the baby so much. For some reason, Savannah and Ellen, Tanner's little sister, were ecstatic about my pregnancy; they couldn't wait to spoil my baby.

It wasn't that Savannah and I weren't close, it was just that I was so much older than her. Six years was a big gap, and she'd only been twelve when I'd left. Kids recovered from things quicker, I guessed. She'd had other things to focus on rather than be angry at me for leaving. But she *would* be mad at me once she found out about the nonexistent baby. She'd be crushed.

So maybe it would be a bit tougher facing everyone than I thought. My heart sank. I had just gotten here, yet I was already exhausted from simply thinking about facing everyone.

"Dad took Josh and Savannah out hiking for the day, but they should be back by dinner. Want to help me cook?"

After I got over the shook that my dad was out hiking with Josh and Savannah, I nodded and stood up to help. Dad had never taken us kids out alone for a day out hiking. But I guess after I left, my dad realized how important family is; he must not have wanted to miss out on the rest of his kids' lives.

I showed off my new cooking skills to which my mom was thoroughly impressed. Fried chicken and fresh mashed potatoes and buttermilk biscuits were my specialty; the one thing I could make without thinking. Mary Beth had seen to that, and my mom eventually put her hands up in the air in surrender and let me take over. She settled at the kitchen table with another cup of coffee to watch me work my magic.

Suddenly, the door opened, and my dad, Josh, and Savannah stumbled into the front room. They were sweaty and dirty but talking loudly and excitedly about all the fun they'd had on their hike. But when Dad rounded the corner to the kitchen, he fell silent. Josh and Savannah laughingly followed Dad into the kitchen, but when they saw me, they too fell silent.

No one said anything, and the ticking of the clock bounced off the walls. My dad stepped forward then, tears sliding down his face and onto the floor. He stayed silent as he gathered me into his arms and hugged me so tightly I couldn't breathe.

That's when it got crazy with everyone responding all at once to the emotional reunion. Everyone was hugging and crying, rejoicing at my homecoming.

We settled down to dinner; everyone smacking their lips appreciatively at my cooking. We danced around the subject of why I'd left and then suddenly decided to come back. But conversation lulled, and my family was exchanging curious looks. I knew I had to tell them, so I started the horrible story all over again.

Because my mother had just heard me tell it, she kept her emotions more in check this time, simply nodding and grimacing at the hard parts. My dad never looked up from his plate, Josh was clenching his teeth tightly and avoiding my gaze, and Savannah fidgeted nervously. My cheeks burned as I told them about how Jason had date-raped me. I tried to get them to understand how terrified and ashamed I'd been when I'd first found out I was pregnant, that I felt that it was my fault, and I couldn't tell anyone about the rape. But as I tried to explain how Jason had manipulated me, how he had made me feel so low, dirty, and unworthy, I could see that Josh didn't quite believe me. I told them how Tanner had betrayed me, and again, Josh didn't buy it. He'd always thought of Tanner as a big brother, someone he looked up to with all his heart. He didn't believe Tanner could do something that heartless, but he had.

Finally, I told them about the fight, how it had been the final straw, and I'd snapped. I'd made a bad decision in my emotionally distraught state of mind, and the bad choices kept on coming. I didn't want to tell them the rest, but the story just kept spilling out. I hung my head as I told them about the abortion, barely whispering what I had done.

Josh had had enough. He pushed back from the table, his chair loudly scraping the new wooden floors in the kitchen. He threw his napkin down and stormed out of the room, completely disgusted.

I sat there, in shock, for a few minutes but then finished the story for my dad and Savannah. I told them all about Mary Beth, how she had opened up her heart completely to me and introduced me to the best friend I'd ever had, Delilah. They smiled when I told them about little Luke, about that amazing Easter Sunday, and the rainy night later that week that I had reopened my wounded heart to God.

Once it was all out in the open, my dad got up and motioned my mom and sister to follow his lead, surrounding me and laying hands on my shoulders. Then, my dad did something he'd never done before. He prayed for me out loud with my mom's and sister's hands squeezing me supportively.

Tears leaked out of my already red and swollen eyes as my dad prayed, "Lord Jesus, we praise you for the return of our lost daughter and friend. We mourn for all she has gone through, but we thank you that you brought her through safely. Please help all of us heal from all that's happened in the past three years. We don't understand why some of these things happened, Lord, but we trust that you have a bigger plan for Molly. Thank you again for her return, Lord, and help all of us to rally around her and strengthen her. And finally, Lord, we ask that you would continue drawing Molly closer and closer to you. The most important thing is that she is your child, and that her sins are forgiven because of your work on the cross, that *all* of our sins are forgiven because of you. We know that we all have fallen short, but we praise you for bringing each of us back home and adopting us into your wonderful family."

My mom sniffed and everyone was quiet until my dad finally said, "Amen."

I didn't go to Josh that night. Instead, I let him mourn for all that he'd lost when I ran away; I let him process all of his emotions. I spent that night in my old room, which my mom had completely changed as well. All my stuff was boxed up and in the basement storage room, and the purple walls had been painted a soft, calming green. A friendly quilt was spread on my old bed and the posters and pictures frames I'd had on the walls had been replaced with family pictures and framed Bible verses. It was a guest room. It hurt a bit that they'd boxed up and removed all traces of me, but I suppose, it had helped them move on. After all, I'd been gone for three years.

But I knew the next few days would be the most difficult ones of this whole journey. Mom hadn't mentioned Tanner; she'd danced around that subject all night. I had a feeling I'd run into him sooner than I planned. And I still needed to make things right with Josh. Savannah had opened right back up to me, even though she was disappointed that I didn't have a drooling toddler with me.

Josh, however, was a grudge holder. I'd need all the strength God could give me to make things right with him.

Twenty-Seven

"I just don't see how you could have made such a stupid decision, Molly. What were you thinking?" Josh asked, pushing scrambled eggs around on his plate. I'd taken him out to breakfast so we could have this discussion in public. This way, if he got mad, he couldn't explode and start yelling. At least, I hoped he had the decency not to explode in public…Josh was pretty strong willed.

I sighed and took a long sip of orange juice. "I have no real good excuse, Josh." I explained with a shrug. "No one knew about the rape, and I felt so alone. And after Jason cornered me in the janitor's closet that one Friday, I panicked. No one else knew what he was capable of, but when he threatened all of you and Tanner, I freaked out."

"What did he exactly threaten?" Josh asked skeptically. He didn't think Jason could hold so much power over me.

I closed my eyes and tried to remember what had happened that awful afternoon, every terrible thing Jason had said to me.

"He just said he'd make sure Tanner could never be with me. And then he threatened to come after you guys."

Josh rolled his eyes. "And you believed him?"

"Yes, Josh, I did!" I cried, completely exasperated. Why was it so hard for him to understand my fear of my rapist?

"He *raped* me. I hated him, and I was terrified of him. I knew he was capable of awful things. If Jason could rape me, then come after me and demand I get an abortion, you better believe I thought he was serious about those threats, Josh. He had *that* much power over me. Don't you understand?"

He sighed. "Yeah, I guess I can see how that would be scary. But really, if you'd just told us about it, we would have made sure he stayed away from you."

I nodded. "I know. But at the time, I couldn't see that. And I was furious at Tanner. He didn't trust me enough to tell Jason myself or to know that telling him was a bad idea. Jason didn't have to know—if he hadn't found out, I would have stayed. But Tanner went behind my back then lied to me about it. And I was furious. The fight was the final straw for me. I snapped. I finally had a reason to run."

Josh was silent for a few beats, then, said quietly, "You could have at least left a note. Something to let us know it was hard for you…that you were sorry." His eyes shone with unshed tears. He was trying so hard not to cry.

"I know." I admitted. "I should have, and I'm sorry. I was self-ish. I just wanted to disappear, to get out of there with no strings attached. I had to completely cut off all emotional ties if I was going to leave. I know that wasn't fair to you."

We finished breakfast, the conversation tense and awkward, but in the end, I knew we would be okay. Eventually, Josh would come to terms with what had happened. He disagreed with my decision to get an abortion, and he was angry. But just like I had, he'd have to realize that it was in the past and I couldn't change it, couldn't take it back. If he wanted to heal, if he wanted to restore our broken relationship as much as I did, he'd have to forgive me, just as I had forgiven myself, and then work on healing. Of course, we'd always have a scar from all the emotional damage the abortion had done, but at least, it wouldn't be a huge, gaping wound anymore. I knew Josh would get there too. Someday, we'd be dancing in the rains together, finally out of the dry and weary desert we'd both been wandering in since the night I left.

I understood, too, why my mom thought Josh and Caitlin would eventually end up married. When he talked about her, his eyes just shone with love, the exact same way Tanner's eyes had shone when he loved me with everything he had. I was happy for Josh. I just hoped nothing would tear him and Caitlin apart like Tanner and I had been torn apart.

On Sunday, I joined my family at church, which was more than a little awkward. Everyone was surprised and overjoyed to see me, but of course, their eyes held burning questions. They wanted to know why I had left so suddenly and without warning. No one knew I had been pregnant, which helped, because then, I didn't have to explain to anyone why I didn't have a toddler following me around.

Before the service started, I was doing my best to make conversation with the hordes of people who kept coming up to me and asking me how I was doing. But soon my head was spinning, and I simply wanted to go home. And that's when I saw him.

Tanner.

My heart slammed against my chest as I saw him standing in a small group of people, laughing and smiling as though he didn't have a care in the world. Maybe he was home visiting this weekend, taking a break from his studies at Iowa State. It figured that I'd picked the one weekend to come home that he was here too. I didn't know if I was ready to face him, but all of a sudden, he was turning around, and our eyes locked.

It looked like his knees buckled a bit, and he looked hard at me, trying to see if it was actually me standing right in front of him.

"Molly?" he called out, unsure of himself.

I nodded and swallowed the huge marble in my throat. I couldn't speak.

He made his way over to me slowly, and my heart was still pounding. So many emotions were swirling in my head right now, but mostly, I was excited to see him again. No matter how angry I'd been at him, deep down, I still loved him. And maybe he could learn to love me again too. Maybe he'd give me a second chance.

Suddenly, I was in his arms, and his tears were wetting my shoulder. His whole body was shaking from deep sobs. I broke down too and cried. It was so nice to finally be in his arms again. This is where I had always belonged. Why had I given this up?

He pulled back and tried to compose himself because, at this point, we were starting to make a scene and people were staring. Most of them remembered how close we had been and how much Tanner had loved me. A few people even had tears of their own in their eyes, touched at his beautiful reunion.

"Hey," he said with a little laugh. "Hey. Wow. I can't believe you're here."

I shrugged. "Figured it was time to stop running and come home."

He looked around, and I knew what he was looking for. "Where's...I mean...when you left..." He couldn't come up with the right words to ask me where my child was. His child, in a way. It had been more of Tanner's child than Jason's.

I let out all my air, defeated, because I knew I'd have to tell Tanner the whole story too. "It's a long story, Tanner."

A petite blond girl walked over and tapped Tanner on the shoulder. "Hey, what's going on?"

I didn't recognize her at first, but all of a sudden, I remembered who she was. Leah. We'd gone to youth group together in middle and high school. She was also the girl Kristina had fallen back on when our friendship came to a crashing end. She didn't recognize me either, but I didn't expect her to. We'd never been close or spent any amount of time together.

Tanner turned back to me. "Molly, you remember Leah, right? From youth group?"

I nodded, confused why she was intruding in this private conversation. "We…uh…got married last year," Tanner stammered.

I took a few haltering steps backward. "Really?" I squeaked. "That's…wonderful. Really great. Congratulations, you guys."

I turned to leave, but Tanner grabbed my arm. "Molly, wait! Here, just give me a second."

He gently led Leah away and whispered something, and she nodded. She didn't look too happy, but Tanner's eyes danced, and he kissed her on the cheek.

"Let's go," he said when he returned.

"What? Where?"

"We need to talk this out, Molly. Why wait? It's a beautiful day. Leah's fine. Really, I promise."

"Okay," I said reluctantly, unsure if I really wanted to tell the story again. It was exhausting.

But the next thing I knew, I was climbing into Tanner's SUV and heading out to the lake. To my favorite spot, probably.

"Finally got a new car, huh?" I joked, remembering back to his old piece of junk that we'd drove around in all through high school. So many good memories in that little car.

He laughed. "Yup. Figured I needed a big boy car now that I'm married and whatnot."

And that's where conversation ended. The news of Tanner's marriage had come as such a shock; I definitely hadn't planned on that. Well, at least I knew for sure now that Tanner had moved on when I'd left. That's what I'd always wanted, right?

So we drove the rest of the way in silence until Tanner pulled into the deserted parking lot. The weather was still gorgeous, but the heavy summer traffic was gone. Now that school was in session, the families had packed up their campers and tents and left for the season. In the early fall, mostly local families came out and used the lake, but everyone in my tiny town was at church. That's what happens in a little Christian town. Everything besides churches are dead on Sunday mornings.

We settled onto my little bench, and Tanner turned to face me. "I kind of adopted your bench after you left. Hope that's okay."

"Yeah. That's cool."

"I came out here a lot during those first months you left. I spent graduation morning out here, thinking about you. Wondering where you were and what you were doing. And I came out here a few days a week that first summer…because I missed you so much and being here…it was like you were here too. If I closed my eyes, I could almost hear your laugh." I let him talk through all these emotions. I was learning that talking was a huge step in the healing process.

"Came out on your due date too, and I prayed that you were doing well. That the baby was healthy. I wished you were here… that I was the one at your hospital bed coaching you."

He fell silent, and I didn't say anything. It dawned on me that he thought I'd given birth. Of course he did. We'd never talked about abortion or even considered it.

"Who was by your bed that day, Molly? You did have someone there with you, right?"

Tears leaked out of my eyes, and I shook my head. "Tanner… I…I don't know how to tell you this…"

He took my hands gently in his. "Let me go first then, okay? Let me tell you everything that's happened to me since you left."

I nodded.

"When you left," he started out, slowly, "you took a part of me with you. It was so surreal at first, and I had to convince myself every day that it wasn't just some bad dream. It was real…you were really gone. So I just kind of lived in a daze for the longest time. Graduation was tough. Your parents came to the ceremony still. For me. And they helped my parents put on my graduation party. They're amazing, Molly. In the midst of all that, they came together. They've never been stronger or more in love."

I smiled. "I know…it's so great. I never expected that."

"Yeah, so that was cool. But it was still really hard for everyone. Especially Josh. I hope you can work it out with him, Moll. He was pretty broken up."

"We talked through it all. We're on our way."

"Good," he said, satisfied. "Well, after graduation, the summer just sort of dragged on. I thought about going to Iowa State, but I'd already rejected my scholarship deal from them, so I just went off to Central Christian College, like we'd planned on."

I shook my head, disappointed.

He shrugged. "I didn't want to go to Iowa State without you. And I wanted to be close to home…in case you decided to come back," he admitted.

My heart was breaking. Tanner *had* waited for me!

"But when you didn't, I knew I had to move on. And that's when I started seeing Leah. We had a class together, and we were partners for a project. Then, we started hanging out a bunch, and it just kind of went from there. We started dating in March of our freshman year, and I asked her to marry me on our first anniversary. We got married this past August."

I started really crying then. I was glad Tanner had moved on, I really was. But deep down, I had wished that he would still be waiting for me, and we could pick up where we left off. But what a foolish hope that had been. I had left without a warning; it was ridiculous to think that he would wait three years for me.

"I'm sorry…I just…for some reason, I was clinging to the hope that you'd forgiven me and that you were still waiting for me. Leah was quite a shock, Tanner. I know it's silly. But…I don't know. I'm still in shock."

"I understand. But you have to understand too, that if I wanted to carry on, I needed to put you behind me. I *did* wait, but then, I got to know Leah, and it was like God sent her to me, to fill the hole you'd left me with. And I prayed long and hard about it because I didn't want to use her just to get over you. But it all worked out. We clicked right away…and I love her."

I nodded.

"One more thing though, Molly. You never let me explain myself the night you ran away. Every time I tried to tell you I didn't tell Jason about the baby, you cut me off, just assuming I was lying. But I wasn't lying, Molly. I wasn't," he insisted.

"How else could he have found out, Jason?" I whispered. "And he *told* me it was you!" Frustration was welling up inside me again…I didn't want to have this fight.

"You should have known what a liar he was, Moll. He over-heard Kristina talking about it to some of her friends at the water fountain that day. He figured if he got you to believe that I had told, you'd get mad enough to leave. Guess he was right, huh?"

My eyes were darting all over the place, trying to piece all of this together. All this time I'd been so furious at Tanner, con-vinced all my problems were because of him. But of course, Jason had been behind this as well! What a brilliant plot, turning me against Tanner like that. He knew I'd never forgive Tanner, and then, he'd threatened me too, just to make sure I left and got rid of the baby.

"I…I…can't believe it. Well, actually I *can*." I stammered. I looked straight into his eyes. "I'm so sorry. I should have let you explain."

So much pain could have been avoided if I'd stuck around to let Tanner explain. We could have faced Jason together, and I could have kept the baby! My heart sank, and I squeezed my eyes shut.

He gave me a weak smile, and I could see the depth of pain in his eyes. We'd both lost so much because I'd walked out without letting Tanner explain himself.

With this new information weighing me down, I said weakly, "My turn. Let me warn you though…it's not pretty."

"I'm ready." Tanner reassured.

"Okay, well, first I need to confess something about Jason and me. That night I crawled into your bed and told you Jason broke up with me…we never had sex that night, Tanner."

He looked so confused. "But…you got pregnant…was it another night?"

"No. Sorry, I'm doing a bad job explaining. What I mean is," I paused and took a deep breath, the words stuck in my throat. "He raped me." Those were the hardest words I'd ever uttered. Telling Delilah and my family had been one thing. But saying it to Tanner was awful. And the pain and anger immediately flooded into his eyes. He reeled back, shock widening his eyes, but all he could stammer was "What?"

I swallowed hard and continued, trying to explain again why it had been impossible for me to tell anyone. Tanner nodded. He understood better than anyone else had. He'd always understood me better than anyone else. But he broke down when I told him about the abortion, letting deep sobs escape without shame.

"I figured when you left," he said between sobs, "it was because you wanted to protect the baby. I didn't think abortion was even an option! When you didn't have a toddler with you today, I kind of figured you'd gone with adoption. But…wow…I just—"

"I'm so sorry." I interrupted. "That was your baby too…it never belonged to Jason. You loved it, I know you did, and I'm so sorry."

He stayed silent for the longest time, then, heaved himself off the bench and wandered off for a bit, kicking at dirt clods and wiping at his face. I waited. Of course he would take this the hardest. Finally he returned and slouched down, defeated. With his face in his hands he asked quietly, "Boy or girl?"

"I don't know," I answered. "They never told me. But I've always believed it was a little girl. Our little Eden."

He nodded and then stared off into space as I told him the rest of the story. I ended with my newfound courage to come back home and stop running.

"I kind of felt like Jesus those years I was gone. You know, when he goes out into the wilderness to be tempted by Satan for forty days? So tired…and weak…vulnerable. It was an absolute desert, Tanner. There's no better way to explain it. But I'm taking the first steps out…I'm healing."

He turned to me again and gave me a lopsided smile, though I could still see the raw pain in his eyes. "I'm glad. You made the right choice coming back and facing all this. I'm glad you're back."

I smiled. "Me too." He leaned in to hug me and then kissed me gently on the head.

"I'll always love you, you know that, right?" he whispered. "Maybe not in the same way I once did, but we have a bond that I doubt anything will ever break."

I gave a sad laugh and shook my head.

"What?" he asked.

"I'm just…a little sad, I guess. Since the rape, it feels like no matter which way I turn, I keep hitting dead ends."

"What do you mean?" he asked, confused.

"Well, I felt like I couldn't tell anyone about it. And it felt like the ending of my innocence. Then, I got pregnant, and it felt like the end of my whole life. There was no way I could ever hope to return back to normal, to the way I'd been before Jason. Then, things didn't work out in Minnesota, and when I finally found a family in Kansas, I had to leave them too. And now here…with you…it just feels like another ending, you know?"

He turned to me and lifted my chin with his fingers. "Hey now…that's not true."

"But you're married now…you have a new life. And everyone's moved on without me. Everyone has a new life."

"That doesn't matter," he whispered. "Yeah, I moved on, Molly. Now I want you to do the same. You've been on this roller-coaster journey for so long, but the hardest parts are over now. Now it's the beginning of your new life…the life God's always wanted you to live. How many people get a second chance at life, huh? Don't you see?"

I ducked my head and sniffed, tears running off my face and into my lap.

Tanner lifted my head again and wiped my tears away with his thumbs. "It's not an ending, Molly. It's just the beginning."

Epilogue

December

My mom gave me one more bear hug before releasing me and taking a few faltering steps into the hallway.

"Are you sure you had to come back to Kansas? You finally came home, and now, you're leaving us again." Her voice was shaking and tears threatened to spill onto her cheeks.

I nodded. "Oak Ridge isn't home anymore, Mom. It hasn't been for years."

"I know," she whispered. "But it's still hard."

We said our last good-byes, and I turned around and took in my new apartment. I'd stuck it out for a few months in Oak Ridge, but I found that moving back was just too painful for me. Every street, every building, held memories of a long-gone happy childhood. Oak Ridge was where the rape still lived for me. It was where Leah was living out my happily ever after with Tanner.

I'm happy for them, I really am. But it's time for me to move on, just as everyone else has moved on. It's time for me to start figuring out how to start over for real, now that I've faced every fear and unfinished ending. With all the loose ends neatly tied up now, I'm free to live out the wonderful second chance I've been given.

Twenty minutes later, I stuffed the last piece of newspaper into a black garbage bag and then sat down with a huff on the sofa. I was officially moved into the apartment, and it had been a crazy day. My family had frantically helped me move in all day, afraid we'd get caught in the snow that threatened to fall from the fat wintery clouds that hovered lowly in the sky. I'd spent the last twenty minutes picking up newspaper scraps that we'd used as packing paper and straightening up though. While I appreciated the help of my family, they'd left me with quite a mess to clean up.

But it was fine with me. Cleaning always helps me clear my head. I looked around at my new home and smiled appreciatively. What I needed was a nice cup of apple cinnamon tea and some music to really feel settled in here. Right on cue, the teakettle began to sing, so I ventured into my fully stocked cupboards—courtesy of my mother—and pulled out my box of tea and some honey. When I had my tea all prepared, I slipped in the CD that Delilah had given me into my stereo and settled into my second-hand couch. I closed my eyes and let the lyrics of my favorite new song wash over me.

It was a song I'd sang at summer camp every year I'd gone, and the lyrics never really made sense to me. They sure made sense now though, so I closed my eyes and softly sang along.

Purify my heart
Let me be as gold, pure gold

Refiner's fire
My heart's one desire
Is to be holy
Set apart for you, Lord.
I chose to be holy
Set apart for you, my Master
Ready to do your will

That was my daily prayer these days. It finally dawned on me that all this time in the desert, all the time I'd spent wandering around in that wilderness, God had been refining my heart. I hadn't just been absently wandering; I'd been walking through God's holy fire. He had been burning away every part of my life that had tainted me. And if I wanted my heart to be pure, untainted gold, fire had been necessary. So each day I prayed that God would continue purifying me. This time, though, I was ready to follow him anywhere, even into more fire. Just like the song, I was ready to do his will. Finally.

And because of that, I finally felt like I was on the right track. I'd been working on getting my GED and was hoping to start college classes at a community college just down the road from Green Lake. I planned on majoring in psychology. I wanted to be a counselor to help girls who had been sexually abused like I had. No one should have to go through the pain of rape all alone like I had, so I wanted to commit my life making sure I was there for as many girls as I could. I wanted them to see what I hadn't seen going through all of it. That it wasn't their fault, that they weren't dirty and cheap and worthless because of it. That they could heal and move on and have a normal, happy life.

And maybe I could save other girls' babies in the process. I couldn't do anything to get mine back, but if I could help save others, I'd be the happiest person on earth. I just hope my baby girl can be proud of her mommy from up in heaven. I hope she knows I love her, and that I'm sorry. I hope she knows that I'm going to do everything in my power to stop other scared girls from making the mistake I had. And one day, I'll hold her in my arms. I'll love her and kiss her face like I was supposed to be doing now.

I'd done some research on rape and learned that I was not the only one who thought they couldn't tell anyone about it. I found out that 54 percent of sexual assaults go unreported, meaning, girls were too scared like I had been and their rapists were simply getting away with this horrible abuse. And 97 percent of those rapists will never spend a day in jail.

Tanner told me though that Jason had finally been reported and was now facing some jail time. The victim had been a fourteen-year-old girl from the Christian School; a girl I used to babysit when I was in middle school. Before I left town, we met up for coffee; and now, we talk on the phone every few weeks just to chat about life and to help each other heal. She's a sweet girl, and luckily, she hadn't gotten pregnant from the rape. She had a bright, promising future ahead of her, and it was all because she'd been brave enough to say something. Speaking up really was the key to escaping from the dark prison of rape. I was so proud of her.

Life was looking up for me too. Josh and I were still working through the emotional mess I'd caused, but he was slowly and surely softening up to me. He was now going to Iowa State with Caitlin, and just like mom predicted, they're getting married next June. I'm a bridesmaid. And I'm already planning a sappy speech for the reception, full of embarrassing stories from our childhood.

Tanner and I are still close, though not in the same way we used to be because he's married now. We got the chance to really catch up in the few short weeks I was in Oak Ridge, and I left feeling good about us. My heart is still stinging from the way things had turned out with him, but I'm happy for him and Leah. I hope that one day I can find the love that they share.

I glanced at the clock. Luke and Delilah should be swinging by any moment, probably with a big plate of chocolate chip cookies as a housewarming gift. They had been delighted at my choice to move back, but to me, it seemed the only logical thing to do. They were my family, and this was the only place that truly felt like home to me. It was where I was going to live out my second chance.

I got up from the coach and padded over to my favorite corner of the living room. Mom bought me a little wooden stand to set decorations on as a housewarming gift, and sitting proudly on the top shelf is the photo of me and Tanner as giddy teenagers. That picture isn't a bitter memory anymore. It's a happy one. Hanging right above it on the wall is the black and white photo of me, the one Tyler took. My mom said it was too pretty not to display. It's hard to argue against that; it's a breathtaking piece. I reached out and traced me and Tanner's happy faces, smiling at the happy memories that thinking of Tanner always brings.

I let out a happy sigh. Life is fuller now than it ever has been. I can finally say with confidence that I have stepped out of the desert for good, and I'm learning to dance in the rain that God is drenching me in. Sometimes at night, I just cry—happy tears, of course—at the way things are turning out. God is good.

I wandered over to the window peeked out of the blinds to examine the view from my second story apartment. I gave a small laugh at what I saw and threw the blinds wide open.

It was snowing.

Huge fat flakes drifted lazily down, blanketing the dirty land-scape with its fresh whiteness. Everything looked clean and pure. It was like God's promise to me that Tanner's words were true. This wasn't an ending, not in the least bit.

This was just the beginning.